DARK

of

NIGHT

By A.M. Paoletti

Published by Minerva Press, an imprint of Mad Hatter Publishing, Inc.

For information or bulk purchases:
Mad Hatter Publishing, Inc.
P.O. Box 20973
Ferndale, MI 48220
MadHatterPublishingInc.com

A.M. Paoletti
ISBN # 9781696942720

Notice: This is a work of fiction. Although its form is that of an autobiography, it is not one. The characters involved are wholly imaginary. Space and time have been rearranged to suit the convenience of the story, and except for public figures, places, and organizations, any resemblance to persons living or dead is coincidental. The opinions expressed are those of the characters and should not be confused with the authors or publishers.

Dedication

For Mom

Contents

Prologue

Alan Jaysen Thorstein III is an accountant in his father's Chicago-based firm. The only son of a wealthy, successful executive, he suffers from a glorified sense of self. He sees himself as the best and brightest while his co-workers and underlings see him as a spoiled, entitled brat. Scoffing and laughing at him behind his back and steering clear of his tempter and ability to fire them on a whim.

His dirty blonde hair is not that of his Swedish father but sits in a greasy comb-over atop his receding hairline. His clothes hang loosely on his five-foot-six skeleton. His drawn, blotchy face and swollen belly lend credence to rumors of heavy alcohol and drug use making him look older than his 35 years. He has the haunted look of a heroin user and the yellow pallor of an abused and failing liver. A penchant for young girls and large gambling debts have him on the verge of trouble with the knee-breakers.

Fueling his sense of entitlement is his position in his father's firm. For the last seven years, he's had only one client – his father's good friend, Antonio Giamo Andiamo, the alleged head of Detroit's criminal underworld. Recently, Alan's begun to think he can leave the family business, a life that's too stuffy, too confining, and too conservative for his taste. He knows he deserves more. He deserves to be his own man. To accomplish that goal, Alan devised a plan to skim money from Andiamo's vast enterprise, siphoning small amounts at a time into multiple dummy accounts used to fund his lavish lifestyle through illegal weapon and drug exchanges.

The small amounts made it harder to detect, but Andiamo's security is tight and well-developed. And detect it I did. He didn't cover his tracks as well as he thought. He figured Andiamo would take the blame when everything fell apart; a natural conclusion under the circumstances.

Unfortunately for Alan, *I* oversee Mr. Andiamo's security and that means his money as well. After all, Antonio Andiamo is my Uncle. He's also my Godfather both literally and figuratively.

So, no. Alan's plan did not go without notice. My unique set of security checks and balances pinged almost immediately, telling me something was wrong. And I thoroughly investigated every aspect of the theft. Once we identified the origin, my team followed every scrap, every breadcrumb Alan unknowingly left behind.

It was a brilliant plan, so I knew Alan wasn't the mastermind. We knew he wasn't that bright when we agreed with his father to let him manage the account. No, it wasn't' him which meant there was someone else, someone highly capable, and I had to find out who. So far, they'd siphoned off about $45 million, $10M in small amounts and another $35M more recently and more brazenly. As if they wanted to be caught. I knew I had to make my move.

I have a network watching every movement Alan makes. I know he renewed his passport. I know he closed his bank account and emptied his deposit boxes, even the one he kept under an alias. And, I know he has a one-way ticket to the Cayman Islands leaving in the morning.

Tonight, I finish my business with Mr. Alan Jaysen Thorstein III.

***

Now, instead of spending time with my favorite busty brunette, Susan, I'm sitting in Alan's bedroom alcove, waiting. He's out shopping for Christ sakes. I guess he thinks people are going to love seeing his scabbed and mottled skin on the beach in the Caymans. I shudder at the thought. His arrogance ends tonight.

I hear the front door open and the sound of keys hitting the foyer table. The rustling of expensive wrapping announces a successful shopping trip and I hear his footsteps land on the stairwell leading to his bedroom. He passes by me without a look, throws the bags on his bed, and heads straight for the bathroom.

I hear the shower start and settle back in to wait in one of the wing-backed leather chairs next to the fireplace. They're comfortable for my purposes. The water stops and I hear him singing along with the radio, nothing I can make out, such a shame to waste a somewhat decent voice.

He opens the door and my eyes follow as he passes heading for the closet opposite me. He's so happy and focused on what he's doing he still has no idea of my presence. Unfortunately, he's stark naked and the image makes me shudder. I think I spared the women of the Cayman Islands a huge disappointment. His desirables are not very desirable.

I spend a moment thinking of Elaine, a generously endowed woman I was with on my last trip there. Sorry Alan, you won't have the chance to create that same happy memory. Time for business. I leave my seat. Softly and silently I move in closer and lean against the wall behind him.

"Hello Alan," I startle him. He jumps, turns and loses what color he had in his face. "You know who I am? You remember, don't you?" I ask and he nods. "Good. You've been very naughty Alan and my Uncle has a message for you. He's not happy with what you've been doing."

Alan gulps nervously looking for an escape but does not find one. He tries to flee back to the bathroom but I easily cut off his naked trip.

"How…how did you find out?" he nervously stammers.

"Well, you were very sloppy and left a trail a third grader could follow," I say as I slowly back him up to the chair I just vacated. He falls into it easily and frantically looks about for an escape.

"Alan," I speak calmly as he turns his eyes back to me, then widen as I slowly twist a silencer onto a throwaway 9mm pistol. He sits naked shaking not knowing what to do. He looks like a scared puppy backed into a corner with his gaunt and sallow body swallowed by the high wing-backed chair.

"Color me surprised when the alerts showed that someone had tripped my uncles' security measures. It was very clever of you Alan, very clever." I pour him a glass of a 12-year-old Glenlivet from the small bar nearby and hand it to him. He doesn't suspect that I laced the glass with a fatal mixture of heroin and fentanyl. It works, but not right away. There's time for a few questions – a little trick I learned as a mercenary for the government. No one will suspect anything more than a drug addict's accidental overdose. Alan gulps down the Scotch then holds the glass out for another. I oblige.

"Alan," I continue as I sit down opposite him. "I need you to talk to me."

I'd found Alan's works earlier and slowly pull them from my pocket. He drools at the as only an addict would and shouts," It's not my fault! It wasn't my idea! I did it for...," he trails off, the heroin/fentanyl mixture taking effect too quickly. Damn it! I give him a few shakes trying to get more information.

"It wasn't my idea," he slurs, "it was..."

Another shake, "Tell me, Alan!"

"...al Hake..." he gurgled, fading into the drugs.

No! If I heard him right then that meant ... ah, shit! Shit! Shit! As his final words sink in, a bad feeling takes up residence in the pit of my stomach and the scars on my back begin to burn.

This was bad. Real, stinking, bad. I sigh heavily shaking my head as I clean up and set the stage for his overdosed death. Alan breathes his last as I set the needle in his arm.

"Dannazione!" I yell at his open-eyed unseeing corpse.

Alan sang his last but never got to use his newly found wealth nor be his own man. And now I know his deception brought something foul and very dangerous with it.

Chapter One

Friday 26 June

The sun is playing hide and seek as storm clouds release their fury across the Motor City. The winds are so fierce they have the streetlights begging for mercy, flying parallel to the wires that suspend them. Those who are brave enough to wander outside meet the onslaught of raindrops sharp enough to pierce through the thickest of protective gear. They scurry about like rats trying to find shelter as quickly as they can. Paper flies high around the tall buildings of Detroit and dance wildly to the rhythm of nature's rage.

Thunder shakes the windows of Bellisio's Ristorante where I sit in the back, waiting for my Uncle, and grateful to be out of the storm. From here I can see everything that goes on both inside and out. I can slip out to the back alley, if necessary, and easily defend any threat in front of me.

Franco Bellisio owns my favorite Italian restaurant. He brought his crew from Tuscany to start this ristorante with the help of my Godfather and it does well here. My family introduced me when I was just a little girl and though it looks like another little hole in the wall diner amongst the crumbling ruins of Detroit, inside holds all the old-world charms of Italy.

The small but efficient kitchen is behind me to my right and through the wooden slatted swinging doors. Restrooms are on the opposite side and down a small hallway. Just beyond my table are floor to ceiling windows running the length of the ristorante, still bearing the remnants of the winds and rain outside.

Slate lines the floors large fireplace in the middle of the room and a toasty fire takes the slight chill out of the air. Shadows and light from the fire dance across pictures of the Italian countryside, vineyards, olives and wine bottles that on the walls while Italian love songs play quietly from well-hidden speakers. I was mesmerized by this place when I was a little girl and I still am.

Franco, a skinny, little mouse of a man, always in a rush, hurries out from the kitchen with my loaf of freshly baked Italian bread and a dish of olive oil with garlic and herbs

"Miss Toni, the usual for you today?" Franco pours me a glass of wine, Dago Red, while he waits for my order.

"Si Franco, Grazie," I tell him, and he disappears back through the swinging doors.

While I dip my bread in the oil and herbs, a headline in the Detroit Free Press catches my eye:

Renowned Accountant Dead of Heart Attack

Alan Jaysen Thorstein II, of Thorstein and Hewell Financial Services of Chicago, dies of a heart attack at the age of sixty-nine. Mr. Thorstein suffered a massive heart attack several weeks ago after finding his thirty-five-year-old son dead from an apparent drug overdose.

*Thorstein II had gone to his son's house
for a family function when he discovered the
body. He was rushed to an undisclosed
hospital where he remained in seclusion until
he passed away last evening.*

*Thorstein II started his accounting
practice with Thomas Hewell in Chicago,
Illinois fifty years ago at the age of nineteen
and has had many influential clients
throughout his illustrious career.*

*Rights of survivorship turn the firm over
to partner and best friend Thomas Hewell. He
current client list includes Antonio Giamo
Andiamo, the alleged crime boss from Detroit.*

*The firm will be closed for the rest of the
week to grieve the loss of the founder.*

I frown, shaking my head. There's going to be a lot of trouble stemming from the III's meddling. Damn him! It was obvious that they wanted him caught, wanted me to find out who was behind the theft. Now it's a matter of tracking where the money went and see what their next move is.

He was an idiot. He believed he was invincible and found out the hard way he wasn't. He was way out of his league. The poor sap didn't have a clue what it was like to deal with these people. If the man heading this is who I think it is then I'm in serious trouble. The scars on my back begin to sear something fierce. I sigh.

Lately, I often wish I could tell my Uncle to find someone else to do his dirty work, but the 'Business' is not that easy to walk away from, especially for family. Besides, I'm indebted to him for pointing me in the right direction and helping me make a life out of my miserable, troubled youth. Anyway, I probably should tell you exactly who I am.

My name is Antonia Maria Frances Patricia Elizabeth Andiamo. Don't ask me about all the names, it's a Catholic thing. You choose a name each time you pass a sacrament such as your First Communion, First Confession, and Confirmation. But, you? You can call me Toni, everyone else does.

My parents named me after my Uncle, Antonio Giamo Andiamo, my Godfather. I'm the oldest of eight kids, six girls and two boys. I happen to be the black sheep of the family because I'm gay, though it doesn't bother my Uncle. The mafia doesn't look favorably on homosexuals, in general, but I believe I'm valuable because of certain skills I possess. Skills my uncle saw and helped me hone.

At 12 years old, I was a spotty enforcer for some loosely organized gangs. We prowled the streets looking for a way to score dope or make money. I was an angry kid and that drug-fueled rage got me into some big trouble when I killed someone. Yes, it was self-defense as the bastard thought he could rape me and take the money I'd collected that day. He was wrong.

I caught a break from the judge because of my age and a word or two from my uncle. After a couple of years in the juvenile justice system, my uncle aimed me down the path I take today. He gave me a job, taught me how to control my fury, and when I was old enough, sent me to Mercenary School after which I joined the Army.

Now, I'm his secret weapon. When he wants absolute discretion and deniability, he comes to me. What those would call murder I call work, which I happen to do extremely well. Alan Thorstein III is just an example of what I do for my Godfather.

For the past twenty years, I've also worked as a private mercenary for the government and anyone who could afford my services. Sounds like I'm a lady of the evening. I suppose I am in a way. In the dark of night, I come alive and do my best work.

My parents have no idea what I do for my Godfather. They're regular, hard-working, honest people. My father, Marco, is a mechanical engineer for General Motors (GM) and my mother, Francesca, works for an insurance company part-time to 'get out of the house'.

My Great Grandfather moved the family from Italy to get away from vendettas and the mafia. He would turn over in his grave if he knew we were back (or still) in the family business. My brother Alessandro and my cousin Alfonso, my uncle's son, are the only ones in the family who know about my work. They also work with him and have other talents my uncle finds useful.

Time for business as the door opens and my Uncle walks in with his security detail. Each one has been personally vetted and trained by me and my team. He's known as 'Big Tony', not because he's overweight but he has a presence that fills the room. He commands attention.

He sees me and smiles, it's infectious and I smile. His eases his six-foot frame out of the raincoat, hands it to his right-hand man, Bruno, and sits across from me. The rest of his men sit in strategic places around the ristorante.

Franco appears as if on cue with plates of angel hair pasta with roasted garlic, artichokes, peppers, and olive oil in one hand and gnocchi in the other. Wine is poured for my uncle, his staff take care of the security team, and they disappear back into the kitchen without saying a word. I wait while my uncle takes a bite and a sip of wine. Pleasantries always come first.

"Mi Bella Antonia, I trust your mother is well?"

"Si Padrino she's very well. I don't know how she puts up with all of us." My mother is a Saint putting up with all six of us throughout the years.

"Mi Fratello?" My uncle spoons more gnocchi in his mouth and takes another sip of wine as he refers to my father. He's been with GM for more than forty years and will be there until his death, I think. I'm not sure my Pop would know what to do if he ever retired.

"He's staying busy on the designs for a new motor. Even with all the troubles and layoffs, they want him to finish and have working prototypes within six months," I say between mouthfuls. We enjoy our lunch chatting about this and that.

When we finish, Franco is there to take our plates and give us fresh cannoli. God bless Franco. He always makes fresh cannoli for me and is the most discreet and thoughtful man. He disappears in a flurry and I know he won't surface again until our business is finished.

"Grazie, Antonia, for dealing with my latest troubles, I can always count on you. I trust there will be no repercussions," he stated getting down to business. It was not an inquiry. My Uncle Tony is not a man who inquires. This is code for 'you took care of these problems for me'.

"Prego, Padrino, but as for repercussions we'll have to see. As far as I could find out, Alan had a nasty drug habit that he hid from his father, though everyone in his office suspected. He tried to hide his track marks in the nailbeds of his fingers and toes. You know Mr. Thorstein was heartbroken when he learned of his son's indiscretions."

It seriously rips at me that he was the one to find his son. I thought someone else would find him like his housekeeper, not his father. His death nags me to no end. At least he left quietly in his sleep and, though his death was not by my hand, it still feels as if it was. It doesn't sit well with my conscience.

"Mr. Hewell understands your needs and will have no trouble looking after the assets personally. I've had stricter security measures put in place. Even the government doesn't have this technology, at least not until I finish negotiating the contract," a feral smile crosses my face.

"Bene, bene, it is hard to lose such a good man as Mr. Thorstein. He was a dear friend. It saddens my heart his son did such things to disgrace his father's good name." My Uncle takes a moment to grieve and makes a sign of the cross. He finishes off his cannoli and more wine before he continues.

"Now speaking of the government there is another little security matter I need you to take care of. This is of much importance and stems from the previous trouble."

He hands me a folder produced by his head of security, Bruno and I tuck it into my briefcase. I won't peruse it here. I always review them at work, behind my locked office door. I know this won't be pretty. Any 'matter' involving the government always sets off my alarms.

I rarely take on government work nowadays. Not only do they tend to leave your backside unprotected. They've left me stranded in some of the most ungodly situations and places no human should ever venture. I've also tried to reduce the work I do for my uncle. I have legitimate work and it's growing, taking up more and more of my time and attention.

After I returned from the first Gulf War, Desert Shield/Storm, my uncle helped me set up several companies. Now, I have a very successful security firm that includes consulting and investigation and a company that creates new gadgets and cybersecurity for the spy, military and corporate industries. This is the firm that produces the technology for security protocols I've set up for my uncle's financial group. We also started a company that trains mercenaries, bodyguards, and high-level security personnel for the government, celebrities, and big corporations.

For the first few years, it was good cover for my past work, but the good causes became fewer and fewer. The government left my fifth point of contact (my ass) swinging in the wind and my uncle needed me more and more.

"I would like to have this matter cleared up by the end of next week, so I need to know what you think by tonight." He likes to give the illusion that his assignments are a choice though he understands there are lines I will not cross. I have standards, such as they are.

"You'll have my answer by end of business today Padrino," I won't keep him waiting.

"Bene, bene, are you spending time with your mother this weekend?" Now that we've concluded our business, we become less formal.

"Si, Uncle Tony, for Sunday dinner as always. How she handles us all is something of a miracle. Will you be there?" My Godmother, Aunt Sofia, Uncle Tony's wife, died several years ago and though he doesn't need it, we take turns watching out for him.

"No, I have to be in Italy tomorrow." He catches the look of confusion and concern on my face as I usually accompany him on his trips abroad.

"Now don't worry. It will be a quick trip and I need you to take care of this thing with the government more than I need you taking care of my fat ass," he laughs at himself. He knows he's fit, healthy, and handsome. I nod and finish the last of my cannoli.

"So, what's going on in Italy," and what's the real reason you don't want me there, I wonder. I can read people and situations exceptionally well. You must in my line of work. So, this feeling in my gut says bad things are coming and it's getting stronger with each passing minute.

"Just routine business. A quick trip. Nothing more than a turnaround. You'll hardly notice I'm gone." And, now the scars on my back again start burning again. Not good.

"If you're sure then," I tell my Uncle hiding my skepticism. "I must get back to my office now, Padrino. I have a lot to do if I'm to give you an answer tonight," I stand and wait for my Uncle's acknowledgment.

He stands, hugs me, kisses both my cheeks, and tells me to give his best to my mother and father. I wish him success in Italy and tell him to have a safe trip.

As I head back to my office, shoulders hunched against the weather, I know that this new business can't be good. If it's stemming from Thorstein's mess, could it have anything to do with Mansur al-Hakeem? Was that the name Thorstein was trying to utter? A chill runs through me as his image flashes in my mind. Mansur al-Hakeem. My scars burn. I curse and continue on my way.

**

The noise of ringing phones, tapping keys and voices softly talking in the background, hits my ears as I step off the elevator. Life is good when the office is busy. Here is the heart of my enterprises and where I run Storm Investigations and Security, Inc., Andiamo Security Concepts, and The Training Facility.

It's hard to believe I started out in a little hole in the wall, nothing but a few dollars in my pocket and a dream my uncle helped bring to fruition. Now, learning from his acute sense of business and a desire to share my skills, I have these three flourishing companies, four partners, more than three hundred investigators, all ex-law enforcement, almost forty-five hundred employees total.

My executive offices take up the penthouse floor in the old Penobscot building, right in the heart of Detroit's financial district. My four partners and I share this floor with the bulk of Storm investigations take up the next couple of floors below us. Francie and Donald hold down the reception area. Behind the reception area are the offices of Karl Birstadt, in charge of the company's foreign relations, and Carolyn Carmichael, our intelligence expert.

Down the hall from them is Murray Sikes, head of general security, and Mitchell Evers, my second in command. The floor also hosts our library, break room, kitchen and a customized S.C.I.F. (Secured Compartmentalized Information Facility) also doubles as our main conference room.

Along the back hallway sits Miss Edna, my secretary, office manager, and surrogate mother. She rules our little roost and sits directly in front of my office, protecting my privacy as well as my sanity. When I open the glass doors to my outer office, Miss Edna hands me my messages and tells me there's a visitor waiting in my office.

"Oh goody," I respond sarcastically as I roll my eyes. I didn't need unexpected visitors today with so much to do but I know it's someone important or she wouldn't have let them in my office alone. My eyes grow wide and instantly I light up as I open my door and see who my visitor is.

"Alex!" I squeal and hug my brother. My brother is the only one who can make me squeal. It's embarrassing. "What brings you here on such a day?"

"Sis, I was just in the neighborhood and wanted to say hi and bye. I'm leaving with Uncle Tony for Italy."

"You're going with Uncle Tony? Do you know why he doesn't want me along this trip? Is something going on I need to know about Alex?" We're close and I know he'd fill me in if there was something I needed to know.

"Nah, it's just a routine trip. He'll be introducing me to people. Apparently, I'm being groomed," he rolls his eyes for effect. "I figure he doesn't want to embarrass me in front of my 'old' Sis."

"Watch it about that 'old' shit, brother. You're only eleven months behind me."

"Yeah, but I'll always be younger," he grins.

"Yeah, but I'll always be prettier," he replies and we both laugh.

At 6'2", his olive skin, brown eyes, thick dark hair, and the physique of a former Navy Seal, he got all the good looks in the family and he knows it. The dimple in his chin deepens when he smiles.

I can hold my own, of course, you can ask any of the lovelies I spend time with. They love my brown eyes, long dark hair and olive skin, looks like I have a tan year-round. That, and the solid athletic body that comes with years of training.

Though we both have brown eyes, his are always twinkling and happy. Mine, on the other hand, are serious, never giving away. Granted, they'll give off a warning when I'm about to unleash my rage upon you. If you see them turn black – run, don't walk. You do not want to be around me then.

Growing up people often thought we were twins; some still think we are though I stopped growing at 5'7". When we can, we run together along the Detroit River. We've done just about everything together and, no matter what we do, we always have fun. We're close, best of friends even. He had my back even when I was into some bad shit. He was smarter, though. He managed to learn from my mistakes and stay out of trouble.

It's hard to believe that not so long ago I was smearing peanut butter on his face and he was chasing me down the street with a handful of liverwurst in revenge. He never caught me. I almost laugh aloud at the memory. Never tell me I don't have the guts.

Then my eyes cloud over with the reality I'll have to deal with at the dinner table on Sunday.

"So, I take it you're not going to be at Sunday dinner. Damn it, Mama's going to be disappointed and you know I'm not going to hear the end of it. Thanks bunches, Bro."

Alex had the grace to grimace and give me his sad puppy dog look. "Sorry about that, but you know Uncle Tony. See him today?"

"Just came from lunch with him. Why?" I lean against my desk and fold my arms as the burning in my back continues.

"Then you haven't had a chance to look at the file yet," he nods. "This one's important Toni, really important," my brother stresses.

I hate when I'm the last one clued in on things.

"Well, then, you better let me get to it. I told uncle Tony I'd have an answer for him by tonight." Alex knows I won't look at anything in front of him even though he's the only person I blindly trust. He knows we need deniability and to cover both of our asses. In this business, everything is about covering your ass.

"Okay, Sis, have fun with the folks. Is Mia going?"

He's referring to my latest conquest, Mia. I'd been seeing her for the last week which is a record for me. Most don't get beyond that first night, not since Maggie. Not since she cheated and left after eight years together. That was what ten years ago, now. My walls are firmly in place.

"No, we're done. You know what it's like Bro, I spend too much time working, and she got clingy."

"Really? Of all the nerve, well I never liked her anyway." My brother scrunches his face.

"You are so full of shit your eyes are brown. You were drooling after her yourself," I laugh, punch his shoulder playfully, and he does his famous eyebrow dance.

"Maybe now I'll have a shot at her. Think she could go for my brawn and forget your beauty and brains?" He flexes his biceps and we burst out laughing. Once we catch our breath, I hug him hard.

"You have a safe trip and I know you won't embarrass me. You're an Andiamo. I'm missing you already."

"I'll miss you, too, Sis. I'll call when we get back in town. Ciao."

He walks out of the office, takes Miss Edna's hand, kisses it, and saunters down the hall to the elevator. I shake my head and smile. We Andiamo's are a charming bunch.

Miss Edna stares after him for a few moments then walks into my office, the beam on her face taking the edge off her years.

"Ms. Andiamo, your brother is certainly a charmer isn't he."

Miss Edna is a sixty-nine-year-old woman whose ebony skin is in direct contrast to her white hair. God love her, I'd be lost without her. She's been with me almost since the beginning and though she's not quite 5' she keeps everyone well-organized and runs my office with the efficiency of a well-trained company of soldiers.

Everyone adores Miss Edna, and no one would dare cross her. She's earned their respect and I often tell her she's the best thing that's ever happened to me and to this company.

"Miss Edna, after all the years you worked for me, how many times do I have to tell you to call me Toni?"

"Now you know that wouldn't be proper, Ms. Andiamo," she gives me a look that's mildly scolding over her reading glasses. Miss Edna is a very proper woman.

"You and Charlie come to my house for dinner when I try out new recipes. You call me Toni then."

"Young lady don't be arguing with Miss Edna now. There's a difference between the professional and the personal. They are two entirely different situations. Proper is proper, you'll do well to remember that."

"Yes ma'am, Miss Edna." Much to her chagrin, I can't help but give her a great big salute and with the withering look she gives me, I clear my throat.

"What do you have that I need to get done before our dinner arrives?" Miss Edna hands me a stack of papers in order of priority.

"Well, I see I'm going to be busy," I groan shuffling the papers. "I need you to push back the office meeting an hour. I have some new work to review before I handle this stack."

"I'll let everyone know. Hold all calls?" she asks.

"Yeah, I'll let you know how long. Thanks."

She leaves, closing the door behind her. My office is my sanctuary and she knows it. Outfitted in mahogany and leather, it hosts a bank of tall windows looking over the

Detroit River, with a great view the Ambassador Bridge, the bridge to Windsor, Canada.

I keep my private files here, behind my desk. My private conference room, another S.C.I.F., sits behind a hidden door in the paneling. On the opposite wall is a second hidden door that leads to my private library; floor to ceiling shelves stacked with books ranging from self-defense to law, from business to private investigation. A lifetime of studying and research.

Long nights happen all too often, and Miss Edna knows to keep fresh clothes stocked in my dressing area. These private access points provide options for a quick escape if needed including the private express elevator hidden by the supply closet. Call me paranoid but this is dangerous work and I like to be prepared.

Leafing through the stack Miss Edna handed me, I lean back at my desk, tap the button to flip the locks, and kick off my shoes. I open the file my uncle provided and start to scan through.

"HOLY SHIT!" Scrambling to keep from falling out of my chair, I hit the intercom, "Get my Uncle on the secure line, NOW!" Not waiting for Miss Edna to reply I shake my head, looking at the file again in disbelief. "Holy shit. Holy shit."

Sinking back into my chair, still staring at the file, I know this is going to be one big shit storm. The other shoe just dropped and kicked me in the fucking ass.

CHAPTER TWO

Friday Night 26 June

It takes a lot of work, but my uncle finally calms me down. Family business will have to wait until I meet with him again after dinner and stuff the file into my office safe. I turn my attention to office matters, return the phone calls that Miss Edna handed me and make it to my office meeting feeling harried.

There's good news and it's time to celebrate after our two-hour meeting. We just secured a contract to handle the security for the new professional hockey arena. It's a coup and we were up against a host of other companies, so the win is even sweeter. Everyone moves to the break room where Bellisio's catering (of course) is setting up for our celebration feast.

Miss Edna stays behind to clean up against my advice and shoos me off like a fly. "I'll join you in a few minutes, Ms. Andiamo. It won't take me long. Go tend to your flock."

My executive team and their partners are waiting in the break room along with the rest of the staff involved with garnering the new contract. Murray and his life partner, Larry, Mitch and his wife Andrea, Carolyn and her wife Olga, Karl introduced us to Wendell, Miss Edna's husband Charlie, Francie and her boyfriend Jamal, Donald, and all the admin assistants Millie, Carmen, Daniel, and Jennifer. The aroma wafting down the hall is more than tempting and everyone forms a line preparing to fill their plates.

There's chicken primavera, vegetable lasagna, roasted chicken, prime rib, assorted vegetables, antipasto salad, plus fresh baked bread and breadsticks.

I wait for Miss Edna to join us before getting my plate. The Cassata Cake with a red-piped image of our hockey team's logo and message of Congratulations is in the fridge waiting to be unveiled.

After everyone finishes eating, Miss Edna and Donald fetch the cake and silence ensues throughout the room while I stand to make a speech.

"I want to take this opportunity to acknowledge Murray and Mitch as well as their teams." Hoots and hollers go around the room.

"This contract comes from long hours of work that I'm sure had everyone's respective spouses, boyfriends and girlfriends complaining," a chorus of laughter erupts. "But at the end of a hard-fought battle, they won the day. Congratulations to all. Saluti," I say raising my glass of champagne in a toast.

Cheers and toasts break out around the room then speeches ensue. When the party dies down and everyone starts to leave, I pull my second in command man aside.

"Mitch, we have a problem developing. I need you to pull everything we know about Mansur al-Hakeem." Mitch's face goes ghost white.

"What the ...?" Mitch starts.

"It doesn't sit well with me either but I have a bad feeling about this. I'll explain tomorrow when I know more."

"I don't like this Toni."

"I know, I know, neither do I. Just get the info. We'll need it."

"Alright, but you better explain this soon."

"I will, tomorrow." I watch as Mitch walks away. It's time to meet with my uncle for the second time.

***

As we walk along the river, I take him to task.

"Respectfully, Padrino, you've got to be out of your mind. I can't believe this. There are too many government agencies wanting a piece of you. What the hell is going on?"

"Antonia, ..." my Uncle tries unsuccessfully to interrupt.

"All they want to do is use me to trap you and put both of us behind bars. I won't allow them to get to you through me. I can't believe this. Something is very wrong here, Godfather. Why me? You know I don't do government jobs anymore. They don't like it when they have to listen to a civilian and they leave you hanging. How did we end up being in the middle of this crap?"

I look to uncle Tony. He didn't reply. He's seething, barely keeping his temper in check. If it were anyone else yelling at him he would be toast by now. He's my uncle and we're close but no one speaks to him this way. To make matters worse, I continue my tirade complete with waving arms and hand gestures.

"Man, I knew it was bad news when I found out who Thorstein partnered with, but this? This is not right Padrino. I'm not sure I could do this, even if I tell them yes. You know what Al-Hakeem did to me," my scars turn from burning to searing pain as I remember the man who inflicted them upon me. I'm shaking so I continue my rant to cover it.

"You know they won't let me run the show. I'll have to insist on it and more they'll likely pretend to go along while running their own op behind my back! Then, they'll hang us both out to dry. Padrino, this is the..."

"Basta!" He finally yells. "You dare speak to me this way! You think I don't know what is at stake!" He takes a deep breath and continues in a calmer tone.

"Antonia, I am letting you know what I was given. If I did not have complete trust in you and if I did not think it was the most important thing, I would somehow keep them from coming to you. I know it's the hardest thing I will ever ask, and you will have to avoid all the traps. I'm sure they will set obstacles in your way, but you must deal with this. This is still part of the earlier trouble with the Thorstein's' God rest their souls" My Uncle makes the sign of the cross. "He put us in a grave situation with the persons he dealt with. This could end us if you don't help straighten things out."

"Oh, Padrino, don't say that to me. You know I wouldn't let that happen. I know I owe you everything for what you've done for me," I spout, the Catholic guilt hard at work.

"I know how hard this is for you, but this is going to happen whether you want it to or not." My Uncle stops and looks at his watch. I turn to stare at the river leaning on the rail. After a few moments of hard thinking, I turn back and give my answer.

"Alright, Padrino, I'll do as you ask. When they come to me, if they come to me, I'll take the job. God, I'm an idiot. You take extra care of my brother while you're in Italy. How many know?" I turn back to the river, my mind racing, and stare blankly at the Windsor Lights.

"Only you, Alessandro, and Alfonso know. I'll always take care of you. You are mi famiglia. I do not let famiglia suffer just for the business sake. I do what's best for the famiglia and this is best for the famiglia," my Uncle answers.

Alfonso is Uncle Toni's oldest son and God forgive me I can't stand him. He's a puffed-up pompous ass who thinks he deserves everything on a silver platter because he's the heir apparent. If he knows, everyone knows. He has a mouth that won't shut up. He likes to brag about everything he and his father are doing.

"Great, that means it's no secret." I hold up my hands before he could say anything.

"I'm sorry Godfather. I know you'll take care of us. You taught me how to take care, too. You can't blame me for wanting you safe as well." I sigh, rub my face, and turn from the river, my anger and fear dissipating.

"You know I won't let you down. I want you taken care of. I'm going to put some extra personnel on security around your house. I'll brief your team and have them check in at The Training Facility for a refresh on their terrorist training. We'll roll them through in small batches.

"Now Antonia, I know you want me safe, but my team is briefed and well trained, as you know. You trained them yourself, after all. Your brother will be perfectly safe in Italy. I agree to put extra security on the house. Now my dear, sweet niece, give your padrino a hug for luck and I'll be on my way."

"Uncle Tony..." I just shake my head and sigh. What's the point trying to argue with him? "You stay safe and keep my brother out of trouble." We do the prerequisite kisses on the cheek and then I give my uncle a hug. I hold on a little longer than proper.

"Ciao."

"Ciao," he replies as he walks away from the river, security team in tow. I watch while he maneuvers into a black SUV and his team whisks him to the airport.

I can't move yet and turn back to the river, brooding. Normally I love watching the river. Tonight, the water is stirred and angry from the earlier storms matching the emotions running through me. I lean on the rail and focus on the lights of Windsor, Canada, across the river. The rain had stopped again, and the clouds disappeared leaving a beautiful breezy night. After a deep breath, then two, I sigh and flip out my cell phone.

"Mitch, I need you to double security at my uncle's house within the hour. Make sure they're hidden. I don't want anyone alerted. Schedule a team briefing for 0600 hrs. I'll explain everything then." I wait for his reply, "Good, I'll leave you to it then, a presto, Mitch."

Another breath, and another, trying to clear my head. I need a drink and I need to relax before the hell that Al-Hakeem has planned is unleashed. I take one last look at the river and head off down the road.

***

I take Jefferson to Seven Mile Rd. and head for a little bar I know. Music blares, it's not packed but there's a crowd. People are talking, dancing, drinking, and making out. This is a place where I can blow off the stress of the day.

This place has a nightly drag show that must have ended before I arrived. Things were just starting to settle down again, just the way I like it. I don't like being so crowded you can't move anything but your big toe on the dance floor. I like to move a little, not be so claustrophobic.

The bartender had my drink ready before I could take my seat at the back corner. The same people have worked here for as long as I can remember. It's a mixed crowd here: gay, straight, lesbian, bi, and those who can't decide. When I was younger this kind of mixed crowd scene didn't exist. I took my very first date to a locked-door lesbian club on Eight Mile Rd. She was a postal worker. The police raided the place all the time. Eventually, it opened to all the LGBT community. We've made a lot of progress since the locked door days.

I scan the crowd looking for someone to relieve my anxiety for the night. Then it hits me, punches me in the gut more like, and steals my breath. In the corner, across the bar talking to a few women I know, is the most beautiful woman I've ever laid eyes on and I've laid eyes on more than a few. I stared at her, breathless. Holy moly!

Her eyes catch mine, eyes the color of clear ice, the kind that looks right through you, devours you. Wolf eyes. Her hair lay in waves past her shoulders with several shades of brown; rich, dark, and deep. Her sensual curves flow gracefully and there's obvious power in her moves. She smiles. Captivating. Hypnotizing.

I sip my drink, at a loss to explain what's grabbed my gut and slammed it to the floor. Okay, stop. Take a deep breath. Get a grip girl.

Taking another sip, I try to ignore the tugging at my chest. I chat up a woman who next to me but quickly lose interest. She notices my attention is elsewhere and sidles up to someone else.

I ask another woman to dance and once again my interest wanes as I steal another glance at that lovely little wolf. Should I go over to talk with and talk with my friends? Why not.

Across the room, Jessica zeroes in on the dark-eyed woman she'd been waiting for. Lean and athletic to be sure. Her pictures certainly don't show the power, the sensuality, the confidence this woman seems to wear. Jessica can't help but look. She's sleek, in control, so, so…wow.

Caught staring, Jessica's cheeks blush as red and hot as the blood rushing through her veins. "Damn look at me," she thought. "I'm actually drooling. What the hell? Shit, she's coming over here. I don't know if I can speak."

Jessica locks eyes with Toni as she approaches the table, the darkest, sparkling brown eyes she'd ever seen.

"Hey Erica, Judy, how have you guys been?" I croon, hoping I sound casual. "Who's this lovely lady with you?" I ask after exchanging our hello's.

"Hey, Toni, we were wondering when you were going to make it our way," her friend, Erica, says with half a laugh.

Judy elbows her partner. "This is Jessica. She doesn't get out much. We had to pull teeth for her to meet us here. Jessica this is Toni. Watch out for her, she's a heartbreaker," she warns Jessica.

"Gee, thanks guys," I whine with a wink.

"Hi, Toni. Call me Jess." Her gravelly voice melts me like snow in spring. Now, even I think that's corny. Get a grip Andiamo!

"Jessica, Jess," I shake her hand. Nice grip, strong, but almost delicate at the same time.

I know Erica and Judy from a biker group, and we ride together from time-to-time. Judy works at GM in the same department as my father and Erica's an aspiring artist. Nice people. Normal people.

"So how are the plans for the show coming along," I ask Erica about her upcoming art show.

"Great, keeps me on my toes."

"I bet. So, how long have you known these two bums, Jess?"

"Oh, a few years I guess," she beams and the pair groan. I give them the eye. A good song starts playing so I decided to take a chance and ask.

"Would you like to dance?" You could knock me over with a feather as she purrs a 'yes'. Oh, my. Tonight, Andiamo, you're going down in flames. For the next few hours, the four of us talk dance and joke around. We close the joint and I ask Jess to follow me to a secluded place along the river where we might continue the evening.

***

We pull into an abandoned parking lot and park at the far end near a trail that leads to a stretch of earth at the river's edge. Jessica pulls a blanket from the trunk of her car and we spread it close to the water. The streets of the city are behind us and the lights of Windsor stare at us from across the river. It's one of my favorite spots in the city.

The moon shines her pale light on the water as Jessica shines her pale eyes on me. I feel a shudder move through me, reminding me of the kind of excitement I felt when I first kissed girl at twelve years old; a sweet, nervous kind of excitement.

The coolness of the night mist tries to chill our heat but failed. Jessica seems nervous, hesitant, as we slowly kiss.

Soon my nerve endings are sitting on the farthest edges of desire.

We explore one another and she sets small fires wherever she touches. I cup her round muscled bottom slowly lower us to the blanket. I feel her long legs wrap around me; our eyes locked. I feel lost and found in those eyes.

She traces the scars that mar my body leaving the sensitive skin raw. I manage to establish some semblance of control. No one has ever made me believe I could reach up and touch the moon before, not even Maggie.

With the dawn approaching, she moves on top, riding me so slowly I want to explode. I hold her hips as if afraid she'd disappear if I let go, keeping me hypnotized with her eyes.

Our ride is rhythmic, keeping beat with the lapping waves. As the sun breaks through the morning clouds we break through gasping for air. I hold onto her unable to suppress my fire. We remain there, waiting to catch our breath before we collapse back on the blanket. Holy shit!

"I think I'm paralyzed. I'm not going to move for the next hundred years," I say, managing to find my voice.

I have a strange feeling in the pit of my stomach as if a bunch of butterflies has taken up residence. I think I'm in trouble here. Yep, I went down in flames.

"Me neither," she replies still breathless, her leg draped over my body.

"Damn," I said. "What the hell? I believe this is the most incredible night I've ever spent." Did she have to know that? That alone is unusual. I maintain control, maintain my distance. I'm not in the habit of letting others pleasure me. Then no one gets too close, no one can get to my heart. I made that mistake once with Maggie.

"This woman is nothing like her and I won't ruin perfectly wonderful evening. I dismiss Maggie and turn my attention back to Jessica.

"Look at me," she chooses to ignore my words thank God. "I'm a bowl of Jell-O." She laughs.

We lie in each other's arms and watch as the sun begin its journey; dressing as the lights across the river fade and the sound of traffic grows.

We hold hands 'til we reach our cars. She draws me in for one last soul-searing kiss then drives away. I try to clear my head and realize that I have definitely gone down in flames. I try to shake off the tug at my heart but Jessica refuses to leave my mind.

Chapter Three

Saturday 27 June

Jessica drives home, ears still buzzing and skin still tingling. "What in the world did I just do?" She asked herself. She'd never done anything like this, never, and wondered how this woman had captivated her.

She touched her lips bringing back the sensation of Toni's kisses. It had been years. Toni felt something, too, she knew.

"Take it easy girl," she tried to talk herself down. "Don't get ahead of yourself here. It was just a tryst in the night, and with a suspected mob assassin." She shook her head at lapse in judgment. "Some agent you are."

She couldn't believe she'd just had her way with Toni Andiamo, one of the FBI's unofficial most wanted. She laughed at herself wondering what in the world she was going to do. Being an FBI agent could be hell on dating but sleeping with a suspected mob assassin could tank your career.

"And, all those scars?" she thought. The FBI had reams of paper in their files and she'd read all of them. There was nothing that hinted at a history that created scars like those.

Jessica drove through the gates of the large, empty estate in Grosse Pointe. She'd come back to this place, this home her parents left her, this city where her parents died; an FBI sting gone bad.

They'd been investigating the Andiamo's and other families, trying to find a way to take them down. They'd failed and now it was her turn. When they offered her the assignment to lead the Organized Crime/Drug Division in Metro Detroit, she jumped at the chance. This was her chance to walk in her parent's footsteps and finally put an end to the Andiamo's.

She parked her car trying to shake off the despair of this place and focused instead on Toni and their night of pure, unadulterated lust. Was this the "in" to the family that she needed? No, she hadn't been undercover at the bar and there's the problem.

It wasn't "just business", their night of lust. She felt something. She felt something for Toni Andiamo, and, for a moment, she hated herself for betraying her parents.

"Nothing you can do about it now. What's done is done. Just be smart and play it out," she thought as she ran into the house to shower, realizing she was already running late. Her boss had texted for an early meeting. He didn't say what it was about, but they never do. The less information sent out the better. She knew she'd soon find out.

***

It's 0500 hours and I arrive at my office with an hour to get cleaned up before my first meeting. Miss Edna's already here with fresh coffee. God bless Miss Edna but, knowing exactly when to stand by the elevator is truly scary.

"Thanks. Sorry to drag you into the office so early and on a Saturday but this is urgent." She looks at my bedraggled appearance and arches a brow at the same clothes I left in yesterday evening.

"That's quite alright, Ms. Andiamo. You must have had an interesting evening to be dragging yourself in looking like that," she admonishes. I smile and stare off into space recalling the night and reply.

"Yes, interesting, very interesting, indeed. I'll be in the shower if you need me. Has the extra security detail checked in this morning?"

"Yes, Ms. Andiamo, just a few minutes ago. Everything is as it's supposed to be. Shifts just changed over and there were no reports of any incidents during the night."

"Okay, good."

"Your uncle's family is taken care of. Go get yourself washed up and I'll get the conference room set," she disappears down the hall and I disappear into my office.

***

Miss Edna is all business as she gets the staff in order. Not a lot of people would take a chance on an older woman, give them a job with no experience, let alone trust them to run anything. She owed her life and the life of her husband to Ms. Andiamo.

She smiles as she remembers the terrible office she walked into that fateful day. God answered her prayers when she found Ms. Andiamo and now, she thinks proudly, Ms. Andiamo owns this whole building. Falling apart and in need of demolition, she helped Ms. Andiamo save this place from the wrecking ball.

She comes out of her reverie, thanks God once again, and barks more orders at the staff. She will not tolerate anything that will inconvenience her boss. Everything must be in exact order.

***

In the conference room my team – my partners Mitch Evers, Murray Sikes, Karl Birstadt, and Carolyn Carmichael are ready to go. I trust them with my life as they trust me with theirs. We've been through some of the worst situations together, from the jungle of Panama to the arid desert in Kuwait to some of the worst places in South America, Israel, Africa and many hellholes most cannot imagine.

The airlock on the steel doors shut and motors silently slide steel into place over the windows. I gaze around the table at this motley crew as they turn their attention to me.

"Good morning. I appreciate you being here on short notice. I'm going to warn you now, this is going to be a shit assignment. Miss Edna, hand out the folders, please."

I give them five minutes to skim over the material my uncle gave me. A stream of 'Oh Shit!' hits my ears. I chuckle to myself.

"That was my reaction when I first read the file," I said, pacing the front of the room.

"I know the intel's thin, a lot thin. I won't know exactly what they have or what they're planning until they call but I don't want to wait. I'm not walking into this blind and I sure as shit would hate walking into a trap."

"In your file is a picture of Mansur al-Hakeem. Last known whereabouts thought to be New York. How he got into the country is unknown. They know he's gone under and supposedly he's on his way here although that cannot be confirmed at this time."

"What the hell is he doing here, how did he get past the No-fly list, and what does this have to do with the government and your uncle?" Murray asks, his cigar smoke swirling around his head before disappearing into the ventilation system.

"You know it's easy to forge a document and get past the No-fly list. The point is, we know he's a sick, sadistic, son of a bitch. Whether the Feds call or not, we must take him out. We're going to do whatever it takes to find him, prevent whatever he's come here to do, and take him down."

"Look, I know all of us have a problem trusting our government and agencies with initials. They've left us swinging in the wind on more than one occasion, but this goes beyond that and you all know it." I look at each one of them.

"They have my ass on the line as well as my uncle and his family. I don't know for sure if the Feds are going to turn to me or want our help, but assuming my uncle is correct we need to be prepared. I want you guys to work behind the scenes until this is figured out.

"So, you have a decision to make. You can stay and help me and my uncle out of this shit situation or you can walk out of this room right now." I scan my team.

"That sits just fine with us," Mitch snorts and the sounds of agreements follow. Then a hush falls over the room as each takes the time to think seriously. One by one they lift their eyes and look to me.

"I'm in." Carrie is the first to state.

"Same here," Murray follows.

"Ya, in all da the way Sarge," Karl is the next to reply.

Everyone looks to Mitch. He fidgets and stares at everyone in the room.

Finally, he looks at me and says, "Alright! Alright, I'm in. Shit. I'm out of my mind. Just thinking about al-Hakeem makes my scars hurt and you know I hate working with the feds." He tosses his pen down on the pad of paper in front of him and crosses his arms.

"But, damn it, I like your ass too damn much to let you go this alone," he sighs and picks up the pen he threw.

He knows more than anyone here that the government can play an ugly game. During Desert Storm, they set us up for ambush and capture. Only thing was, we didn't know. Mitch had to watch as our captors did some horrific things to me. I think it affected him more than me, but those flashbacks are murder when they hit.

I let out the breath I didn't know I was holding and sent many thanks to God. I couldn't have done this without Mitch. He's the one I count on the most, the one I'm closest to. I know he's not happy about this an I can't blame him. It's why I was so mad at my uncle.

"So, here's what I know. About five weeks ago, my private alerts were tripped when my uncle's accountant, Thorstein, launched a scheme to siphon small amounts into dummy accounts. I wanted to let it unfold a bit and trace all the transactions, so I didn't do anything right away. Good thing, too, as it gave me a head start.

"I found out he was the one who our systems, at least it was set up to look that way, but I kept digging. I knew he wasn't smart enough or brave enough to do this on his own. Now, I haven't found everyone he was working with yet, but I do know that one of these people is Al-Hakeem. You know he isn't a techie so had to have someone extremely tech savvy to come up with this scheme and get through our security. I'm just glad they were working on old info and didn't know about the hidden security measures I'd installed.

"I wish I could tell you what else is involved but I haven't found much out and won't know how he and the government connect until I'm briefed. If I'm briefed. I do know that he made a business offer to my uncle, but of course, my uncle refused him, so he found a weak spot in my uncle's accountant.

Carrie speaks up, "Has the accountant said anything as to why, how, or who?"

"No all he said was that it wasn't his idea," I answer. "Now he's not saying anything. He's dead from a drug overdose." I didn't tell them I'm the one that caused said overdose. They didn't need to know.

"So, I'm trying to follow the money which they've been bouncing different amounts to various banks around the world. Trying to track the real IP address that set off the alert is proving even more difficult.

"I know it's not much to go on. We need to use everything at our disposal to find out what and who's involved. I want to know more than the powers that be when, and if, they summon. We're all familiar with how they work – on a need to know basis. They won't tell me anything even if I really do need to know.

"We also know they won't like a civilian running roughshod over their territory let alone running their operation. We've got to count on them making us the scenery in their little play once they get what they want out of us," I pause as everyone agrees.

"So, if we're going to need to know more than them. I want deep background on this guy and I mean everything there is to know besides what we personally experienced at his hand." Damn scars. I unconsciously reach around my back to scratch at them. The burning hasn't let up.

"This is it people. We finally get to have our day. I need GPS trackers in all our vehicles as well as video and audio burst recorders that searches won't pick up. Karl, will you come up with something the scanners won't find?"

"Ya."

Karl is just a chatterbox this morning.

"Good I want it tested before Monday morning. I also want you to take over tracking that originating IP address responsible for our breach. Coordinate and work with Roger and the team at Andiamo Security Concepts.

"Carrie, I need you in charge of surveillance. I want to know if anyone follows me. I want to know who they are and who they work for. Also, I want any and all intelligence you can gather from inside any agencies with initials would be helpful."

Carrie replies, "No problem, I'll get to work on that right away. I'll set something up with Karl as well as grab you a little beauty that can detect one if they decide to put it on you or any of our vehicles."

"If we're short of equipment, again, see Roger. He'll provide you with whatever we need." Carrie nods her head as she busies herself with notes and equations. "Also see if you can find out who will be in charge of the task force and who's in it will you? I want to know everything about the people we have to deal with."

"Will do Sarge."

"Good. If they do come to me, you know they'll want my skills but also want to put me on a short leash. They don't want the wildcard too wild or they'll have to answer to somebody.

Everyone nods in agreement on that fact. They all know what happens when those in power think you're too wild. They eliminate. I don't like being dead, so unfortunately if they tried, they'd be wasting perfectly good lives for nothing.

"They'll also try and put ears anywhere they can in hopes I'll somehow incriminate my uncle. Murray, I want to make sure we know where every single bug is. We cannot afford to miss even one. We'll decide later which ones we keep active and we're activating this room as a S.C.I.F.F. from now on."

"Right, I take it you want your condo swept as well?"

"Yeah, I know they'll bug my place, without a doubt. You should sweep over there now and randomly throughout the day. They'll try to plant them while we're here. You sweep in here?" I inquire of him on the afterthought, knowing full well this room is up to code according to Intelligence Community Directive (ICD) regulation 705, and Intelligence Community Standards 705-1 and 705-2. It's mandatory to stay on top (or even ahead of) security standards.

"I certainly did," he acknowledges.

"They haven't had too much of a chance to plant anything here. Mitch and I spent most of the night going over the Book Cadillac Hotel Paintball Sniper deal," Murray continues.

"There still a problem with that guy? I thought that was almost wrapped up."

"It was supposed to be but apparently he hit again last night. They tried to set a trap for him, but didn't even come close," Murray chortles and I give him a look. "I know this isn't funny but I can't help it. This twit is smarter than they're giving him credit for and they wouldn't listen to anything we tried to tell them. It ended in disaster so now instead of a couple of extra security officers, they're begging us to take over and get this guy."

"Okay. Okay," I sigh. "We'll map out a strategy after we finish with this. I want this guy put to bed tonight. I don't want anything interfering with this federal deal. It's too volatile. Got it?"

"Got it, Sarge," Murray beams.

"Also, you are the one coordinating personnel for whatever we need starting with those guarding my uncle's place," I tell him.

"You got it."

"Alright, next, Mitch I want you coordinating everything from the office while you are coming up with all there is to know about Al-Hakeem." Mitch nods.

"I'll get on it as soon as we're done here," he states without a glance my way. He's upset and I can't afford that. Damn.

"We need to clear everything that can be cleared, delayed, or delegated for a couple of weeks until this mission is done. You all have good people on staff, see to it they get the extra work." I look around the room to find everyone nodding in agreement while dividing their work on paper.

"Okay, I think that finishes up the feds for now. Let's look at our paintball sniper."

For the next hour, we go through maps, strategies, and set-ups. We finally agree on a plan and a time to play it out.

"301 will be the communications center where Mitch will be set up. Karl, Carrie, you'll be here and here," I point to two areas on the wall screen we set up. "Murray, I want you on a scaffold here." He nods. "Alright, are we clear on everything?" I look around and all nod. "Good. Let's do it to it. Thanks all. Mitch, can I have a moment?"

"Alright," he seethes and we wait until everyone clears out.

"I know what you're going to say, but damn it all to hell Toni, this could put all of us out of business permanently. This is playing with our lives. Despite my obsession with keeping your ass out of the fire, I'm not sure I can do this, not this guy. It could end up bad for us Toni, really bad and you know why."

"I know what you're saying, Mitch. Don't you think I yelled, screamed, and cursed? I told him he was insane, that I would be insane for doing this. Nevertheless, if the intel's correct and the Feds come to me, you know I need to do this, and I can't do it without you. I wouldn't want to, but if I must, I will. There's too much at stake for my family, Mitch. This guy too dangerous to let loose on this city. I need to put him down like a rabid dog and you know it. This is our chance to get some of ourselves back."

"Damn it, Toni, you're insane. What in the Sam Hill am I going to do with you?" He shakes his head. "No, don't answer that. I know what I want to do but you'd enjoy it too much," and just like that, the tension breaks into insignificant little pieces.

"Alright. Alright. I'll go along with this, for now. Someone has to keep that pretty ass of yours out of trouble."

"Thanks, Mitch. I really can't do this without you."

"Yeah, yeah, yeah" he turns and leaves the conference room.

I smile to myself. We'll be all right now. I exit the conference room and head to my office, letting Miss Edna know that I'm heading to the hotel to check on the set-up for the operation tonight. I check out the area Murray booked and return to the office to rest. As soon as I close my eyes the demons come. Suddenly, I'm in the desert of Kuwait...

***

I hear the whoosh of blades as the Medivac chopper comes over the horizon. It's been more than two hours and I don't know if this kid is going to make it. Damn shame. Somebody's going to pay for this kid getting hurt. I hear myself telling him he's going to be okay, to hang in there and everything will be okay.

Suddenly, the sand underneath my feet shakes like an earthquake. I instinctively cover the kid and look around me to see what's happening. Mortar rounds are exploding all around us. Son of a bitch! I feel the heat of one that explodes a little too close for comfort.

Next thing I know Sergeant First Class (SFC) Evers is on top of me slapping out flames. I'm on fire. Son of a bitch! There's a slight lull in the action and I take stock of my troops. I didn't lose anyone yet. Please, God, don't let me lose anyone, not here. My troops try and pin down where the mortars are coming from.

The Medivac is coming closer. I tell Carmichael to get on the radio and tell them to hold off because the LZ is too hot. The stupid idiot either didn't hear or thought we were joking. The pilot keeps coming. Fucking idiot!

The next thing I know, the chopper explodes. Flames shrapnel, and debris burst everywhere. I yell "cover" as bits and pieces of the Huey fly all over. I hear SFC Evers yell out an obscenity as blood starts flowing from his leg. I jump up and rip off part of my uniform to wrap around his leg.

Looking around, I see two others hurt. I look after Carmichael. She has a piece of shrapnel sticking out of her back but it's small and not dug in too far to cause much damage. A quick yank and she was good to go. The young kid under her is fine. Another mortar and more pieces fly, one hitting me in the head.

On the other side of me lies Karmicki, eyes open, a piece of rotor sticking out of his chest. Ty! Oh no, not Ty! I feel tears stream down my face. Ty Karmicki and I are best of buds. We grew up together, signed up together, have been deployed and survived in lots of conflicts together. He lived two houses down from me. How am I going to explain this to his mama?

I hear SFC Evers curse again. I hear shouts of 'I want them alive' then through the smoke comes the blackest, most lifeless set of eyes I will never forget before everything turned grey then faded to black.

***

Jessica worked her way up through the ranks to earn her spot as Assistant Special Agent in Charge (Assistant SAIC) of Detroit's Organized Crime/Drug Division. She's meeting with the Assistant SAIC of the Counterterrorism Division, Calvin Sheppard, SAIC of the Detroit Field Office, Sean "Spence" Spencer, and the Deputy Director, Malcomb Davis.

This operation must be damned important for the Deputy Director to get involved personally and on a weekend. Malcomb Davis is her mentor, the one she turns to when she's troubled or needs someone to guide her.

He knew her parents well and she grew up calling him "uncle". When they died 'Uncle' Malcomb saved her soul and helped choose the path that led to her successful career. He took her under his wing when she joined the Bureau and he keeps in touch regularly. He had not let her know he was going to be here for this briefing, and she wondered why.

She let all thoughts drain away to concentrate on this meeting as she enters SAC Spencer's office. Jessica smiles at her Uncle Malcomb warmly.

"Director Davis it's so good to see you," she addresses her mentor formally. "What's so important to bring you to our neck of the woods?"

"My child, you look as radiant as ever. You become more beautiful every time I lay eyes on you. Your parents would be so proud of you. Have a seat. I'll give you as much information as I can. You'll receive a second briefing on Monday with the full task force. It should be interesting work."

"Okay, let's get started," she sits and opens her notebook. Formality aside, the heartfelt exchange was not lost on Calvin Sheppard.

***

The team and I are at our positions around the hotel. For the last two hours, I could think of nothing else but Jessica. I go back and forth arguing, telling myself she's just another one-night stand. Maybe it could go a week, maybe two. Who knows? Should I really get to know her? Thinking about her helped when I came out of my nightmare earlier. In that way, it was good, but this could be a dangerous distraction. Why can't I get her out of my head? Down in flames, I'm telling you Andiamo, you are going down in flames.

Breaking from my reverie, we finally get a little action. I dismiss the image of Jessica as Mitch barks in my ear. It's time to go to work.

"He's coming from your nine Toni, wearing black TAC clothes and a black ball cap that's turned backward. Jesus, he looks like maybe he could be in Grade School."

"Got him, Mitch, everyone ready to move?" One by one I hear whispers of 'roger that'.

"On my signal, I'll mark him after which you move in for the capture." Our subject is setting up to scope out his target for the night's entertainment. I patiently wait until he has his target in sight before I gently squeeze the trigger of my own rifle.

"Now," I urgently whisper. All move in on the target. He's looking thoroughly confused as to why he was covered in paint.

"What da fuck? I'll get whoever did this, feel me? Hey mother fuckers, let go of me! I ain't done nuttin'." He keeps screaming at my team. "Let me the fuck alone." They quickly take the kicking and screaming target into the office security had set aside.

I come down from my perch and join our little delinquent and Karl in the security office. The others remain outside the door. His curses assault my ears.

"Mitch, are the police on their way?" I ask receiving the affirmative. "Thanks, let's break it down."

I turn to our little sniper. "Well, that's a hell of a mouth you have kid. What are you, twelve? You in a gang?"

"What da fuck's it to ya, bitch. You got no cause holding me here. I ain't done nuttin', dawg."

"That's why you have this paintball apparatus. What you been doing with this?" I ask, admiring his rifle. I receive an angry glare as my response. "What's your name kid?"

"Fuck you. Ya ain't got no rights dissing me, girl."

"Okay Mr. Fuck You, I'm Toni. I'm the *girl* who sniped your sorry ass." He did not like hearing that. He wasn't happy that a girl captured him.

"How long did you think you'd get away with the sniping? You think you're that smart, punk? They asked me today to find you. It didn't take us ten minutes to figure your punk ass out." To tell the truth a little longer than that but he doesn't have to know.

"Fuck you, bitch. I don't have nuttin to say to your ass and you'll regret this, feel me?"

"They're going to throw your punk ass in jail for the rest of your natural life, feel me? Why you may ask? Because they're going to argue that you were practicing for a terrorist attack and in this day and age, they'll try you as an adult and put you away for good. We're just waiting for the cops to get here."

"Wait da fuck a minute. I ain't no terrorist dawg. I just doing this for fun. I got bored and wanted somethin' to do. They can't put me in no jail. They can't put me in no fuckin' jail! I ain't hurt nobody. I was just having fun. Can't put me in no jail!"

"Well then Mr. Fuck-you, I suggest you start talking to me and convince me your sorry ass is worth keeping out of the slammer for the rest of your pathetic no good life." He glares at me and sits in silence for a good several seconds then nervously scans the room looking for an escape.

"Okay, cops should be here any minute," I shrug my shoulders. "Karl, watch him and make sure he gets turned over when they show. Tell them I'll meet them at the precinct to fill out the paperwork for the hotel."

"Ya, good, I tell them, Sarge." Karl sets his sights and stares daggers at our little sniper. He can be quite intimidating with his six foot seven well-cut body and a hard face. I move toward the door of the office when the kid starts shouting.

"Hey, Bitch, you can't do this! Don't leave me with this Nazi mother fucker!" He definitely has quite a nasty attitude. I'm starting to admire his spirit and Karl is foaming at the mouth because, though he is from Germany with the requisite blonde hair and beautiful blue eyes, he is as far from being a Nazi as I am.

The spunk in this kid reminds me of the way I was once. That fire could get him into deeper trouble than he is now. I stop at the door and slowly turn around.

"Kid, you are pissing me the hell off. I can guarantee you won't like me when I'm pissed off. I can be quite nasty. You need to clean up that mouth of yours buddy or I will clean it for you." I give him the 'look' and it put terror in his eyes along with a wet stain down the leg of his trousers.

"Well now, ain't this a switch. If you can't handle a look from me, how the hell are you going to handle the box? "You're going to be someone's bitch inside a couple hours punk. Are you sure you want to mess with me? Now, I want your name."

"Frankie Tee," he looks at me with rage and fear in his eyes then stares holes in the wall next to him. "I ain't in no gang. Don't need 'em."

"Well Frankie, that's a start. Now I need to be convinced that your ass is worth keeping out of prison. How old are you Frankie?"

"I'm fourteen. You gonna really keep me out of trouble, dawg? My Grams is going to kill me." Frankie loses his bravado.

Well, this kid has some semblance of manners after all.

"Frankie, you had to know that you'd get caught eventually. Didn't you think about what you were going to tell your Grandmother? I know you're not stupid enough to believe you could get away with this for long."

"I planned on moving someplace else before they got close to me. I had them idiots running around in circles, dawg. I figured two more nights of target practice before I bounced. I didn't count on a bitch would figure it all," he spouts off.

He had to save a little face, so I let the last remark slide.

"Uh-huh, so tell me, Frankie, what do you think I should do with you now?" His face drops. He hangs his head, shrugs his shoulders. I shake my head and look at Karl who's still staring holes into Frankie for the Nazi remark.

"What do you think I should do with Frankie, Karl?"

"String him up by bootstraps." Karl nods his head once.

"Well Karl, I don't know. I think there may be something worth saving somewhere in all that attitude. I know his Grandmother taught him better than to go shooting people with paint just for the fun of it. Though this is a sweet setup you have here, Tippman A-5 right?" Same setup I used on him.

"Yeah," he nods.

"Nice, it's pricey though, top of the line. Where'd you get it?"

"My Grams got it for me for Christmas thought it would keep me out of trouble."

"Well, that certainly backfired didn't it," I challenge.

Carrie walks into the office before he can answer and whispers in my ear that the cops are in the waiting area.

"Okay, thanks. Tell them to give me a couple minutes with the kid. Then let them in. I turn to Frankie who by now is petrified.

"Okay Frankie, let me tell you what's going to happen. You are going with the officers to be charged and booked." When he starts to say something, I cut him off.

"Look, you are going to have to trust me, Frankie. I know it's a hard thing to do because you don't know dick about me, but you will listen to what I'm saying. Otherwise, I don't give a damn what happens to you." I stare at him and again he hangs his head.

"You're going to be charged and booked. Your Grandmother will be notified."

"Fuck, this sucks. Why they call my Grams for?" He has a pleading look in his tearing eyes.

"Why? I'll tell you why, because you are a minor, Frankie." He turns his head and stares at the wall again. "Look at me, Frankie. Look at me." He shoots venom from those big brown eyes of his and his dark ebony skin somehow seems darker.

"I'm telling you how this is going down and how I want you to handle yourself because I'm going to cut you a break Frankie. I don't know why I think you fucking deserve one, but I'm giving it to you."

I tell Frankie everything that's going to happen to him for the rest of the weekend and once he gets out on Monday, where he needs to report.

Mitch comes up behind me and puts his hand on my shoulder. I almost rip him apart. I tend to be on high alert especially after a trip down memory lane and he knows better than to come up behind me. He's always brave enough to do it anyway.

"Take it easy there kiddo." He hangs the offending arm over my shoulder as we watch the cops put Frankie in the squad car. He whispers in my ear, "Softie."

"Fuck you, Mitch," I scowl while he laughs.

"You know, that kid reminds me of someone."

"Yeah, he reminds me of someone too. I have to get to the precinct and do all the paperwork. I notified Tyrell. He'll be there to represent Frankie. Will you take care of things here and our office report? I need some shuteye before I totally collapse." The scant couple of restless hours I took this afternoon seem but a distant nightmare.

"Sure kid. I'll take care of it. You know, I think you'll do that kid a world of good. You did the right thing, Toni."

"Thanks, Mitch. I owe you one. I have a feeling this kid is going to give me a run for my money. See you later."

Trying to take my brain from Frankie, thoughts of Jessica sneak into my head yet again. Damn it. You spent one night with this girl and you're acting like a love-starved puppy.

Mitch looks after me as I make my way to the parking garage. "Do it to it kid." He shakes his head and walks away smiling.

Arriving home shortly after four in the morning, I drop everything I'm carrying, step over my mess, and strip on the way to my bedroom to collapse on my oh-so-comfortable   bed.

CHAPTER FOUR

Sunday 28 June

I wake late Sunday morning groggy from a restless sleep filled with haunting visions. I live in historic Indian Village built between 1875 and 1924. Most were built-in 1894 like mine. There are House and Garden tours throughout the village, and no, I'm not on the tour circuit. Some of these houses are as much as 12,000 square feet. Though my place isn't quite that large, I do live comfortably in my brick colonial.

To observers, it looks like your basic city house. What no one would know is that I hired and fired contractor after contractor to build secret rooms and open old passages when restoring the place. No one knows what's here now. The official record shows a typical three-bedroom, three and a half baths, with living room, family room, library, kitchen, dining room, and basement. In my line of work, it's important to have several means of escape available.

It's a nice sized property sitting on a third acre corner lot. Large enough to maintain privacy. I've surrounded it with a wrought iron fence and gates at the front and sides and an eight-foot privacy fence creates a secluded are out back.

My parents helped with the landscaping, so it has a special place in my heart. There are Maple, Oak, and Black Walnut trees across the property. Shrubbery and assorted blooms form a border around the pool hot tub, and outdoor kitchen area.

The signature columns of the colonial period line the big north-facing front porch and double glass doors. I love the foyer. In fact, I fell in love with this property when I first laid eyes on it with its custom spiral handrail, 10' ceilings and oak-paneled walls running the full length of the house.

The cleverly disguised panels and decorative hide the escape paths that lead outside or to the basement tunnel system for those times when I might have to make a hasty exit.

The living room is immediately to the left off the great hall, with its great fireplace sitting handsomely along the east wall opposite a set of bay windows. The library is off the hall to the right and the kitchen and formal dining area at the rear of the house. Double French doors lead from the dining room out onto the back patio. My rooms are on the top floor along with office.

Downstairs is partially underground with my weight room, on-site security ops, and my personal armory safely tucked behind the mirrored bar.

We found the entrance to the old Underground Railroad tunnel system during one of the renovations. I did some investigating when we found it and discovered that the system leads out to the river and spanned across the city.

The railroad ended in 1865, before this place existed and was later used by rum runners during Prohibition. More than three-quarters of the liquor that fueled underground speakeasies across the country came across the Detroit River. That meant business was exceptional for our family.

I throw myself into a hard workout and finish with fifty laps in the pool and enjoy the midafternoon while I can. I head back in for a shower with my muscles singing. The pulsating spray feels wonderful and I let out a low groan as I leave the cool spray.

As I throw on some old comfortable jeans and a tank top, the phone rings.

"Ms. Andiamo, its Edna. I'm just letting you know the report for the night. It was a still night. No incidents."

"Thanks, Miss Edna. I appreciate the update, as always. Enjoy your Sunday." She's probably been to and from her church by now.

"No problem Ms. Andiamo. Be good for your Mama and I'll see you in the morning."

I start to hang up, then change my mind and dial the office, hoping to catch Mitch. He picks up after several rings.

"Storm Investigations, this is Mitch. How can I help you?"

"Ciao, Mitch. Been there all night or get there this morning?"

"Afternoon to you too, sunshine. I've been here since nine. Get everything squared away with the kid last night?" I roll my eyes even though I know he can't see me.

"I hate cop shops, but yeah I got everything squared away. Didn't get home until four this morning. If he gets to the office before me, keep him busy until I get there."

"Sure, I can think of several things I can bog him down with and stop rolling those eyes at me." How the hell did he know?

"Find out anything about Al-Hakeem?" Changing the subject and silently hoping he's found something we can use to find Al-Hakeem.

"Not much and because I know you kid." Damn, he's just too good.

"It's slow going. I've set bots to search and called in a few favors. I have a feeling the Feds have put up some smoke screens that we're going to have to work our way through before we gain any real traction. We'll find out soon enough either way. I can get through most of their security eventually if it's them." He waits for my reply.

"Good. Keep it under the radar. We don't need them coming down on our ass for hacking along with all this other shit right now."

"No problem. I'll handle it. What've you been working on today? You want to grab some dinner or something? Andrea's with her family and I desperately want to get out of it." I laugh. Sundays are for big family dinners.

"Sorry Mitch, I'm heading to my folks soon for Sunday dinner. I'd rather not with all that's going on but my brothers out of town and I don't dare say no to Mama."

"Oh, that's no joke, I wouldn't say no to your mother either. That would be a very scary situation," Mitch replies. He's met my mother and is deathly afraid of her.

"Ok guess I can't get out of it with Andrea," he sighs. I could imagine the look on his face at that though. Andrea's family was great, but they could talk your ear off. "Talk at you later then."

"Ciao, Mitch. Good luck." We hang up and I get ready to leave.

***

It takes me only 15 minutes to get to my parents' house. They live on the eastside in East Detroit, in what used to be 'Little Italy' back in the day. Now only a handful of the Italian families are left.

My parent's place is a three-bedroom ranch style house. God knows how we all survived growing up in this small house. The lawn is well-manicured as with all the lawns on the street. The front porch takes three steps to reach and is just big enough for the two lounge chairs that sit empty now.

My parents like to sit on the front stoop in the evenings and watch the world go by. I try to tell them it's not safe anymore because gangs have taken over the neighborhood but they still enjoy it. What's there to do? They've been sitting out there since they got married fifty-one years ago and bought the house. I doubt if they'll break their habit anytime soon.

The back door has a porch that again takes three steps to get to and opens into a small dining room. Bushes, mostly roses, surround the porch and backyard. My father grew roses for as long as I can remember.

There's a detached garage behind the house and he has a garden where he grows all his own cucumbers, lettuce, carrots, parsley, thyme, rosemary, peppers, and tomatoes. His tomatoes are legendary throughout the neighborhood. Across the drive from the side door in the neighbor's fence is a pole still bent from when I ran into it with a 1968 Delta 88 Oldsmobile after I returned from juvie.

I walk in the side door off the driveway and call out to my mother. She's busy stirring some marvelous concoction on the stove and my mind instantly flashes back to when I was a kid and the smell of dinner cooking. Back then, I was full of trouble and lived mostly on the streets. I didn't realize how desperately I could miss the taste and flavor of my mother's cooking until I sat in juvie.

The sweet smell hits me and I wipe the drool off my chin, take the three steps to the kitchen, and hug my mother. Taking a risk, I stick a finger in the pot and taste her incredible spaghetti sauce. She's made mostaccioli and meatballs for dinner. My stomach growls as my mother slaps my hand away. Pasta is one of my favorite meals.

"Ma, you shouldn't leave the door unlocked. You never know who's going to walk in."

My mother eyes me a moment as if to say 'yea you for instance' then waves her hand and replies, "yeah, yeah, yeah. So you keep saying. I knew you were on your way so I unlocked the door only a few minutes ago. You have no cause to be yelling at your Mama that way."

"Sorry Mom, I have a key and I don't want anything happening to you. You're my Mother and I love you."

"Oh, my Antonia, I know you protect me, but I know everyone in the neighborhood would never dare hurt us with you, your brother, and your Uncle Tony looking after us."

My mother pinches my cheek then taps it with an open hand a couple times while she's lecturing me. Really? Did she have to pinch my cheek?

Of course, my mother's right. No one would dare go after my family because for fear of my Uncle, but I hate like hell getting my cheek pinched. You'd think I'd have outgrown it considering the life I lead, but I guess you never outgrow your mama and for her, your baby is always your baby.

"Speaking of which, I saw Uncle Tony Friday," I respond to my mother, rubbing my cheek when she turns back to her cooking. "He sends his love and well wishes to you and Papa. I understand that he's in Italy with Alex."

I bring this up now before anyone else gets here so maybe, just maybe, she'll be calm by the time we settle for dinner. But I catch a glimpse of her scowl. Uh-oh, maybe not. She doesn't often give her emotions away unless you screw up. Then, she makes her feelings known in no uncertain terms.

"So your brother told me. I swear I could give your Uncle a good talking to next time I see him. I'm not sure I like your brother being around him so much. Bad enough you travel so much with him but now your brother too?

"You're your Uncle Tony is no good. You both need to watch yourselves around him. You don't need to turn out like him or end up in prison. I couldn't handle it if that happened. Once was enough you hear?"

"Yes, Mama I hear you." I roll my eyes. Yep, I'm not going to hear the end of it tonight, and while my mother launches into a tirade, I try to tune her out by thinking of ways to get back at my brother. I love my mother dearly, but sometimes she goes on and on.

While she's continuing her lecture on the misadventures of my Uncle, I begin to get things out and set the tables while making the appropriate responses when necessary to let my mother know I'm still listening.

My Great-grandfather, Tito Andiamo, brought the family to this country in 1900 from Italy to get away from the Mafia. Nonno, his son Renato and my grandfather, brought us back into the fold. He made his bones during Prohibition, grew powerful and eventually took over as head of the Detroit Family. He didn't hold it very long as he died from a stroke only a few months into his reign. From him, the torch passed to my Uncle Tony at a young age. There were struggles early on, but he proved himself and kept hold of the reigns.

My father never liked the lifestyle and tried to shield all of us from the life. Our family dinners mean a lot to him. They're huge affairs and now have more meaning to me than when I was growing up. Back then I always found excuses to finish in a hurry or not be there at all. I had better things to do, after all. As I said though, I found out the hard way that Mama's dinners were very hard to beat.

Two adults and six kids barely squeeze into my parents' house. When you add spouses and children, to the two youngest who still live at home, the house is overflowing. There's usually twenty-four of us when we get together, unless my brother and I bring a date. Tonight, there'll be twenty-three. My brother's absence will be felt.

We are a family who talks, bickers, and argues almost every day sometimes about stupid, petty stuff. But don't be fooled. We're very close and if you cross one of us you cross all of us. You do not want this bunch as enemies.

I finish setting the tables and putting out the pitchers of wine, water, and bottles of soda, when I hear the first of my siblings arrive. By the sound of only one child, I'm guessing it's my sister Beth. This is confirmed a moment later when little Ashley runs up to me and jumps into my arms.

"Aunt Toni," she screams!

She jumps down again and runs into the living room to turn on the TV. This four-year-old is one little spitfire, just like me. She's fearless, smart, and she would play baseball in a dress if she could. Well, that part is not like me. I certainly wouldn't wear a dress. Jeffrey enters laughing at the antics of his daughter.

"Hi Toni," he kisses me on the cheek, grabs a beer from the fridge, and follows his daughter into the living room. Those two are a pair. I turn to my sister and kiss her on the cheek.

"Hey Sis," I say. "Long time no see."

It's only been two days since I last saw my sister. She's my accountant and handles the financial reporting end of my businesses. She has her own firm and right now, she works part-time because she's due to drop her next bambino at any moment.

"Toni! I didn't think you'd be here tonight. I thought you'd be with Uncle Tony's in Italy."

"I have work here and Alex has the duty this time."

"Oh shit, that means Mama's on the warpath," Beth rolls her eyes.

"Don't worry," I laugh. "I already took the flack. She should be a little subdued for dinner."

"You know sometimes it's quite wonderful having a big sister to take all the crap for you. Where's Mia? Shouldn't she be with you tonight or is she working?"

"You don't want to go there, Beth."

"Uh-oh I'm glad I don't come to big Sis for relationship advice," she starts laughing, shaking her head.

"Hey, I give great advice and since I date a lot I know quite a bit about relationships. I know I'm not going to stay in one for long." She lifts her hands in an 'I give up' gesture. She understands the devastation I went through with Maggie and why I refuse to deal with any emotional bonds.

"Okay, okay. I'll drop the subject, but you know one of these days you're going to fall for someone and fall hard," she gives me a knowing look. "Well, at least you don't have kids or a husband who doesn't know beans about how to keep a checkbook. It's a darn good thing I'm a

CPA. I swear Jeff only married me because I'm good with figures."

"He's not as dumb as he pretends to be. It's only one figure he was after and at least he had the good taste to snatch you up. Besides, why have kids when I have a bunch of nieces and nephews I can spoil? You guys already did the work for me. All I have to do is give them back when I'm through being a bad influence." I grin at her.

"Is that why all these kids love you? All this time, I thought it was your sparkling personality. You sure had me fooled. Now you'll regret ever giving up that secret."

By this point we're laughing so hard we don't notice Ashley in the dining room until she starts pulling on her mom's shirt.

"Mommy, how come you and Aunt Toni are laughing about secrets? Secrets can't be laughed at," she scolds us. "Secrets are kept secret."

We both shake our heads and try to explain the difference between keeping secrets and surprises. I pick her up and put her on my knee. We explain to her if anyone should ask her to keep a secret, even someone she knows, it is not right. Surprises are okay because they're like presents that can be told or given to someone eventually.

"Ashley if someone touches your pee-pee and tells you not to tell anyone, that's bad. Even if you know them and they tell you it's okay to do that, it's not. If your friend tells you someone touches them and tells you to keep that a secret, it's also wrong. If your friend tells you she likes someone and doesn't want you to tell them then that's okay. Can you understand the difference? You don't want to be a snitch but you definitely need to speak up if someone touches your boobies or pee-pee alright Sweetie?" Her mother explains.

You can never be too careful with kids and potential predators like pedophiles, even if they aren't strangers. Ashley's happy with her new understanding and runs off to tell her daddy what she learned.

Dinner is a loud affair, and everyone likes to catch up on each other's lives. Add in the addition of all the little ones and it's almost deafening. I have little John sitting in my lap as I feed him off my plate. For some reason, all the kids like to be around Aunt Toni. I must be a cool aunt.

Charlie Jr. is explaining to me the wonders of biology that he learned in school today and Chris asks me to come over and fix his bike because everyone uses it and breaks his things. Avery is on the floor clinging to my leg. Ashley is clinging to the other leg fighting with Avery. I do so enjoy dinner with my family. It makes me feel so alive and loved. I'm also a sarcastic shit.

Somehow, we all made it through with Mama only saying nasty things about my brother and Uncle twice. It's a good record for her.

My Pop walks in just as I'm just cleaning the last dish. He comes over, kisses my cheek, and thanks me for doing the cleanup. I know he wants something because he hardly ever kisses and thanks me.

"What's up Pop?"

"I'm worried, Antonia. Your brother is spending so much time with your Uncle and I'm not naïve. I know the kind of man my brother is. I'm just not so sure your brother should be taking after him." My father is frowning over his cup of coffee and is has trouble looking me in the eye.

"Papa---" I'm not quite sure what to say to my father. My brother owes me big time since I got this double duty, first Mom now Dad.

"Papa, Alex knows what he's doing. He has a good head for business and Uncle Tony can teach him even more. Look at all he's taught me. He's a big boy Dad and he does well for the famiglia. He learned that from you, who takes good care of all of us. There's no need to worry. He's happy when it comes to his work and that's all it is Papa, work."

"Antonia, I know the work you do for him and I know what he means to you. I don't know," he shakes his head staring into his empty cup of coffee. "I suppose if everybody is doing what they are good at and what they want to do, then that's a good thing.

"Still, you choose a hard life for yourself. I only wish that you and Alex would do the same things as your sisters and your brother, get married and settle down. However, if you two are happy, then I must put up with your mother's lectures. Forgive me! I was just trying to save my own skin."

That's my Pop. He starts out giving me the third degree and ends up asking me to forgive him. He's nobody's fool, though.

"Papa, I know you worry about us, but you didn't raise idiots. Now, you never have to apologize for trying to save your skin from Mama. I think you're safe tonight. I took the brunt of her heat while I was setting up for dinner."

"Well, I do owe you my thanks then. It must be tough being the oldest, having to be the strongest, wisest, and always trying to keep the peace. I don't know what I did wrong to make you a homosexual. I had to have done something to make you turn out that way, but at least I did something right with you. I think I'm going to go to bed. It's been a long day. Goodnight Antonia," and with that my father kisses my cheek and disappears from the kitchen.

I stare after him with tears in my eyes. My Catholic guilt is hard at work now. Don't you know Dad that you did everything right? It breaks my heart to know he believes he did something wrong. He's told me it makes him sick to think about me with another woman and every time I try to speak to him about it, he shuts me down.

Same with my mother only her excuse was I'm just going through a phase. I wish I could explain to them why I am the way I am but I still have no idea myself. I just am and have been since I had a crush on my second-grade teacher. She crushed my heart when she married and moved to Florida.

I ranted, I raved. I slept with as many boys as I could, did drugs, all to no avail. I still couldn't bury these feelings. I believed I had no one to talk to or help me deal with my homosexuality, certainly not my parent's or the Church they strictly clung to.

I was rejected everywhere I turned. With drugs, I didn't have to deal with anything. I could sleep with guys though it did nothing for me and though it made me sick at times, I could control it. I could ignore the rejection and fit in for a time. I was no longer a loner. The drugs clouded my thinking and helped create a lot of anger. That anger had no direction so I pointed it at everyone.

It's why I had my first taste of death at such a young age and I discovered with that first kill, I had an affinity for the extinction of human life without any remorse or feeling. It didn't thrill me. I didn't get any satisfaction from it. I handled a situation.

Eventually, I realized I could do it for money, lots of money. The day I left the Juvenile Detention facility, my Uncle began honing my skills so to blossom into his private deadly weapon. It took me a long time to be at peace, both with being gay and that I could kill without blinking an eye.

Once again, words remain unspoken with my Papa. My parents have never turned me away or treated any of my dates with anything but the utmost respect. But my father doesn't come to me like this. He's not one to bare his soul to his children so it must have taken a lot for him to say something to me.

As I said, he's nobody's fool. We skirted the issue of my Uncle's activities as well as my own. As a bonus, he stirred my Catholic guilt. I shake my head and think about what it was he didn't say. I'm sure he knows more than I should be comfortable with.

With my heart heavy, I sigh, turn back to the sink, wipe the counter, and hang the towel across the edge of the sink to dry. Taking one last look around, I rub my face, lock up, and head for home. Could this night get any worse?

CHAPTER FIVE

Monday 29 June - morning

I wake to buzzing at the front gate as well as my phone. Someone is desperately trying to get hold of me. It's Mitch.

"Yeah, Mitch. What the fuck?" I groggily answer.

"Toni, let me in now! It's important. Come on come on. Hurry!"

"Alright, alright I'm coming. Jesus Mitch."

I hit the buzzer to let him in, trying to clear my head. He. Something is seriously wrong. I meet him at the front door and can't explain the look on his face, but I know it's something bad.

"What's wrong Mitch? Is Andrea ok? What's going on?" I hurriedly inquire of my friend, trying to clear the cobwebs. He's shaking his head never taking his eyes off me.

"Toni, it's your parents," Mitch tells me. A feeling of dread settles in my stomach.

"Shit, shit, shit," I exclaim running up the stairs to get dressed.

"Toni, wait!" Mitch calls out halting me in my tracks with his tone. I turn around.

"There's been an explosion at their house…," he starts to say but trails off. I plop down on the stairs trying to process what he's saying.

"What?" I'm trying to wrap my head around this.

Refusing to believe what he said, I stand up and resume my trip up the stairs to get dressed. I rush around, throwing on the clothes I wore earlier tonight. This night just got worse.

Why did I have to say it? I berate myself, and in a scant two minutes, we're out the door. Mitch driving like a man on fire, barreling our way to my family's home.

We arrive to find both sides of the street cordoned off by police tape. The street if filled with fire engines, police cars, and emergency crews parked everywhere. I get out and start running to get as close to our house as we can get. I stagger just a bit when I see the destruction. Mitch catches and steadies me.

Bricks and shards furniture and everyday items are strewn everywhere. Where our house once stood is now a smoldering, smoking mess. No one stood a chance of survival. The houses on either side are scorched and the torn. The fences are mangled and melted, no longer separating property.

The back corner furthest from the house is all that remains of the garage. My parents' cars are nothing but twisted, molten metal.

I watch as EMT's treat the injured, hoping to see my parents or sisters, not finding them. Then, I drop to my knees as I see tarps covering several bodies. My family. Someone close by identifies himself as ATF. I tell him who I am, ask a bunch of questions and receive what little answers he was able to give. He tells me a detective from the Eastpointe Police will be in touch.

I let him get back to his work as I try to pull myself together. I take the agony, the grief, the sorrow and ball it all up, tucking it away for safe keeping. There'll be time in the future to take it out and process. Right now, I need to get this situation under control and then find the bastard who did this.

The devastation is all around me as the County Morgue's van rolls up to spirit my family away. I turn to stone as I notice Jessica talking to ATF personnel. She notices me just then and her jaw drops. She excuses herself and walks over to me.

"Toni? What are you...," she stops herself as she realizes why I'm here. "Oh no! Oh, Toni, I'm so sorry."

"The question is not why I am here but why you are?" I respond with a hint of disdain.

"I'm with the FBI. I take it this is your family. I have reason to believe this is related to something we're working on."

My mouth drops and for a moment I'm stunned into silence. She's with the fucking FBI? Damn, I slept with a Fed? She sure didn't act like a fed the other night. Well shit. I shake my head. Could this be related? Oh, shit. Shit, shit, shit. Fucking Al-Hakeem... no. I close my eyes trying to keep that ball of grief and building rage contained.

"Related how?" I ask revealing none of my thoughts.

"I can't tell you that right now," she winced. I open my eyes then and stare burning holes of suspicion and anger into her.

"This is about Mansur al-Hakeem isn't it," I claim.

"How...what do you know about this?" She turns on her cop persona now.

"I can't say at this moment. Obviously, you need to get answers from your office," I sneer.

"I see. That's how you want to play this. I'm sorry for your loss Toni. I truly am. I'll talk to you in a few minutes," and with that, she turned on her heel walking away to continue her work. I couldn't do anything but stare.

"What the hell was that all about," Mitch turns to me.

"Long story. Tell me how you heard about this. The cops wouldn't have come to me until they received positive identification," I turn to Mitch, my anger building.

"I was on my way to the office to check some pings from the bots I set up. I usually listen to the police bands, you know, to make sure none of our security sites are involved in any incidents. That's when I heard the talk about your parent's place. I recognized the address and rushed to get you. I'm so sorry Toni." Mitch looks as crushed as I feel.

Suddenly, Miss Edna joins Mitch at my side. Together, they pull me away from the wreckage. I didn't have to say, 'Sorry ass sons of bitches! I'll get every single sack of shit that's responsible for this. I'll fucking fry their asses. I swear to God, every single fucker who had even the slightest little thing to do with this is going to pay.' I didn't have to say it, it rolled off me. As my rage begins to spill, Mitch grabs me, hugs me close.

"Toni, I know you're spitting nails right now," he whispers in my ear. "But there's a mess of cops and Feds who might take it seriously if they know you're about to go on a murder spree. Let's find out who and why first. Okay, kiddo? Let's just take care of family business right now."

Mitch, always the only one who could read me when no one else could. He was right. I couldn't to lose it right here, right now. Holding everything in, I pull back from Mitch, take a deep breath, roll the rage back into a ball, tuck it deep in the pit of my stomach, and pull myself together.

"You're right Mitch." I turn to Miss Edna. She looks grief-stricken, crestfallen. For the first time since I've known her, she looks every bit her age. All the rage I feel turns to ice as I see her mirroring my misery.

"Miss Edna." She turns to me with tears and quiet terror in her eyes.

"I---" I clear my throat to keep my voice from cracking. "I need you to coordinate with Murray and put massive security around the rest of my family. Now, if you would, please."

"It will be taken care of Ms. Andiamo. I'll see to it personally. I already have a list of those we need. I believe the police need to speak to you."

"Yes, I suppose they do," I quip. "I need to contact the rest of my family. Now. I suppose I also better see who's in charge." I take another deep breath and square my shoulders.

Through all this, I forget about Jessica. I let myself be spirited away by a Jr G-man to a command center the Eastpointe Police set up.

"Mitch, you're with me." Jr. G-man looks like he wants to object but one look at my face and he wisely decides to keep his mouth shut.

I spot Jessica heading to the command center, her phone jammed tightly against her ear, arguing with someone on the other end. She gets there just a moment before Mitch and I arrive.

I stifle the anger I feel at her betrayal. Why it feels like a betrayal, I don't know. I only slept with her once for Christ sake. All I know is the fury I feel and the need to put it somewhere.

Jessica looks at us as she settles in a chair bolted to the floor. There's a quick something in her eyes, sorrow maybe, but I ignore it. She gestures to another chair for me to sit. I do so without saying a word, my face hard as stone.

Never taking her eyes off me, she addresses the room in her soft-spoken way. "Thank-you for your help, but I'll take care of Ms. Andiamo now." She looks to Mitch and her Junior G's as she dismisses them. Mitch is having none of it.

I continue to stare in front of me focusing on a small hole in the wall. Looks as if someone put a fist in it. I wouldn't mind putting my own fist through it now. I control the urge.

Two men in bad suits stick out in the far corner, must be the detectives from the Eastpointe PD. A couple of ATF agents sit in bolted down chairs as well. Cramped in this tiny space. Jessica realizes Mitch isn't moving and waits a few moments before speaking.

"She'll be okay," Jessica states kindly. Mitch still doesn't move.

"Let me start off by saying I truly am sorry for your loss," she pauses. "Shit." She sighs, pain in her eyes. "Everybody clear out. I need a few moments alone with Ms. Andiamo." She continues to look helplessly into my eyes. It's almost painful to watch.

I break contact with those eyes and look back at Mitch to give him a nod. We wait until the room clears. She walks forward and boosts her hip on the console next to me; tries to take my hand. I know it's childish, but I pull back. She tries again and this time I let her.

I whisper through clenched teeth, "You knew, didn't you." It wasn't a question.

"You knew when we first met. You knew who I was. Was that part of your job? To seduce me? To get me to sleep with you so I'd spill my secrets? Did you really think because I fucked you that I'd suddenly reveal everything about myself? About my uncle?" Venom spews and another pained expression crosses her face.

"Yes, I knew exactly who I slept with. No, Toni, it wasn't my job to seduce you. I did it because I wanted to, wanted you. I didn't know," she responds quietly. I turn to her with disbelief. Her eyes remain locked with mine as a confirmation of her statement.

"I did not know until you showed up here, that you were the person that's connected to Al-Hakeem. It just didn't register with me. I was just as surprised to see you here as you are about me being with the FBI. Frankly, I'm more surprised you didn't run a background check after we met, didn't take me for a Fed. And, by the Goddess, I prayed this moment wouldn't come."

"Why? Why sleep with me then? No, I didn't run you. I should've. I just thought I could enjoy the feeling I got from it. Why didn't you tell me?

"I have no real answer for you Toni except to say that, like you, I wanted to enjoy it. I enjoyed the night I spent with you and regret nothing. Frankly, I thought once you found out that I'm a Fed you'd disappear without a trace and I didn't want that. I wanted to see you again. It makes this situation all kinds of sticky no matter what angle you look at it." She shook head, lightly squeezing my hand for reassurance.

"Oh, it's sticky alright." I pull my hand free and pace the room. Deal with her later, deal with it later. What's to deal with? Chalk it up to another one-night stand.

"Why? Why go after innocent people? Why go after my family?" I ask not giving Jessica a chance to answer or go into detail as I change the subject.

"I mean, I knew there was a risk. That's why I had an extra security detail at my Uncle's place. I just never thought they'd go after my family. It's my fault. I'm responsible for their deaths." I didn't mean for that last part to slip from my mouth. I throw my head back and fight for air.

Jessica starts to say something but I cut her off. "Don't worry. I'm not going to sit here and feel sorry for myself. I'm not going to wallow in self-pity." Another deep breath. Now, set the steel in place. No, I won't feel sorry for myself. I want the bastards who did this and I will find them. When I find them, I will extract my revenge.

Unsure of what to do next, Jessica hesitates, then puts her arms around me and holds tightly. She knows how much I'm bleeding inside, though for the life of me I don't know how. I give away nothing, but she seems to understand.

I lean back into her and, for a precious moment, I feel safe and protected. For a split second, I forget that my life has been blown apart. That my parents and younger sisters' bodies are in pieces. I pray to God to let me have this little moment. I close my eyes and sigh, not wanting to pull away from Jessica's warm embrace.

For a moment, I glimpse what it's like not to have a bull's eye painted on my back. She gave that gift, if only briefly.

Another deep breath and I quickly break away to continue pacing. She says nothing and waits for me to settle, my nerves radiating in waves. This isn't like me. I'm trained to show nothing; to keep a cool head in all situations. Idiot. It's not usually your family that's killed. I steel myself, turn, and calmly take my seat once again.

"Okay, let's get this over with. I still need to notify the rest of my family."

"All right, this shouldn't take too long." She waits until I turn around. "I'll tell everyone they can come back in. Okay?"

I nod, taking a deep breath and letting it out slowly. I'm confused at the way Jessica is handling all of this. Mitch walks in, interrupting my thoughts. He stands possessively next to me, and rests his hand on my shoulder for support. I reach up and pat it to let him know I'm okay. He keeps his hand there anyway and hands me a bottle of water with the other.

"Thanks, Mitch," I respond. He notices that my eyes are red and believing Jessica is to blame for that, stares daggers into her. He starts to hurl his anger when the rest of the troops come in. They take up positions around the cramped trailer and Jessica takes over the room.

They really didn't have anything to report yet. It's too early in the investigation and blah, blah, blah. Of course, I answered their standard questions, does anyone have a grudge, did they have any enemies? They also wanted to know why the Feds were there.

In the back of my mind, one question kept coming around. How did Al-Hakeem know? Jessica steered all questions to her and didn't answer much of anything. Just like a good

Fed. She made sure she didn't mention anything about Al-Hakeem. When everyone left, I ask Mitch to wait outside for me. He gives an imperceptible nod and disappears through the door.

"Toni, I know you have a lot to do right now but my superiors need to have a word with you at our offices about this whole situation."

"Of course they do," I retorted and before she could say anything, I raise my hands as an apology.

"Alright, I'll let you know when I'm through. Don't worry, it'll be later today." I get out of my chair to leave.

"Toni, I truly am sorry about your family." I nod again and as I take my leave, she steps in my way, gathers me into her arms, and tenderly places her lips to mine. Despite my misgivings, I couldn't help myself, I return her gesture.

***

A half-hour later, I gather the family at my house and let them know what happened to our parents and sisters. Grief, shock and anger ripple through the room. I don't know how to comfort them.

Hell, I don't' know how to comfort myself. I could give them little more than what law enforcement gave me. The only thing I could give them is reassurance and my promise: I *will* find out who and they *will* pay.

"Alex and Uncle Tony are about half an hour out. They called from the plane," Beth tells me. I give her a barely noticeable nod of acknowledgment.

"I've arranged security for all of you," I explain. "You don't go anywhere or do anything without a detail. I'd like to put every single one of you under lock and key, but I know you wouldn't go for it. So, I don't want to hear any bitching about how tight the security is because I'm not losing anyone else."

I look around the room. Nobody's willing to challenge me. They all know what I'm feeling. They all feel the same. I'm not taking any more chances with my family.

"I'll handle security details for the church, funeral procession, and the viewings. Beth will handle all the communications with the funeral home. Mom and Dad had everything planned and paid for so all we have to do is meet at the church to go over the specifics for the service."

I try to pay attention to what I'm saying but everything is spinning around in my head. Al-Hakeem. Jessica. I feel like I don't know which way is up.

Why did he go after *my* family and not Uncle Tony's? How did he know of my involvement before I knew? And this crap with Jessica, this all I need. She's a Fed for Christ's sake and she withheld that knowledge from me.

She probably wants to put you away for the rest of your natural life. So, what is it about her that pulls at me? Why should I trust her to be straight with me? I keep my face hard as stone.

"Keep it cool, kid," Mitch whispers to me as I leave the living room, ready to get work.

"We'll get through this. The rest of the team's together at the office. I'll have Murray help Miss Edna with security details." With a kiss on my cheek, Mitch is out the door.

***

Jessica quickly gathers the rest of her crew and heads back to her office. Her mind wanders to the murder of her own parents during a sting gone bad. The bastards were never caught. She was fifteen.

Shaking off memories of her own loss, she expertly threads traffic on the way to brief those above her. What has she gotten herself into, anyway? How did Toni know about Mansur al-Hakeem? Either there's a leak or she's more involved than she let on. If there's a leak, it's up to me to find out who they are, damn it.

Should she trust Toni? That wasn't just her call. She'd have to go with whatever her boss decided. Shaking her head, she knew that it wasn't' that simple. "You better keep a clear head on this one, girl," she told herself.

***

"Ms. Andiamo, the security arrangements are in place. Your sisters and your brother are on their way to their homes with their guard detail, security teams are stationed around their homes as well."

"Miss Edna, what would I do without you? Thank you for all your work on this."

"Ms. Andiamo, there's no call for thanking me for doing my job, one I should've done better. If I did, if I insisted on protecting your family as well, then nobody would be dead now." She looks down at her shoes, willing the tears away.

"Miss Edna," I take her gently by her shoulders, willing her to look at me. "This is in no way, whatsoever, your fault. There was no reason to believe they were in any real danger. If anything, it's my fault. I take full responsibility. I underestimated Al-Hakeem and my family has paid the price. I'm the one that should've ordered security for my own family. On this point, Miss Edna, you can't argue with me."

Miss Edna looks at me with respect. I'll give her credit. Though tears were in her eyes, she didn't let them fall. I admire Miss Edna as much as she does me. All of us are Miss Edna's family and she treats us as such.

"You are my responsibility, too, Miss Edna. You are one of my family and I won't lose you. Murray will make sure you have a security detail of your own.

"Alright Ms. Andiamo, don't you go worrying about me. Just take care of your family now."

"Miss Edna, you *are* my family." I think I saw her blush as she left my office. Mitch bullied his way in. He hands me a file so thick I hardly believe it.

"They have this much on the guy, and haven't put him away yet? Come on, are these people idiots?" I look at him incredulously.

Mitch answers, "For some reason, he's been one step ahead of every organization that's chasing him. He's a damn ghost. The only way he can do that is if he's got someone on the inside; someone high up"

"Shit. Well, he doesn't have the inside track with anyone in our organization, so the leak had to come from somewhere else. Shit, it could be the NSC or the CIA, or the DHS, or the DOD, or the F fucking B of I or maybe even Interpol. It could be any one of them, and this is a bunch of bullshit!"

I rub my eyes and stare out the window at the river trying to make sense of everything. Trying to keep calm. Trying to will away the sight of four tarp covered bodies lying in the idle of the street.

I tell myself to remember the rules. But, when I find out who's responsible for this, I'm saying to hell with the rules. I feel my rage start to well up and it takes everything I have to swallow it back down again. It sticks in my craw. I know it's just going to fester but I need to keep it contained for just awhile or it'll ruin, not just me, but everyone around me.

"Speaking of the FBI," Mitch starts out with a casual tone. "What's going on with this Jessica agent? Who is she and what's between you two?" He questions me.

"I couldn't believe it myself," I grimace and turn back to face Mitch.

"I ran into her the other night at a bar and we spent some incredible face time together, know what I'm saying? Next thing I know, she's there tonight, at the scene of my family's death. Tells me she didn't know that I'm connected to any of this but I'm not sure I believe her. I can't look at this as pure coincidence. You know how I feel about that."

"Yeah, there ain't such a thing."

"Exactly and thanks Mitch, for everything."

"Sure, someone's got to look after your pretty ass. I've gotten too attached to it to let anything happen to you." He walks out the door.

God bless Mitch. I start tearing. Okay stop this shit, I berate myself. Concentrate on finding this asshole. I roughly rub the tears off my cheeks, pick up the file, and start scanning through it. When I finish, I turn off the light, plop down on a couch, rub my face, and, for a few silent moments, let myself grieve.

I remember playing bocce ball and lawn darts in the backyard and family reunions in the basement; my sisters playing *Gong Show* with the neighborhood kids. My mother cooking just the other night and my father leaning against the kitchen counter worried about my brother and admonishing me.

Rage, sadness, and guilt grate on my nerves. Words will be forever unspoken now. Damn it! Damn it all to hell! I get up and head off to see my Uncle.

***

Taking a circuitous route to my uncle's house, I watch to make sure I don't have a tail. I see no one. Alex greets me at the door and holds on.

"Sis, I don't know what to say…," grief overwhelms my brother and he sobs into my shoulder.

My Uncle is just settling in from his trip and I disappear in his arms as he gathers me in for a hug. "Antonia, I'm so sorry. You are all so special to me. I can't believe this. Do you know what happened?" he questions me.

"It has to be al-Hakeem. Tell me, Padrino, what the hell is going on? What do you know about this guy? The FBI hasn't even called yet. Why does this guy want us so bad?" I fire questions at him, not giving him a chance to answer.

"I have to have an explanation before I meet with this task force. I'm the one that has to answer their questions. I need answers for that, Padrino. I need them now."

He knows I'm grieving as he grieves, or he wouldn't tolerate such treatment. He barely keeps his own anger in check as he answers slowly.

"Antonia,", he puts his big hands on my shoulders. "I wish I had all the answers, but I don't. I've told you what I know," he waves my unspoken words aside, "and I want to tell you that if I knew this was going to happen, I sure as hell would have arranged protection for everyone myself, as I'm sure you would have."

"Damn it, I know that Padrino. You're right, I should've seen it coming as soon as I heard his damn name. He will pay Padrino. I guarantee you that. I will find all those responsible. For now, I need all the intel I can gather. So please, level with me on why he wants our family so bad."

For the next couple of hours, my Uncle answers my questions as I try to understand. We discuss the progress I made following the money or lack thereof and that he may just want payback for what happened in the desert. Finally, we come to agreement that he may just be moving his pawns around, getting into position for something major.

I know he didn't show up here just for simple payback. Me and my family are just a side benefit. So, what's his target? What's he moving his pawns *for* and why? What's important in Detroit? What's here that he wants?

I look at my watch. It's time to meet with the FBI. I'm just so looking forward to this.

CHAPTER SIX

Monday 29 June - afternoon

I walk into the building and they intercept me right away. They search and relieve me of the weapon I forgot I was carrying, a Sig Saur P229 .40 cal. I would never carry in a federal building and if I weren't feeling so offbeat, I wouldn't have. I didn't have anything smart to say so I just gave them a warning.

"I want a receipt for that. I will take it with me when I leave. Don't be taking ballistic tests now without a warrant." I get on the elevator with my escort and silently prepare myself up for the meeting.

When I arrive on the designated floor, they lead me to a conference room about a quarter of the size as the one in my office. It's stark and claustrophobic and makes my scars burn. They pull me to the side to frisk me again, run a wand, check me for bugs and search the leather satchel I'm carrying.

I expected the search and seizure when I entered, but this second one was an insult and I bet, strictly for entertainment. The agents in the room flexing their law enforcement muscle. I'm the criminal don't forget. I roll my eyes.

It's already early evening and I feel scraped raw like the inside of a pumpkin being prepped for carving. There's a deep, underlying exhaustion wanting to drag me to the bottom of a pit. I want to cry, to scream, but I can't. I must focus and keep going – for my family.

"I apologize for showing up late," I quip, my face devoid of expression. "I'm sure you can understand why. Now, who wants to tell me what it is you want."

I sit my satchel with the file on Mansur al-Hakeem, gently on the table in front of me and take a seat. I see Jessica, her Junior Gs in chairs behind hers. One look at me and she can tell something's not right. She straightens in her chair and swivels it to face me directly. Mitch isn't the only one who can read my face it seems. Hmm, interesting, but right now it takes all I have not to show her the betrayal I still feel.

Next to her at the long oval conference table is someone I assume is her boss. He looks like a weasel with his beady brown eyes and blonde wiry hair. He's in his fifties, about my height and dressed like a Fed. His body language surprisingly shows too much for a ranking member. No one looks particularly happy. All in all, I'd say there are around fifteen people stuffed into the room from the different agencies assigned to what amounts to a task force.

"Andiamo, I've got more important things to do than sit here for hours waiting for you. I want your uncle, now!" the snidely weasel jumps up with a look like what he thinks is "the eye". His subordinates around the room shrink, trying to hide under the conference room table. Not Jess. She looks at him in disbelief.

He's a pipsqueak and doesn't manage to intimidate me as he does the others. He picked the wrong tactic to lead with.

"Excuse me, *sir*," I respond. "But you didn't do me the courtesy of introducing yourself. If I don't know who you are, then I cannot help you. If you have more important things to do I can go. I *too* have more important matters to attend to, like the murder of my family for instance. Have a good day, *sir*." All eyes in the room look to him, trying to stifle gasps as I stand to leave.

"I don't deserve to be treated like this. I'll stuff you into a hole for obstruction, then you'll be willing to do what I want," he sputters, trying to save face.

I roll my eyes. "Right, again if I don't know who you are, then I cannot help you." Jessica's elbow is on the table, her hand hiding the disgrace of her boss's behavior. He starts to spout again but I cut him off.

"If anyone here cares to help this poor man out, feel free to open your mouths."

Before Jessica has a chance to speak, a highly polished clean-shaven man with slick blonde hair and green eyes stands up. He's a couple of inches taller than his counterpart and looks paunchy. He reminds me of a snake, a slithering, sneaky, snake.

"My name is Isley, Donald Isley." Oh boy, a James Bond wannabe. He must be the spook.

"Ms. Andiamo, we regret what took place early this morning. If you'll forgive our colleague here, we might be in a position to help each other. After all, you can provide a service that we desperately need. I believe *you* are the best person to help us out of a tough situation," he addresses me.

"What is it, exactly, that you think I can help you with?"

"Ms. Andiamo we understand you've had a prior relationship with a certain terrorist, one named Mansur al-Hakeem."

"Excuse me? Relationship?" I question incredulously. "Do you have any idea what that man did to me? Relationship, my ass," I counter him harshly.

Jessica straightens, a shocked look on her face. Apparently, she wasn't in the loop on such an important detail.

"Yes, I am aware, which is why we would like your help in finding out what he's up to and where we can find him. We need to interrogate him, and you have a unique insight into this man that would be very helpful to us. It seems he's already targeted you." I give him a hard look that has him clearing his throat.

"Then why do you want my Uncle?"

"We know this has everything to do with who and what your Uncle is and what you do for him. We're asking that your Uncle answer questions on this and other matters we have pending." All eyes remain on me. Jessica slowly shakes her head.

"Do you have a warrant for his arrest?" I ask him pointedly. "He's a very successful businessman and I provide his security. I provide security for many of your dignitaries when they come here. In fact, I provide security for most of the city. I happen to be damn good at my job. Why would the CIA want to question him? You have no real jurisdiction on domestic soil. No, let's be honest. I'm here because you lost your boy, am I not?"

Isley grasps his lapels, rocks up on his toes and back down again, and clears his throat, looking very unhappy at my retort. I picture him as the snake that he is, forked tongue preparing for attack.

"Ms. Andiamo, I understand why you want your Uncle and the rest of your family under wraps, but don't presume to hold the high road. We all know your Uncle is head of the Detroit Syndicate with you his enforcer and executioner. You aren't so squeaky clean and the only reason we're here is because of your reputation for circumventing the law." Apparently, he did not appreciate my comment about losing his boy. Oops.

"Mr. Isley, I think I resent that. I performed executions on behalf of this government and was only one of your many assets. I suggest you have proof before you make accusations if you don't want to find yourself the subject of a lawsuit." Pictures of Thorstein's dead eyes float before mine then quickly leave.

"So, let's cut the pretense. Is Al-Hakeem the true objective here or my Uncle and me? Because if you're thinking you can have it all, then I suggest you think again."

"Ms. Andiamo, I understand how this must seem, but you have to look at this from our perspective."

"Okay, let me tell you what I see." I open my leather satchel, pulling out the file and slamming it down on the table with a loud smack.

"Every single one of you assholes had ample opportunity to get this guy, and every single one of you fucked up. Why? You have leaks in your organizations. You have more leaks in your Agencies than the Titanic did before it went down to Davy Jones."

All eyes are trying to look elsewhere, all except Jessica. Her eyes are pure ice looking at the thickness of the file I threw down. She steals a glimpse at her boss before I go on. It was not a pleasant look. I shudder and continue.

"One of you here is the reason why half my family is dead. When I find out which one of you is responsible, and believe me I will, you and I will have a private chat." I didn't directly threaten anyone, but I could tell that everyone in the room understood my intent.

"Until then, this is how things are going to go. Anything I come up with and deem pertinent to you finding Al-Hakeem will be relayed through Agent Caruthers here. You, in turn, will go through her to let me know anything you come up with from your so-called briefings.

"Now Ms. Andiamo..." Isley begins. I cut him off

"Is there anything else Isley?"

"As a matter of fact, there is if you'd please join us in Mr. Sheppard's office where we can discuss this further," he answers shortly and heads down the hall.

"Of course," I exit the conference room after him.

"Hold up a minute Calvin, would you please? Jessica asks. She waits until everyone clears the room before she speaks.

"What did Al-Hakeem do to Ms. Andiamo that has her so upset with us and why the hell don't I know?"

"Need to know Caruthers, you know how this works. I think now it's become necessary for you to see who this woman is so I'll make sure you get a copy."

"Fine, what's going on with you Cal? This isn't like you. Why couldn't we just tell her what we know? This is supposed to be a Joint Anti-Terrorist Task Force not on organized crime."

"Don't you see what an opportunity this is, Caruthers? An opportunity to take down one of the most notorious criminals of our time, put him behind bars for good? This could be such a boon for us, to finally get our office noticed."

"Cal, I've spent years studying, infiltrating, and gathering intelligence on organized crime and gangs. You know this. I understand more than most that putting Big Tony behind bars would be a good thing. It would break the back of the Detroit Partnership. If we can capture Al-Hakeem and grab Big Tony, too, great. But alienating Ms. Andiamo from the start isn't going to accomplish either of those goals. Believe me, this isn't the route to take. This cannot be our priority," Jessica argues.

"I hate the thought of working with this criminal to catch Al-Hakeem. We should be able to do that ourselves. No, she'll be another feather in our cap, too. I'll need your report once you've seen what she has. You've managed earn her trust, maybe she'll let something slip."

"Well, I doubt that. She's not stupid and she's nobody's fool. You're not going to get anywhere this way Cal," she says to his retreating back.

"You'll see Caruthers, you'll see," he rushes off to join the others in his office.

***

"Okay, what's left to discuss that you didn't want the rest of the task force to know," I ask once settled in Sheppard's office.

"Simple, Ms. Andiamo," Sheppard answers. "You in prison along with your Uncle and the rest of your family."

My eyes turn black and I get up to leave.

"Calvin. Ms. Andiamo, please," Isley gestures me back to my seat.

"Look, we know what you went through with this man. Considering your skills and connections we're unofficially giving you a green light to take him out, should it become necessary."

"Unofficially. You think I'm stupid? You want me in prison so you'll use him to get me there. Yeah, that about sums up you and your agencies. Hypocrites." I walk out leaving them with their gaping mouths, staring at empty space.

As I retreat from confines of Sheppard's office, I run into Jessica speaking to her assistant. She asks me to join her in her office. All these secret meetings, it's a wonder they get anything done around here. Nobody knows what anyone else is doing.

I look out her window at the city below. People are shuffling from place to place oblivious to their surroundings. Listening closely, you can hear traffic below.

Jessica takes a seat at her desk and for the second time today, motions me to sit as well. God those legs, don't think about it now. Later, there's too much going on now, too much at risk. It's not the time and but certainly not the place. My emotions are in turmoil I keep telling myself to put it away until later, over, and over like a mantra. She looks at me with confusion in her eyes as I keep talking to myself.

"You want to let me in on the conversation?" she asks.

"Hmm? Uh, no that's okay," I answer still distracted. "How much trouble are you in for me giving that Snidely weasel, flack?" I don't know how this woman ended up in my world. Everything about her screams grace, and purity and righteousness. I can't quite catch the breath I seem to lose any time she's near me.

"Who? You mean Sheppard? Oh, I'm not the one in trouble. He's pointed in the wrong direction. Right now, he's probably trying to get a search warrant for your offices, your home and the homes of your other family members, so he can get to your Uncle. He has no probable cause and he knows it.

"His priorities are out of order, but he refuses to see that your uncle isn't our target. He's periphery right now, and it's not the right time to go after him. He's not our mission. We have to focus on finding al-Hakeem."

I look at her, full of conviction and passion. Yeah, and she's FBI. I could never have a relationship with someone in the FBI. Whoa, relationship? I don't do relationships. Never mind. I need to concentrate on finding al-Hakeem and everyone involved in the murder of my family.

"Toni? Toni! Are you okay?" She comes around the desk to shake me out of my stupor. "You took a little vacation on me there for a moment. Look, we're both exhausted, I know, but I'm concerned about you and that look on your face. Are you all right?"

Jesus, what look on my face?

"I'm okay." I give her a small smile. "Really, I'm just thinking about your gorgeous legs and how they move. I really like those legs." Oh, sweet Jesus. Did I just tell her that? Down in flames, Andiamo. I'm mortified. How could I think like that at a time like this?

"And that puts a look of pure panic on your face? I'd hate to see the look you have when you stare at my behind." I start to laugh. This girl has a sense of humor, too.

"Panic? Uh no, I don't think so, and I can't believe the tone of this conversation." I shake my head. "I should be thinking how to get the bastards who killed my family. Frankly, you have me distracted and I'm not too sure that's a good thing."

"Well, sex is a normal, healthy response to trauma and the perfect outlet for anger." She perches her hips on the desk in front of me, her hands on the edge. She leans over and kisses me gently. Her hands move around the lapels of my suit jacket as she pulls me out of my chair and up to her, but I step away.

"What the hell am I doing? I can't deal with this right now. How am I supposed to get over this feeling that everything we do is a means to an end with you?" She quickly hid the pain at my words but not fast enough that I didn't catch it.

"I don't know, Toni," she replies coolly. "I don't know how to convince you that there's no ulterior motive on my part. Others here? Absolutely, but not me. I'm just someone you met at a bar. I happen to have a job that crossed paths with yours. My reasons for wanting to see you have nothing, I repeat, nothing to do with that job." She pulls me back to her, kissing me again.

All my emotions come to a boil in that kiss. I kick my chair out of the way, picking her up and slamming her into the window. She grunts from the force. I hoarsely whisper in her ear.

"Are you sure you want this?" I shake her slightly. "Do you want me to show you who I really am?" My fire melts the ice of her eyes.

"Show me," she said. It was a challenge and I felt my restraints break. I hold back nothing, and she gives me everything.

I spin her around tearing her blouse open and buttons fly as I grab her. The window chills her nipples erect and sends goose bumps down her arms. I bite into her neck and her moan is a drug driving me on.

Overwhelming need and greed take over as tear at her nylons and fall back against the desk. She moans and I let myself drown in her sweetness.

I ease up a bit and she flip easily takes over, riding me heard. I'm helpless to stop the sensations, pleasure and pain mix as we rock with each other. She tightens her arms as we catch our breath. My rage and hunger satiated for now.

"Fuck me," I curse when I'm able to breathe falling back down to her desk.

"I believe that's just what I did," she says, looking pleased with herself. I couldn't help but snort, then shake my head.

"Damn it," I whisper, knowing this isn't right. I'm barely keeping things in check and there's too much at stake, too much to do. I push her away roughly, make myself presentable, and leave without a look back.

***

"Mitch, office," I yell as I hit the floor, slamming my satchel on my desk when I get to my office.

"They rattle your cage kid?" He stands leaning against the open door with his arms crossed at the chest.

"Sono un po 'di buchi buttati nell figa! They're a bunch of pussy-whipped butt holes! No wonder they had to come to me for their intel; to clean up their mess. They couldn't find their assholes if they pulled their own heads out of them." I continue ranting in Italian waving my arms.

"Pezzi microbo cazzo di merda! Stronzi idiota cazzo! Figli di puttana!" Mitch lets me rage and in a couple of minutes, I run out of steam. I plop my butt into my chair, take a deep breath. He waits patiently while I collect my jumbled thoughts.

"Okay, have Karl and Carrie do a sweep of the conference room. With all these agencies wanting a piece of me, I'm sure they want their own set of ears and we need to cover our asses. They're not going to let us lead this operation, not we rogue civilians. But we are running it and running it on our own. They took me aside Mitch. They want me to off this son of a bitch 'unofficially'," I use air quotes with my fingers.

"My bet is they created this whole damn situation. They want my cooperation and know I wouldn't do them any favors. This way, they knew I'd be motivated to take him out."

"You think they'd pull something that horrific just to get you to kill a target for them? Come on Toni listen to what you're saying."

"You think I'm being paranoid? My parents and sisters are dead Mitch and damn straight I'm going to take out

Al-Hakeem. I would have done it without the extra incentive. And tell me this: Why didn't they advise me he was in country knowing our history? Do you really think I'm being that paranoid?"

"Aw, shit Toni, I don't know. But I'll tell you this. We will find him."

"Right. Now, we need to be extremely careful. They'll be watching every move I make and try to bust me after I kill him. Publicly they want him alive to interrogate him. Unofficially, they give me permission to take him out. Nothing else makes sense. They've set me up."

"Alright, I'll bite on that last point. We'll cover our asses as we've always done."

"Oh, by the way," I look at the river and contemplate. "I don't trust that weasel, Jessica's boss. He has an agenda all his own on this. He's playing at something and I don't think he clued anyone in on what he's doing. Have Carrie do a deep background on him and ask Karl to set me up with a small tracking device I can plant on him."

"I'll get right on it, kid, anything else?"

"Yeah, once the conference room is cleared, we'll meet in there and go over this file."

Mitch nods. "Okay, kiddo. Anything you want."

"Toni? May I come in for a moment?"

I turn to see Jessica standing in my office doorway. Where the hell is Miss Edna? "What the hell are you doing here," I snap.

"You said I was to be your liaison so here I am."

My own words come back to bite me. I sigh, mentally hitting myself in the head. "Right. We're about to meet, just waiting on a few things."

"Toni I..." My intercom buzzes. What now? "Yes?"

"Sorry to disturb you Ms. Andiamo, but there's a Frankie here?" Francine from the reception desk sounds dubious, knowing this kid certainly doesn't belong in these offices.

"Damn, I totally forgot about it."

"Thanks." I let go of the intercom and sigh. "Time to go to work," I groan.

"Who's Frankie?" Jessica asks. How do I explain Frankie?

"Frankie is a fourteen-year-old delinquent I'm keeping out of prison. He's a handful but I do admire him. He kind of reminds me of me when I was his age." Jessica shoots me a half a smirk.

"What?" I replied raising my eyebrows.

"It seems you've got a great big, soft heart for someone who is supposed to be...." and before I know it my mouth is on hers.

"Look about earlier..." I begin when we come up for air. She brings her finger up to my lips.

"Go deal with Frankie," and she turns away. Damn it.

***

Frankie waits in a chair across from Miss Edna's desk. They're eying each other with wariness, sizing each other up. He sees me out of the corner of his eye and a partial grin appears on his face. He gets an eyeful of Jessica and his jaw drops down to his toes. I pluck a couple of tissues out of the box on Miss Edna's desk and toss them at Frankie.

"Wipe the drool off your chin and close your mouth Frankie, it's not polite to ogle women."

"But, damn, she's one hot mama dawg." Frankie catches my look and straightens up. "Sorry."

"Frankie let me introduce you to Special Agent Caruthers of the FBI." His jaw drops again

"No fuckin' way. You really FBI dawg? You be too damn hot for a Fed, mama." Frankie continues to stare at Jessica.

"Well, thank you, Frankie. I think. It's a pleasure to meet you," Jessica replies. She sticks out her hand for Frankie to shake. He continues to stare. I elbow him and he takes Jess's hand and kisses it. That's what I want to see, good manners for a change.

"Frankie, I take it you did okay this weekend. Tyrell said you caused no trouble. How did your Grandmother handle it?"

"Shit, Ms. Toni, she was pissed and I mean really upset." He looks down at the floor, ill at ease. "She says it's a good thing you gonna help me out 'cause second chances don't come along in every life. She told me to be on my best behavior 'cause she raised me right and it's up to me to decide if I use my brains for good or bad. So, I told her I'm gonna use my brains for good, so I don't end up in no more trouble. She bought it so I made her happy," he shrugs his skinny shoulders. Jess and I shake our heads trying not to laugh because we both know he's being totally serious.

"Okay Frankie, when do you have to be in court again?" I ask.

"Uh," Frankie thinks, "Thursday, 8:30 in the morning."

"Okay, I'll make sure I'm there with you. Now let's get you going on your community service before the court orders you. It impresses the judges when you do things like that without being told."

I hand him a piece of paper with an address on it. "This is where you're going. It's a shelter. You missed serving dinner, but you can still make it in time to help hand out blankets for the night. When you're here, I'll start you out slow. It'll loads of shit work at first, but I'll also teach you about this business if you're patient. When you finish school and community service you'll have a career that pays well."

Frankie nods in agreement. I hand him over to Miss Edna with a warning to him that she has soap for his mouth if he doesn't keep it clean and off they go. I turn to Jessica. "What?" I'm saying that quite a bit lately.

"You're really good with kids. Especially juvenile delinquents," she says with a perfectly straight face.

"Ha, ha," I retort. I'll meet you in the conference room. It's just down that hall. You'll find it." I turn in retreat to my office in total embarrassment.

Ten minutes later, I'm in the conference room, composed and serious. I hit the SCIF mode as walk in. Time to get this Al-Hakeem. She's glances at Jessica, pleased to see a note of awe on her face.

"Alright, let's get down to business. First, let me introduce all of you to Assistant Special Agent in Charge of the Organized Crime/Drug Division of the Detroit Field Office and Second in Command of the Joint Terrorist Task Force, Jessica Caruthers. She will be our liaison to the FBI."

"I found seven bugs in here when I swept. Seems our friends are pretty nosy," Mitch says, with a scowl aimed at Jessica. She lifts her hands and shakes her head. "I also found two on Miss Edna's desk, two in the men's room, four in the ladies' room and two in the supply closet."

"Shit, do you think they feel left out of the loop? I wonder when they got in to plant them, sneaky bastards." I look suspiciously at Jessica.

"Which ones did you leave? They'll get a load of Frankie's mouth and shit."

"Not only his mouth but the boss's as well," Mitch replies. He gives me a withering look before moving on. "I left them all. The ones that were in here we pulled and took them apart to trace them to their home Agency. They wouldn't have worked anyway given the technology we have in place."

"When we finish here, run a sweep in my office just to be sure."

"You got it, boss," Mitch replies.

"I received an update from the Detroit PD and the ATF. They're still sifting through the rubble, but they did manage to track the origin of the explosion. It came from the basement. A burnt trail of accelerant poured over the floor led to the furnace. Most likely gasoline triggered by a spark lit the fumes, which quickly spread to the furnace. They must've blown out the pilot. The spark that lit the fire most likely came from a broken light bulb." It horrified me to think that someone in the house smelled the fumes and tried to turn on the lights to investigate.

"They said they've seen this before."

The more I recite the more my anger burns. Shut it down. Contain it. Just for now. I get a handle on the rage and continue.

"Miss Edna, please pass out the copies of the file on Mansur al-Hakeem." Miss Edna hands out the copies.

"My boss doesn't even have a file this extensive. At least not one I've seen. You must have excellent resources," Jess remarks, while everyone studies the file.

Looking Mitch straight in the eye I reply, "Yeah, excellent resources. Sorry, Jess, I won't give them away." I don't think she would appreciate finding out her own organization had all this information and just chose to hide it.

"Hmm, okay. What interests me is if this additional information will help us track him and why we ourselves don't have this much?" Murray pipes in.

"Every little piece of information helps, Agent Caruthers."

"Call me Jessica, please."

"Okay, Jessica. As I was saying, every little bit of information helps. From this file, we're analyzing how many people he has on the payroll. It'll only be a matter of time before we learn who the leaks are and begin to plug them. Once we start to plug the leaks, then we can start gleaning information from those leaks to find our target."

"Thanks, Murray," she laughs. "What I mean is I'm trying to find out if any of this is helpful in figuring out where he went from New York? Do we have any idea where he is?" Jessica didn't take offense by Murray's insinuations. She gives him a knowing smile.

"Sorry Jessica, I'm used to knot heads who think they're better because they are in an agency with initials. As far as finding al-Hakeem, yes it will help and no we don't have a location on him yet." He gives her a smile that's all teeth.

"I have a few sources to contact," Jessica says. "The task force will be combing their databases, listening to the chatter, and tracking down the sources as quickly as possible. If I learn anything, when I learn anything, you'll know it. Now let me bring you up to date on my briefing this weekend."

"I was told we had a tip that Mansur al-Hakeem was in the country and allegedly here to purchase weapons after a deal he was involved in fell apart. We believe he intends to do something here in Detroit. We don't know yet what that might be.

"The Deputy Director personally set the task force and told me a civilian would be consulting with us in order to find him and until the explosion that took your family's lives, I didn't know who that civilian was. We've been trying to track his movements since his arrival in New York City."

"Hmph," I pipe in. "Need to know basis my ass. Okay, I want his whereabouts locked down ASAP. Miss Edna, what's the status of security for my family?"

"Everything is scheduled and in place, Ms. Andiamo. We identified two suspicious vehicles, ran their plates and found they belong to one of the agencies. They've set up surveillance on your family."

"That's fine, let them have their surveillance. As long as they stay safe, I don't care. They won't be getting close to Uncle Tony."

"Your brother needs to talk to you and security is tight as a drum. I checked personally for you," Murray speaks up.

"Thanks, Murray, I appreciate that. Let me know as soon as the report from the sweep comes in."

"You got it, Sarge," he answers.

"Okay, next, Carrie what do we have set up so far?"

"We have vehicles ready to go and the specific things you wanted all checked out and ready for you. I'm sure the powers that be will not be happy with you. Strategies and contingencies are drawn and ready for you to study. Umm, I also have workups on those you wanted earlier in case you care to look those over," she says eying Jessica.

"Great. Thanks. Miss Edna would you put those on my desk, please. Karl, did you get a chance to set up what Mitch asked you to," I inquire, referring to the tracking device for Snidely Weasel.

"Ya, Sarge." Karl is never one to mince his words.

"Okay, I'll see you before I leave. I must speak to my brother and meet with my family for arrangements at the funeral home." I turn to look directly into Jess's pools of ice.

"Jessica, I know your bosses aren't happy with me, but I don't give a shit and I won't be available to them for a while. I know it's going to piss them off, but I can't deal with them now. I need to do some of my own research and I also need time to study al-Hakeem. The more I know and understand him, the more I can get in his brain. That'll give me an advantage, help me anticipate his moves, maybe figure out what he's planning. Then we'll be able to set the stage for the show." Jessica hesitates and gives me a hard look.

"You don't make this easy on a by the book law and order girl do you?" Her ice eyes never waiver and never leave mine. She nods slowly as she comes to a decision.

"I'll handle my bosses for the moment if you keep me in the loop. Just remember, I'm not stupid and I'm not green."

"Point taken and noted. I'm sure we'll have no problem keeping you in the loop, will we team?" A chorus of no's echoes around the room.

"Anyone have any questions?" I look around the room and find Carrie with her hand in the air. "Go," I acknowledge her.

"Why has this guy surfaced now? I mean, we all know his work but why is now? What's so important now?" Carrie asks, squirming from her own scars. "I mean it was pure damn luck he left just an hour before we escaped, so why wait all these years?" Good question.

"Well, hold onto your shorts," I said, "because this guy is the one who coordinates, organizes, recruits and trains men for these terrorist organizations. We suspected it back then, but according to this file, confirmed. He's one big master manipulator who has no trouble finding young impressionable kids to carry out his work.

"He's a Saudi citizen, first recruited by the Taliban when he was fifteen. He worked for the PLO, Hamas, IRA, Al Qaeda, the Taliban, the Elite Iraqi Republican Guard and, hold on to your shorts, the CIA. He doesn't take sides and sells himself to the highest bidder. He's capable of some nasty shit, as all but Karl and Agent Caruthers here know."

I mentally fidget to soothe the scars searing beneath my blouse. "He's the teacher's teacher and the spooks want him back in a big way."

"It was just pure damn luck that they spotted him in New York," chimes in Jessica. "He's managed to stay one step ahead of everyone. He's a ghost."

"He was trained right here in the United States, by our own government when he came of age so you can imagine why they want his ass so badly and why they've managed to keep so tight-lipped about him. He went rogue many years before and skirted everyone's radar since. So, they turned to me, because I was also one of their assets."

"Damn," Carrie responds.

"Right. Listen. We cannot afford any mistakes. This man will take full advantage of any and all opportunities we provide. We've seen him in action, up close and personal. He's a master at his craft. He uses the internet and social media and fosters false propaganda to find young men for these organizations. He looks for kids who are lost and lonely, looking for a family and a place to belong. Kids who, for one reason or another, don't think they belong anywhere, the same way gangs recruit."

"And even though these organizations say they're Muslim in faith, they're not. They took parts that suit their cause, bastardize them, and made their own faith. They use any fear and any slight the public has against the Islamic faith to recruit the disheartened and disillusioned. These people are looking for something to believe in and al-Hakeem provides it. Anyone have any other questions?" I look around the room and all remain silent.

"Good, now let's switch gears and talk about Frankie. You all know what went down the other night and why he's here. I want him taught the ropes. He's a good sniper and can become a better one, but I want him to learn the consequences, the strategies, the planning and the strength of will the boredom of surveillance takes. I want him to learn electronics, stealth, investigation. By the time he graduates I want him to have a trade to be proud of." Everyone agrees they'll take turns with him.

They all file out of the conference room while I sit for a few minutes reflecting on things like Jessica, my parents, my sisters. I must talk to my brother. At least I know the rest of my family is safe. I hope I can continue to keep them that way. I need to see some of my contacts. I don't want to trust a Feeb but I see no other way around it.

I stand, gather my files, and go to my office. Jessica is at my desk making her phone calls. She looks perfectly at home sitting there. Damn. As I walk toward her, she hangs up the phone.

"Sorry to take over your desk, but Miss Edna said I could use your phone."

"It's okay. I don't plan on being in the office much longer." I watch as she walks around my desk while I take her place and lean against the window. My eyes narrow when I notice a drawer slightly open.

She rifled through my desk the fucking shit. Tingling nerves run through me because I'd do the same damn thing and decide to let it go for now.

"Jessica, I'm asking you for a little patience. I'm not sure who to trust right now and I'm not used to working with anyone outside my team."

"Alright, I'll give you that patience as long as you remember I will not be stuffed in the backseat on this and I definitely won't be restrained by a seatbelt," Jessica replies continuing her vehicle analogy.

"Understood."

"I believe we've just come to an accord."

"Yeah, I suppose we have."

"Oh, by the way, Toni, no one from my team has seen your file. Even I haven't seen it, though Sheppard just decided it was pertinent for me to review so I'm sure I'll be getting a copy. I just thought you ought to know that. I'll see you later." She comes around the desk again, leans into me and lays on one hell of a lip lock. It instantly fogs my brain, the windows and leaves the place feeling like a steam bath. Damn it Andiamo, you are definitely going down in flames. Slowly I pack up to leave my office giving me time to clear my head. □

CHAPTER SEVEN

Monday 29 June - evening

I head to my Uncle's place to pick up my brother. I need his expertise.

"What do you need me to do?" he asks as he gets in my car.

"I need your contacts on the Westside. I want you to personally get in touch with every source you know. We need a line on al-Hakeem. I need to know the word on the street, and you know the area better than me."

"No problem. As soon as you drop me off, I'll start on it. I can't take bodyguards with me, but I'll make sure to protect my ass." I start to argue but my brother cuts me off. "I know how to take care of myself, Sis," says the former Navy Seal.

"I know, I know," I sigh. "Just be careful okay?" My brother nods. "Okay then."

I drop him off and finally arrive at my own place, totally spent. I throw off my clothes, crawl into bed and fall into a restless sleep.

***

Jessica works on her report, trying not to think about the woman who might tank her career. "Be real Jessica, she won't mess up anything, you will. It's your choice," she thinks.

She thinks about the briefing at Storm Investigations as she taps the folder holding Toni's file. She opens it and starts reading. Her debrief will just have to wait a few minutes.

She reads through Toni's early scrapes with the law, her time in juvenile detention, and finds nothing until her military service. The Military records are heavily redacted, but she got the gist of Toni's abilities with tours in Panama, Kuwait, Mogadishu, and Bosnia.

She received a Congressional Medal of Honor for her time in Kuwait – the Country's highest honor for Military personnel, three Silver Stars, two Bronze Stars, two Purple Hearts and a host of other medals. She reads on. Several incursions into Israel, Africa, and in different areas of South America as a mercenary, again heavily redacted which means CIA involvement. Her number of confirmed kills is quite impressive.

The meager intel reported other mercenary jobs in a host of location that had no way out, the hardships they endured, torture chambers they escaped. So much death and destruction, so much they went through together that could have destroyed her team. Instead, it made them, solidified them.

What she could not get out of her head was the report on the monstrosity that happened in Kuwait when al-Hakeem captured Toni's team. Horrified by the images her mind conjured, she continued to read. Dear Goddess that woman lived through so much. She now knew why they chose Toni.

"But they have to know that she's not going to be satisfied to see al-Hakeem caught," she thought. "They have to know Toni is going to do everything she can to eliminate him from the face of this earth and do it her way." Light begins to dawn on the strategy those above her put in play. They want this man dead not captured and they want their hands to be clean.

Shaking her head, she sets aside Toni's file and makes herself a copy of the one on al-Hakeem she received at Toni's office. She knew they'd done a hell of a lot of work in such a short time. What she couldn't figure out was how they were able to accomplish so much when it took so long for her office to get good intel.

"Toni seems to have the contacts and the manpower to get further than we can," Jess thought to herself, "and with the way Sheppard's acting, we'll get nowhere. Why does he have this obsession all of a sudden with Big Tony? Can't he see he's not the main problem right now? There is no benefit going after him on this. Nothing would ever stick. But, if we hold on, wait for a bit he might slip up with all that's going on. Then we can reel him in."

"How would she feel about me then? If I haul off her uncle and lock him in a cage? She knows that this is my work. I can't tiptoe around a criminal because I'm sleeping with his niece." Jess weighed the situation she was in and shook her head. She threw caution to the wind for one night. Now, all she can do is keep moving forward.

She finished typing up her report and readied for the blistering she expected at her debrief. She took a deep breath as she stepped into the conference room where the other members of the task force waited to hear all the juicy details of her time with Toni Andiamo. Sheppard is on her before she can take her seat.

"Did she tell you where her uncle is?"

"No Calvin, she definitely did not tell me where her uncle is. Try his home. I don't think he'll go into hiding anytime soon. Anyway, al-Hakeem is a bit more important now, don't you think?"

"Hmm, we'll see. Let's get down to business. What did you come up with Agent Caruthers?"

"I was given a copy of this file on Al-Hakeem. I'd like the time to go through this with a fine-tooth comb."

"Give me that. What else?"

"They're working on locating him and I offered her what little we had from New York. We just tasked this to her so there isn't much to relay yet. Has anyone come up with anything from our end?"

"No, it's frustrating. We're still filtering through the chatter but it looks like no one's talking for the moment and that's unusual. We'll apprise you if something shows up on the grid. That'll be all Caruthers," he dismissed her. On the way back to her office, she runs into Deputy Director Davis.

"Uncle Mal, are you still hanging around? What are you doing here so late?"

"A Director's work is never done. I'll actually be around until the current situation comes to a successful conclusion."

"Good to know. Actually, do you have a few minutes for a heart-to-heart? I have a few issues I need to talk over with you. "

"Sure, what's on your mind, my dear?" Malcolm took a seat in front of her desk.

"Well, it happens to be about Ms. Andiamo."

"Oh?" He raises his eyebrows and leans forward to pay attention.

"Yes, you've known about my sexual preference since before my parents' deaths. Well, I was out on Friday night you know just enjoying a night out with a couple of friends when I met the most amazing woman. We hit it off and I spent the night with her."

"Okay, I don't see what this has to do with Ms. Andiamo or the current case, but continue."

"It was Ms. Andiamo I slept with."

"I see. Well, you certainly know how to make a difficult situation worse little girl."

"Tell me about it. I didn't know she was the civilian that was to work with us until I saw her at the scene the day her family was murdered."

"Really? You're joking. Are we talking about the same Agent Caruthers I've known, loved, and nurtured for years? I don't believe that."

"Uncle Mal," she laughs. "Seriously, I knew exactly who I slept with, so I didn't look into it further. I certainly didn't think I'd see her again let alone be working with her on the Task Force.

"I see. I suggest we keep this to ourselves for now. We can reevaluate later if it becomes an issue. You ended this didn't you?"

"Not exactly," she winces, thinking of what happened in her office earlier.

"What? You can't be serious here. Do you know what this could do to you, to your career?" Malcolm looks incredulous.

"Yes, I know," she grimaces. She hesitates, but only for a moment before continuing.

"Not to change the subject but I don't understand Agent Sheppard's tact he's taking where Ms. Andiamo is concerned. He seems to ignore the fact that her insight and Intel can be invaluable in finding al-Hakeem. He seems to believe the task force can do that without her and he's making Big Tony the priority instead."

"Are you sure it's not your libido talking? Will it interfere with your work on this?"

"I'm quite sure and you know me better than that Uncle Mal. He even has the CIA backing his play and I know it just can't be the right path. Sure, I understand that if we can get him along the way, that'd be great but making him a top priority is a waste of time.

"We've tried to get something on Big Tony for years and failed. Now, with all that's going on around his family right now, he'll slip up. Then, we can nail him. Isn't the goal here to find al-Hakeem so we can interrogate him, find out what he's planning? C'mon, how is sex playing a role in that?"

"Alright, alright young lady I'll have Spencer look into it," Malcolm assures her.

"I don't need you to run interference for me. I just thought you should be aware of what's going on and maybe give me some advice on how to handle Agent Sheppard's lack of interest in his own field of Counterterrorism," she stated upset.

"Okay, take it easy young lady. Do you want my take? Just let it be for now. Keep to your specific assignment and if he becomes intolerable then and only then will Spencer take care of the situation. In the meantime end this with Andiamo."

"Yes Sir," she said to her mentor as he left.

"Dear Goddess, help me," she prayed to an empty office.

***

I wake on a sandy dirt floor my head pounding as if a herd of elephants stomped on my skull. I groan trying to sit without throwing up and I lean back against the wall. As my vision clears, I take stock of my surroundings. There's no furniture and there are two windows about neck high if you're on your feet. One in the wall above me and the other in the wall to the left of me. I hear someone calling out my name. Mitch and Murray are on the other side of the wall, and Carrie is sitting up along the wall to my right. I hold my head in my hands and answer.

"Yeah, I'm okay. Where the fuck are we?" I ask, pulling myself up to look through the hole, seeing a bruised and bloody Mitch. Equally bruised and bloody, Murray is sitting against a wall throwing stones at something in the middle of the floor. There's an underlying smell of urine, blood, and cordite permeating my nose. It doesn't bode well.

"Damn Evers, you look like shit," I tell him holding the side of my head to make sure it stays on.

"Gee, thanks kid, you don't look so pretty yourself," he chides, and I let out a humph. "He's here kiddo. Mansur al-Hakeem, the one we're looking for," he whispers.

"Oh fuck," I reply. "We need to figure a way to get him then get out of here."

"I've seen a few avenues of escape if we can just get out of these rooms," Carrie pipes in. She has a photographic memory and everything she sees imprints on her brain.

From the looks of it, the walls are at least two feet thick. Sundried mud mixed with rock is hard as concrete. Changing my view, I look out the back to see the nearby area mottled with several tents made of heavily woven goat hair, a few vehicles scattered around and soldiers milling about. Well, we're still in the desert. I steady myself before I move to the door that is holding us prisoner in this small room. It's new and made of thick heavy wood with iron hinges drilled and anchored into the wall. The lock and door handle is iron too.

"Shit, we aren't getting out through these doors but I bet you could've told me that." Carrie nods her head in acknowledgment.

I contemplate trying to lift myself and squeeze through the small hole I once again look out. Get real Andiamo. You can't fit. I hear the chatter of a few soldiers coming closer as I sit back down to consider our options. The soldiers stop in front of our door. The door opens and six men rush in, two taking up positions pointing their weapons at Carrie and the rest coming for me. I struggle as they manhandle me through the door, knocking me out once more.

I wake up groaning with my arms tied above my head, my feet dangling about a foot above the ground. I find myself stripped of my BDUs. Shit, this is not a good sign. Someone slaps my face, trying to bring me totally out of my stupor. Razor sharp, white, hot pain goes from one end of my head to the other. I spit on whoever slapped me and receive another for my trouble. My brain feels like it's exploding out of my head and I groan my displeasure.

When my eyes finally focus, I look around. Three men with the Iraqi Republican Guard are standing in front of me, another two on each side of me. I sense a couple behind me too. I smile, flattered that I warrant such heavy guard. My smile disappears as I spot Mitch in the corner forced onto his knees a garrote around his throat and arms tied behind him.

I growl and hear the men laugh. Not the response I wanted, need to work on that. Another slap. I yell my name, rank, and serial number. More laughter. Mitch curses. I realize why they brought him in, what they plan to make him watch. Sorry, Mitch, I'm so sorry you have to watch this.

Mansur al-Hakeem walks into the room and everyone stiffens to attention. He takes up his place in front of me and gives me a wicked grin. My face turns stone cold. I'm looking at pure evil in dead black eyes. He rips my tank top and bra off, takes his knife and slices at my left breast. It's not deep enough to do major damage, but enough to draw blood, fucking sting like hell, and probably leave a scar.

I wince but continue to stare straight ahead. I hear Mitch cursing up a storm. Another slice curving to my right breast. I start to tune myself out when I hear al-Hakeem trying to get information from Mitch, our ranking member.

"Don't you do it, Evers," I speak to Mitch, my voice calm and deadly. "No matter what happens, don't tell them anything. No matter what."

"You are listening to a woman? They are good for nothing but carrying male children and suicide bombings. When you want those willing to kill themselves and you have little choice but to use them." He looks at Mitch and then looks at me.

"Fine. Let us see how you handle this."

I hear the rest of the men cheer. Out of the corner of my eye, I see why. A bullwhip. The first lash lands on my back before I hear the crack. Strange, I thought. Another lash and I groan involuntarily, gritting my teeth against the pain. The third one has me screaming out an obscenity that would have made my uncle proud. Mitch is frothing at the mouth; nothing he can do with the thin wire digging into his throat.

The fourth lash spins me around and my head falls forward. By the fifth one, my body takes over and numbs the pain. I'm in my own world, now, distanced, feeling nothing. I think it took them another five or six lashes to realize it no longer phased me.

They drop the whip and rip my boxers off me. Mitch tries to drop his head, but his guards wrench his head up and tighten the garrote, forcing him to watch their torture.

Al-Hakeem speaks to Mitch then to me, but at this point, I can't understand what he's saying. He slaps me, I feel his blade once again, lower this time, on my belly. His soldiers spread my legs and tie them apart. I see the iron rings cemented in the dirt and dark stains beneath me, my blood staining the dirt. I steel my mind for what's to come but instead of pulling out his manhood, he says something to one of the guards who runs out and returns with a broom handle.

My eyes widen for a moment as he breaks the handle in two. I feel and hear my ribs crack as he beats me. I never once answer a single question and neither does Mitch. I repeat my name, rank and serial number one more time, knowing I'm pissing these guys off. No. I'm not cooperating, matter what they do to me.

In their eyes, women aren't supposed to be strong. He shoves one broomstick up my vagina with enough force to make me scream in pain. He enjoyed it so much he slammed the other half in my ass, and I let out another scream against the onslaught. He laughs. A laugh so evil, the devil himself would've shuddered in fear.

"Women are not warriors," he tells me. "They crumble and fall apart without men. You are nothing, a whore, a failure, a piece of shit in the eyes of Allah. Infidel!"

Al-Hakeem performs for his men, slamming those broom-handles home with each word. What they don't understand, what they refuse to see, is the will to live, to survive growing stronger with each thrust. Poor Mitch. He looks both horrified and resigned. Don't worry. I'm still here. I *will* survive this.

When he tires, they cut me down and leave me lying naked in my own piss, shit, and blood. When I come to, I see Mitch still kneeling in the corner, blood dripping down his neck from the garrote cutting into his flesh. It feels like hours before I can get to my knees. My back raked raw and my insides a scrambled mess, burning like hellfire.

It hurts to breathe, and saliva pours from my nose and mouth from the pain. Scusate, figlio di puttana! Sorry ass sons of bitches! Fottuti Stronzi di Madre, fucking motherfuckers aren't going to get away with this. Assholes are going to get what's coming to them. I swear it. I spit blood trying to clear my nose and throat.

I crawl toward Mitch, each movement agonizing. He's in shock, his eyes looking far away. I yell at him, slap him with what little strength I can muster. It takes every ounce of energy I have but, finally, he turns to face me. I tell him it's time to go. He nods and helps me stand, taking several moments to catch my breath.

Shredding my uniform to tie around my broken ribs, I slowly get dressed. The cloth grate again my ripped and torn flesh like a coat of spikes. Motherfuckers are going to pay for this I swear. Mitch, encouraged by my foul mouth, comes fully back to his senses.

He steadies me as we check on the door and find it unlocked. Either they didn't expect me to recover much or it's a trap. Either way, I'm heading out, pure rage and hatred the only things keeping me upright. I imagine getting my hands on al-Hakeem and all the unspeakable things I'll do to him. It keeps me going, pushing forward. I grab the sullied, bloody broom handles and we head out the door to find our comrades.

We make our way quietly through the building, killing every guard we find and releasing prisoners along the way. We find Murray and Carrie. It was obvious they found this wasn't the Ritz either.

"Come on, Carrie, find us a way out of here." Helping her to her feet, groaning through my own pain. We ended up with a few grenades, knives, and Ak-47's from the guards we took out. So armed, we battle our way out looking for our target until we realize he was no longer here.

***

I fight my way out of my nightmare, sweat soaking my sheets, covers twisted into knots and my scars alive and blazing with fresh insult. Fuck. That was a vivid one, like reliving it all again. Falling back on the bed with silent tears stinging my eyes, I try to settle myself. Time helped the flashbacks and nightmares dwindle, but the past couple of days brought them back, a terrible, painful reminder of my past. □

CHAPTER EIGHT

Tuesday 30 June

Stripping the bed and adding fresh linens, I head downstairs to the gym hoping a good work out and long shower will rid me of my unsettled feelings.

I start with yoga, but meditation is nearly impossible with so many thoughts running through my head. Along with the nightmarish hell I live through day to day because of al-Hakeem, I knew I'd let my guard down. Finding out he was behind the attack on my uncle's finances had me reeling and I hadn't seen things clearly.

That lapse cost me half my family. Now I find out he's in the U.S. and know that I should've looked for him specifically from the start instead of just trying to track the money. It troubles me that the CIA or FBI didn't alert me as soon as they found out he was in New York. That also contributed to the murder of my family. Blood is on their hands. While I can pretty much figure out their deadly game, it's hers I can't fully understand.

Who is this woman? Is she on the level? Or, is she playing me? But, there's something in her that speaks to the very essence of me. Something that makes me feel safe in her arms. Seeing her puts butterflies in my stomach and makes me catch my breath. Can I trust that she has no hidden agenda? What does she want from me, to get to my uncle, to bury me? I mean, she's a cop, after all.

Shaking my head, I know there are too many unanswered questions. She seemed sincere when she said she had no ulterior motives, but I don't think I can trust that right now. There's too much at stake, too much has already been lost.

I give up on yoga and switch to my free weights. Trying to focus. Thinking of this woman is distracting me from the real problem and I can't let anything jeopardize my goal: eliminate al-Hakeem.

First, I need to find him. I consider my network. Alex is already hunting down his contacts. I know, between the two of us, we'll find what the street's saying.

I put away the weights and finally empty my mind after several miles on the treadmill. When I hit the shower, I'm more settled and ready to meet my family at the church and discuss the services with our pastor.

***

The services will be held at our family's church. Our parents married here. We were all baptized here. My brother and sisters were married here, and we've had many of our family's funerals here. It's hard to fathom that it's my sisters and parents' funeral mass we're about to plan. I join my remaining family and we head into one of the rooms off the vestibule. It's a small room, typically used for the brides and grooms during weddings, small gatherings, or meetings of this particular nature.

Father Tommissino greets us somberly and offers us comfort with his words and tells us it shouldn't take too long. We pick out the music and the piece the Choir

Director will sing. Next, we pick the two readings from the Bible, decide who'll recite them, and who'll represent the family and give the eulogy. Father Tommissino will do the reading of the gospel and give his homily, introduce the eulogy and then invite others to share their stories. The grandkids will bring gifts to the altar and roses from my father's backyard to place on each casket.

When we're done, Father Tommissino leaves us to grieve privately. I elect not to hang back with the others and take my leave. I need to get back to work. My sister, Beth, as the executor of my parents' estate, already took care of the details at the funeral home. From setting up the times for the viewings on Wednesday and Rosary on Thursday to picking out the caskets, flowers, sayings, and pictures on the little cards, my sister handled it all, even what's to go in the obituary. Mass and burial will take place on Friday with a luncheon at Bellisio's after.

Alex and I stop outside to discuss his plans for the day and the buzz he put on the street last night. As usual, I surveil the parking lot and surrounding area and notice a van moving slowly down the road, too slowly. Suddenly picking up speed, the side door slides open and gunfire sprays the lot, taking out our vehicles and wounding two of our security detail. We hit the ground behind and come up firing as the van speeds from view.

"Merda! Damn tutto all'inferno!" I yell, kicking my flattened tires in frustration. A church, they shoot up a damn church to get to me. Cazzo di cazzo! Fucking assholes! Father Tommissimo and the family come rushing out and we reassure everyone that we're okay.

We can already hear sirens as we check everyone and tend to the wounded. When the cops arrive, I give them the plate number and description of the van and they radio out while one of the squad cars on the scene rushes off to try and intercept. One guy, as big as a tree trunk, confiscates our weapons while others cordon off the area and take statements.

My blouse is in shreds from scraping the ground and flying glass and I take stock. There's a graze on my left side and right arm, cuts on my face and arms but the worst of it is the gash on my side. It'll probably take some staples to close it up, a few more scars to add to the trophy count.

The officers finish taking our statements and Officer Tree Trunk advises that others will be talking to us. While EMT's are treating us, Jessica pulls up. Her eyes hidden by the tactical shades most Feds wear. She's appropriate in her dark suit and crisp white shirt. Her blazer flies open with a gust of wind, showing her weapon and shield as she is walking toward us, stopping for a few quick words with Officer Tree Trunk.

"Are you alright?" she asks. "Officer Tito says you were hit," her concern genuine.

"I'm fine," I quip and sigh, feeling her eyes bore into me.

"Really, I'm fine. Just a couple of scrapes," I wince as the last staple bites into my skin.

She looks at the gash on my arm and the staples on my side. Her fingers brush my forehead as she moves the hair off my face, looking at my cuts. She gently cups my cheek momentarily, satisfied I'm okay.

"How'd you get here so fast, Caruthers?" I ask.

"Surveillance notified me from first bang as they chased the van. They lost the perps, but we got the van. It's going through a thorough exam right now. I'll be heading over as soon as I'm done here. ATF should be here in a few."

"I can't believe they lost them. I don't know what's worse, me missing them or your guys losing them." Anger's getting the better of me and I know I need to tone it down.

"I understand," Jessica answers gruffly her arms crossed obviously miffed by my statement.

"I'm going to be tied up for a bit here and I know you'll be, too. We need to debrief after. Your office or mine?" I ask.

"Mine," she turns on her heel to do her work.

Merda. Damn Feds were right there and still couldn't do anything and all my security useless against a van coming down a road spraying gunfire. It's already been a long day. It's going to be an even longer night.

***

Jessica heart raced when she heard of the attack. Images of Lace being pulled out of the river flitted through her mind until she saw Toni safely sitting with the paramedics. She knew Toni would be cold, but, still, the attitude bothered her.

Now, she went to meet the two ATF agents, her friend Sam Bernakker, the shorter of the two, and Jerry

Federlin. The crime scene techs are numbering and photographing everything. Every detail is recorded.

"What do you know Bernakker?" she asks.

"Agent Caruthers, we seem to be having a busy couple of days," Bernakker replies.

"Yeah, too busy. Vic says Micro UZI and she knows her weapons. What's your take?"

"Won't know until we examine everything but given who you think is behind all of this, your victim is most likely correct. Uzi's are pretty easy to get."

"Looks like 9mm rounds, not armor piercing."

"Right, see how this round mushrooms out?" He points to one of the many rounds in the door of Toni's car. "They used hollow point rounds. The 9mm are more readily available than .45 and much cheaper than armor piercing rounds."

"Okay, let me know when the report's ready. I'm headed to the van."

"Caruthers," Bernakker stops Jessica.

"Yeah?"

"I noticed your exchange with the Vic." He takes his sunglasses off and continues. "Be careful with that one."

"Yeah," she continues to her vehicle. Damn, she sighs to herself.

***

By the time we finish, its late evening. Carrie brought one of the heavily armored SUVs from our fleet, generally used for transporting dignitaries. She also brought another Sig P229 which I leave locked in the glove box when I head into the building that houses the FBI. I clear the metal detectors, the pat down and head up to Jessica's office. Even at night the building is still alive with the late shift.

Jessica is studying something in her hand and looks up as I enter. I can't read her eyes as she gestures me to one of the chairs in front of her desk. I can't help but picture naked on top of that desk. Was it just yesterday? God, get it out of your head, Andiamo. I rub the image out of my eyes realizing she was speaking to me.

"I'm sorry can you repeat that please my brain just took a breather," I tell her.

"Understandable considering everything that's happened in the past couple of days. I was asking how you're holding up." I tilt my head and scrunch my eyebrows trying to read her once again. I still can't.

"I'm fine. What did you find out?"

"Not much really. 9mm hollow point rounds, four grooves, one twist that spells Uzi, which you already knew. Thought we caught a break. Seems a round hit one of the perps in the back of the van. We found a spray of blood and a small trail leading away from the van where it ended at a dead body. It's still waiting to be identified.

"Everything's been sent to Quantico for analysis and the body's at the Wayne County Coroner with FBI forensic pathologists doing the post." This is a surprise. I didn't think we hit a damn thing. Jess continues.

"The van was reported stolen two days ago, of course. We're looking into the owner, a contractor. Questioning him, his associates and his employees as we speak. Wish we had more but the forensics will take time, same with the digging."

"I need to see the dead one. I may recognize him. If not, then I need a picture to show some of my people, see if they know him."

"I can arrange that. Do you need to change first?" She looks at my ragged state, still in my wrecked clothes, no time to change.

"Soon. We need to hit my office before we meet my contacts. I keep clothes there. First, I need to see what we can find out about that body." Jessica's perfectly shaped mouth drops open.

"You're taking me to meet contacts?" she asks incredulously.

"Yes, and believe me, I'd prefer not to, but we don't have time for bullshit. We need to intel fast and that means you're with me."

"Ouch, bet that hurt."

"More than you will ever know, Agent Caruthers, more than you know.

"I need you to forget the people you see. Keep your mouth shut about being a Fed. Most are going to smell cop anyway but please if they know you're a Fed they'll never trust me again." She nods her agreement.

"This ain't my first rodeo, you know. I know how to blend in undercover."

I nod. "Good. Then let's get out of here. Being in this place twice in one week gives me the heebie-jeebies." I get up and exit, leaving Jessica to catch up.

***

We're on the streets in Greektown after a brief stop at my office to change. My informants wouldn't give me the time of day without the right look. Right now, my guy is late, not unusual for him.

I didn't recognize the young guy in the morgue, and they haven't identified him yet. Jessica brought a couple snapshots along. While we wait, I try to explain what al-Hakeem has to do with my uncle but she's buying the shit I'm shoveling.

"So, what you're telling me is, you have a nutcase terrorist on your ass because your uncle wouldn't sell him arms? That's crazy, Toni. Do you think my bosses are going to buy this?" she asks.

"I don't care what they buy. This guy tried to launder his money through one of my uncle's import/export businesses in Italy. When my Uncle caught it, al-Hakeem tried a take-over. When he thwarted the take-over, al-Hakeem was pissed. He tried to take over other businesses after

137

that, unsuccessfully. We had an accountant who tried to work with people al-Hakeem trusted to launder his money and buy weapons. This is what I found out. "

"Uh-huh, keep going," she's obviously having a hard time buying it. Can't say I blame her.

"The straw, as they say, that broke the camel's back, was when my Uncle caught one of his associates selling al-Hakeem the weapons he wanted. Something my Uncle wanted nothing to do with so threw a fit and put a stop to it, quick."

"Needless to say. This associate is he still among the living?" she raises her eyebrows inquiringly.

"It may seem pretty simple to you there in your safe little world, but things are different here in real life. Yes, he's still amongst the living," I snap. "The accountant, however, had a nasty drug habit and overdosed, stupid idiot, instead of facing the consequences. He was the one siphoning money and that's how I found out it was Mansur al-Hakeem I was dealing with." Most of that was the truth. She didn't have to know I was the one who caused said overdose and I found out it was al-Hakeem as I watched his life slip away.

"So tell me why he wants your family so much. You, I can understand, but the rest of your family? I know it's personal for you and I know why but why is it personal for him?"

"If you know why it's personal for me then I assume you read my file." She nods for me to continue.

"I was the woman he couldn't break, that he couldn't kill. I believe when he found out who my uncle was, he tried to get to me through him, just like you are. He should've known it wouldn't work. What he did to my parents, my sisters? That did work. That I will not forgive or forget. It's him or me now and you can either help or get out of my way." I don't give her a chance to respond and changed the subject.

"I wish you would've accepted a change of clothes. You're a sitting duck out here and you scream Fed." Just then a couple of mean looking characters approach, hoping for a quick thrill. They didn't notice me, and I can tell that one of them is packing. Damn it. I don't have time to deal with these two idiots.

"Hey baby, we just be wantin to get down tonight," ugly number one dribbles spit down his chin and bubbles out. Ugly two grunts his agreement. "We get down wit' you, hot mama." He rubs his hand down her arm, licking his chops. I start to move out of the shadows when Jess holds up her hand to stop me.

"Now gentlemen, what makes you think I would just fall into your arms, handsome as you two are?" She smiles and a feral grin spreads across my face. I think I'm in for a treat, so are the gentlemen in question.

"Come on, baby, you don't even have to take us home. We do this right here, right now," ugly two pipes up while ugly one moves in on the other side stroking his manhood. Jessica positioned herself to put them exactly where she wants them.

"Gee, as romantic as that sounds, I'm going to have to decline." She still looks casual leaning against the building. Ugly one grabs her from one side, as ugly two advances from the other.

"We don't like the 'tude chica, so we just take what we want," two says. She moves so fast I hardly believe it, a wolf catching her prey. They're both on the ground before I could even move.

"I'm impressed. For a Fed, you sure move well," I tell her as she brushes off her hands.

"Thanks," she snarls.

"What you want to do with these two? I know them. I don't think they're going to be trying this again anytime soon." I kick over ugly one, recognizing him, and grab the front of his shirt. I relieve him of his piece and slap him awake.

"Hey stupid, wake up. Come on. That's it. Wakie, wakie." He starts stirring. "Marvell, you know this is not the proper way to impress a woman."

His vision starts clearing. "Storm? You? Shit, what da fuck she hit me with, a brick?"

"No, dumbass. She used her hands," I chuckle. "What the hell. Are you trying to get yourself killed?"

"Shit dawg, I just wanted to find myself some boo-tae, ya know?"

"Marvell, what part of 'no' you don't understand? You tryin' to get locked-up on purpose?" Marvell shakes his head.

"Naw, not goin back to the box, dawg."

"Shit, Brah," I shake my head, "you done screwed yourself big time 'cause you just messed with a fucking Fed man."

"Aw shit, for reals?" A look of terror comes over his face then his eyes focus on me.

"What you doin' wit' a Fed?" My expression hardens and I don't say a word as I flash him a look. He gulps loudly.

"Never mind, dawg."

"If you and your butt buddy Cole make it right, she might, you know, let it go, man." I look over at Jess as she picked Cole up off the ground. Cole had the same look of terror.

"Well, gentlemen are you very, very sorry?" Jess inquires.

"Yeah," they reply in unison.

"Do you promise not to hit on a lady like that ever again?"

"Yeah!"

"Okay, I'll tell you what. Since you promise, I'll give you the benefit of the doubt and let you off the hook, this time, and I'll be sure to stop by from time to time just to make sure you're keeping your word." She stares at the two miscreants, knowing she just picked up two new informants.

"Yeah," they had the good sense to say one more time. She gathers their contact information before she dismisses them.

"Scram," Jess says calmly and didn't have to tell them twice. I never saw guys with pants hanging to their knees run so fast.

"As I was saying," I stole a sideways glance, "not bad for a Fed."

"Hmm. I thought you didn't want anyone to learn I was a Fed." She backs me into the wall of the building. We look into each other searching for what I couldn't tell you. Lies. Truth. She has my stomach twisting in knots as she penetrates my soul with those eyes. Getting uncomfortable, I break contact first and turn the tables on her. Now her back is against the wall.

"I don't but I found it prudent for those two. Just so you know, Agent Caruthers, I do have a few moves of my own." With that, I make another quick twist and spin her around so that her belly was against the wall. She starts to counter and I whisper in her ear.

"Be cool, my guy is here." I half turn to the approaching footsteps.

"Stutter, what took you so damn long? You shouldn't be sneaking up on me while I'm trying to have me some fun."

"S-sorry St-St-Storm, I d-didn't mean nuttin. I'm j-just making s-s-sure it was you." I chose him because he's Muslim and the Mosque where he prays is the one al-Hakeem would most likely use to recruit. Plus, I know Stutter can pick up bits of info once he knows about my family.

"Don't let it happen again. I want to know the word Stutter; you hear any chatter about the explosion that happened on the Eastside?"

"N-n-now you d-d-don't wanna get m-m-mixed up, t-t-too d-dangerous. I don't wanna g-g-get in on th-this." He turns to leave, but Jessica's not the only one with fast moves. I grab him by the neck and shove him against the building. He just confirmed he knows what's going on.

"You don't want to fuck with me on this one, Stutter. Whoever did it, killed my fucking parents and two of my sisters. I'm pissed off, could be I take my anger out on you. "

"Pleas-s-se, St-Storm, I d-didn't know they were yours! Sh-shit!" The fear in his eyes tells me part of what I want to know. He's not just scared of me.

"What do you know? I need to find the sorry ass son of a bitch who blew my family to pieces. They tried for the rest of my family at the church, Stutter, a fucking church."

"I d-d-don't know anything. I s-s-swear. I didn't want t-t-to know."

"I don't believe you." I tighten my grip on his neck and shove his face into the rough brick. "I want answers Stutter. Now."

"S-s-shit, the only thing I heard is that they are l-l-l-looking for peop-p-ple willing to follow instructions with no que-questions asked. Young kids with nothing to l-l-lose; ya know, kids who are wi-l-l-lling to die for Allah."

"Where?"

"I d-d-don't know."

I shove his face against the wall again. "Where?" I lower my voice slightly. "I'm a patient person, Stutter, but I'm losing it quick. I won't ask again. Where?" I shove him one more time.

"Shit, F-fuckin bitch. A p-p-place on Caniff, near the Mosque."

"That's better and it better be good info, otherwise, I will come back and find you. Remember, they killed mine." I ease up a bit, letting him straighten up. "Now, I want you to look at a photo. Do you know him?"

"Yeah," he sighs. "T-T-Tariq, Tariq ibn Khalil al-Askari, he's a f-friend. He g-got c-c-c-caught up in the hype I just t-t-told you. I told him..." Tears form in his eyes.

"I'm sorry for the loss of your friend, Stutter, but if I find out you had anything to do with this, you best believe we'll have another chat and it won't be as pleasant as this one. Now, you're going to do some work for me. You're going to find out anything you can about this group. And, stay available, Stutter. Don't make me come looking for you."

"S-s-s-shit." I give him a c-note for his trouble and he takes off like a scared rabbit.

"Storm?" Jessica comes away from the wall. "Ah, Storm Investigations, I see." But I didn't see. I didn't see it coming until it was too late. I was paying attention to the radiance she projected with her feral grin and before I could move, she had me against the wall with the side of my face scraping brick.

"Well now, Storm," she spreads my legs wide to frisk me. Damn what she can do with those hands.

"I'll just have to calm that storm won't I," her mouth whispers into my ear, her breath hot. Payback, I suppose, point taken.

"Um," I clear my throat. "Agent Caruthers, while I, uh, must admit you, uh, have a superior frisking technique," my heart is racing – in a good way. "I must remind you that we, uh, do have work to do, people to see, places to go – terrorists to catch." Fuck me, payback delivered. Whew!

"You don't look like much of a storm now but yes you're right. Remember this next time you want to play me. You're not the only bad ass in town." Just as abruptly, she pulls away. Damn, Andiamo, I think you've met your match.

Jessica turns to head out of the alley. I take a moment to watch her then shake my head and follow this lovely wolf out into the night.

For the next few hours, we visit source after source across town. I know every inch of these streets. I should, as often as I got into trouble here. Every contact we talk to is scared right down to the bone. None of them want to have anything to do with the active recruiting that's happening. Fear keeps them quiet even with the promise of big money. Jessica's informants were the same. By the time we get through with the last one, I'm trying not to close my eyes.

"We need to go over all of this. I'd prefer my offices this time, if you don't mind," I address her.

"I see what I can work out. Not sure what time I'll be able to get away or how long it'll take brief them on all the information we got. Do you want them to know about the place on Caniff?"

"No, not just yet. I want surveillance set up, then we'll pay a visit."

"Alright, I'll let you know when I'm free then," she says wearily. I leave her at her office and head home.

As the gates open, someone steps out of the shadows onto the drive. Sheppard. He follows my car inside the gates. I stop and step out to confront him, weapon drawn and in sight. With my other hand, I feel for the tracker I picked up earlier at the office.

"What the hell? This is trespassing, Agent Sheppard. I didn't invite you and I know you don't have a warrant."

"I'm here to warn you, Andiamo. I am in the FBI. I can make your life a living hell, which I *will* do if I can't get what I want, and what I want is your uncle. Now!" he yells, standing his ground. Whoa. Left field.

"Sheppard, there's something you don't seem to get. You see, I can make your life much more of a living hell than you could ever make mine. And, frankly, this makes me quite suspicious of you. Have you been a naughty little agent, Sheppard? Are you the one leaking information to al-Hakeem?"

"No, of course not," he sputters nervously. Hmph. No, shit. Now, I *am* suspicious. I just tossed that out there to get him off my back. I can't believe what I'm thinking; this pathetic, snide, weasel? Could he be one who caused the murder of my family? Or, maybe he knows who did? Yeah, that's more likely the case, I nod to myself. I must know for sure.

"Agent Sheppard," I mock. "Why is it that I don't believe you? What are you hiding?" At that, his anger took over.

"You bitch. I'm going to get you and your uncle one way or another. Nothing is going to stop me, not you and especially not that bitch you're sleeping with. She's a disgrace. I don't know how she ever got past her profiling with the sick things she does with you. I'm in charge here and I won't tolerate such behavior."

"Excuse me? Sheppard, I have no idea how you got your position or how you keep it. Obviously, someone misread your profile. How did you ever manage to sneak by your superiors? Who'd you sleep with on your way, huh?" He starts to sputter again but I cut him off.

"Let me remind you, Sheppard, that you're on my property illegally," I move closer to him. "You're without a warrant," closer still. "I'm holding a weapon. If you want to survive this night, I suggest you take your leave, or I won't be responsible for my actions."

"You and your so-called girlfriend will pay. I swear to you." He comes at me. While still holding my weapon down at my side, I counter his move and inject the small tracker into his neck. I don't think he even felt it. He looked surprised and a bit panicked that I could so easily thwart his attack and he hurriedly left.

He reminds me of why I don't work for the government anymore. Idiots like him got people killed, people I knew. People who were just doing their jobs and following orders from buttheads like this Snidely Weasel.

So, he knows Jessica and I were together intimately, but he doesn't know that it was only a couple of times. I sigh and apologize to her for having to put up with an idiot boss.

I dial Mitch knowing I'm going to have to deal with Andrea for waking them up. I wince not looking forward to the wrath I'll have to endure later.

"Mitch, we have a situation, get to the office, I'm on my way." I hang up and make two more calls.

CHAPTER NINE

Wednesday 1 July

Taking more precaution than usual, I park in the hidden garage, deep under the building, taking my private elevator up to the sanctity of my office. Once I change and start the coffee, I open my office door knowing Mitch and Jessica are already there waiting. I let them skirt around me and take up the two chairs in front of my desk.

Now, I need to explain to Jessica why I believe her boss should be off this case *and* that he had something to do with the murder of my family. It won't be easy for her accept and probably piss her off.

"I had a little surprise waiting for me when I got home this morning," I tell them glancing at Jessica.

"What happened?" she demands.

"I had a visitor. Sheppard. He was waiting for me."

"What? Shit. Idiot. What did he do?" She sounds resigned, frustrated.

"He made it clear he wants my uncle and me and that nothing will stand in his way. He threatened everyone and promised to make my life, as well as yours, a living hell."

She gets out of her chair and paces around the office. Mitch looks to me with a 'what's going on' look on his face. I shake my head, slightly. She starts to say something, stops, decides to grab a coffee and continues her pacing, coming to a stop at the windows behind me, staring out at the river below.

"I see. So, he said included me in this threat?"

"Yes."

"What else?" She knows what's coming. Mitch looks like he wants to get the hell out of here as she sips at her coffee.

"Do you want me to leave, Agent Caruthers? I could let Toni tell you in private," Mitch pleads.

"No, that's okay. I prefer that you stay and listen. Maybe you can help me figure out how save my career after he does what he plans to do," she says, turning again to stare out the window. "And please, Mitch, call me Jessica." Mitch's heart softens and I get up to pace, feeling uncomfortable talking to her back.

"Jess," I pause as her shoulders stiffen, "he knows." She looks down and lets her forehead lightly hit the window.

"Well, I figured as much. It was bound to happen."

"Yeah. He knows and plans to use that as leverage to get you out and to get my uncle. He doesn't give a shit about al-Hakeem. He wants us behind bars or dead. He's dangerous, Jess. I could see it in his eyes. I hate to say it, but I think he's one of your moles." Her eyes widen in disbelief.

"He about gave himself away, that he knows who the mole is and used them for his own purpose. He hasn't reported his suspicions and definitely doesn't feel any remorse about keeping his mouth shut."

"No, that's impossible. It's simply not true. I've known him for years and worked closely with him. He's a good agent and usually a good leader. He just loves his work too much."

"That's the whole thing, in a nutshell, Jess. He doesn't love his job; he's obsessed with one aspect of it. He's obsessed," I say again when she turns from the window to stare me down.

"He's stuck between the horror and the power of it right now. He's scared and obsessed and doesn't know what else to do. He's striking at whatever and whoever he can to get his way and, right now, his way is to have my Uncle and me. He's like a little kid throwing temper tantrums and that makes him extremely dangerous."

She continues to stare at me for a moment. She's upset now, can't say I blame her. I hope she'll come to her senses, otherwise she has no career left and I have a feeling she'd be lost without it. She turns back toward the window to stares at the river again. Mitch and I turn to each other and shrug. It's totally up to her now. We wait in silence for a few minutes, letting the ramifications sink in. Finally, she turns around to speak.

"Well, I must admit, as unbelievable as this is, it makes a certain kind of sense. So tell me, what can we do to get my boss headed in the right direction, get the bad guy, save my career, and keep the girl at the same time?"

Mitch and I burst out laughing. God, despite myself, I think I'm falling for this woman. She's got guts. Damn it, Andiamo.

"First things first, I'm going to have to deal with my superiors when I stagger in this morning. I didn't think anyone knew what happened between us except for the Deputy Director. I need to see how that goes since I only spoke to him about it yesterday. I better check my office for listening devices," she sighs. "I have an idea, but I need to run it by you before I make myself look like a bitch who'd do anything to advance her career, including sleeping with the woman we need cooperation from," she looks at me for assurance.

I nod in agreement though I'm disturbed the Deputy Director knew about us. This makes him another suspect in my eyes, but I keep that suspicion to myself. I'd need solid proof first or she'd never believe it.

We go over the possibilities, looking for a plan. We know that Sheppard will pull out all the stops when she confronts him about what he did at my place. He'll throw her under the bus by bringing up the fact we have been intimate. When he does, she's prepared to own up to it and say that she spoke to the Deputy Director about it seeking his advice.

She's on solid ground on her end but Sheppard isn't, and he knows it. There's just no spinning the facts. He not only illegally entered private property, but threatened and attacked someone enlisted to help find a very dangerous man. She could be reprimanded for not following the chain of command when she spoke with the Deputy Director instead of Spencer but if the Special Agent in Charge is a stand-up guy, he'll understand she was having a conversation with the man she calls Uncle. But, there's just no telling what they'll do with Sheppard. Damn right, I'm going to do everything in my power to make his life a living hell.

When Mitch retires to his office, I lock the doors hoping to have a private conversation with Jess.

"Look Jess...," I start to say.

"Toni, I know what you feel about Agent Sheppard, but he's a solid agent, one of the good guys. I know we planned for the worst, but I don't think he'll do it. I don't know what's going on with him right now. This just isn't like him. I think with a little guidance, he'll get back on track."

"He's a weasel, Jess. Don't be fooled. You're a much better judge of character than that. He'll turn on you in a heartbeat, so you need to watch your back."

With that, I change the subject.

"On this place by the Mosque, I think we should head over to watch it before I place someone on the inside. When we gather more intel and confirm it's the right place, then we can pull in the full weight of the task force."

"Sounds like a plan if we can get past all this other crap. Well, I best get busy," she starts for the door.

"Jessica?" I don't know quite what I'm doing. I've never been in a position like this. She turns back toward me.

"I..." Why does she always have me at a loss for words? She nods her head, understanding what it is I'm not saying.

"I'd like ... Merda," someone tries the door, interrupting me. Finding it locked, they start pounding on it.

"Cazzo!" The pounding continues. "Alright, alright, keep your pantyhose on. I'll be right there," I yell. I walk over to the desk and flip the locks. There, in all his beauty, stands my brother.

"Hey Sis, what's the haps?" He looks over at Jess. "Oops, looks like I interrupted something." He walks over to Jessica and introduces himself.

"Buon Giorno, mi chiamo Allesandro Andiamo." He grabs her hand and doing his eyebrow dance, kisses it lightly.

"We're finally introduced, Mr. Andiamo. I'm Special Agent Jessica Caruthers, pleased to meet you." Jessica's amused.

My charming brother's smile froze, a look of terror coming into his eyes. I burst into laughter. Jessica walks to me and draws me into a lip lock heavy and full of promise. Puttana.

She looks back at my brother, still frozen with a panicked look on his face, then focuses those eyes of ice at me, winks, and disappears. I laugh so hard I fall back into my chair. My brother just stares at me like I've gone completely mad. It feels good to laugh about something.

"Are you insane? A Feeb just kissed you. What the hell is going on?" He flops down on the couch, looks from one side of the couch to the other and jumps up so quickly, you'd think his ass was on fire.

"You didn't like just finish doing anything on this thing did you?" I laugh even harder at that. He shakes his head at me while I try to catch my breath.

"No, nothing happened." I said, still trying to catch my breath. He sits back down on the couch.

"Here I am all ready to report to you on my exploits on the Westside last night and I find you trying to screw a Fed? One hot Fed, I'll give you that, but damn Sis, what the fuck?"

"Now, now, getting jealous won't do you any good Bro, besides, she was just messing with me. We hooked up before I knew she was a Fed and you know more than anyone it's not going to go anywhere." My brother shakes his head again.

"Hey, look, I don't have to explain myself to my younger brother, especially one who just tried to charm the socks off her. I thought you were better than that Bro." He rolls his eyes at me.

"Got the point Sis, but what can you do with something that looks that good? If the Feds are hiring babes like that nowadays, I'm a goner. Shit." He props his feet up on the arm of the couch, lying down with his hands behind his head.

"Gees Bro, you're making my heart bleed for you. Let's get to work here kiddo, we're running on a tight schedule."

"Yeah, yeah, yeah." He sits back up. "I don't know what's going on but my sources are scared to death. Lips are shut tight on this one, even when money's talking."

"Yeah, I got the same thing."

"When I did get a few to talk, I came up with a recurring thing---" my brother pauses. I interrupt him before he could finish his sentence.

"Place on Caniff. Yeah, I got the word last night on our trek through the jungle."

"You took a Feeb with you to talk to your informants? You must be insane. What other explanation could there be? You've lost it. That's the only reason I can think of for you to trust a Fed. What the fuck are you thinking, Sis? You feeling okay?"

"No, I'm heartbroken, Alex. Our parents and baby sisters have been murdered and we don't have time to mess around, Bro. For what it's worth, she also took me to meet her CI's and we found essentially the same thing. So, let's keep trying to track his movements from New York and find his ass."

"You're right, Sis. I'll keep at it."

He stands up and comes toward me. I heave myself out of my chair and give him a big hug. Miss Edna's typing reports at her desk and he stops to take her hand, kissing it lightly before heading to the elevator. I shake my head. Don't ever change Bro. Don't ever change.

"Good morning, Miss Edna. I hope you got some sleep last night because we've got a long, hard, road today. I have some things that need to be ready for the morning briefing. I want everyone ready in an hour. We've got a lot to go through."

"Yes, of course, Ms. Andiamo." She smiles sweetly at me. "The surveillance vehicles are still dogging your family. Other than that, the teams are reporting no problems."

"Thanks, Miss Edna. They can keep an eye on my family as long as they want." I went back to my office to shower and change. An hour later, everyone's sitting in the conference room.

"Alrightie then, we have a lot to get through. Miss Edna, please pass out the updates. Mitch, why don't you start the briefing, how many bugs you find this morning?

"Nothing new and I just got the sweep results of your place." Everyone looks to him quizzically. "They found nothing."

"Ok great, my security remains intact."

"Thanks, Mitch. Let's go over these new developments. We have an Agent who's gone rogue, though he believes he's doing the right thing – trying to capture me and my uncle. He's a danger to this mission. I believe he set in motion the events leading to the murder of my parents and sisters. I believe he knows who the mole is, that it's someone higher up the food chain, and that he used that mole to instigate the murders to try and draw me out, to get to my uncle. Now, after talking to Agent Caruthers, I have reason to believe the mole is the Deputy Director himself. Now, I can't bring this to Agent Caruthers without proof, so we'll have to dig deep on him.

Right now, Agent Sheppard believes he has the upper hand and that the mole, one of his superiors, will have his back on this."

For the next two hours, Mitch and I relay developments to the rest of the crew. We discuss everything the others came up with as well. When we finally come out of the conference room, we have loads of work and everyone heads their separate ways. Miss Edna hands me a stack of paperwork and messages that require my attention.

I spend the next couple of hours on business, after which I call a contact over at US Customs. There are several ways to cross the border from Canada to Michigan. If I can find out where he crossed, then I might be able to track him to where he's hiding.

I call everyone I can think of and fax sketches asking them to let me know if they see or hear anything. Though I know in my gut that he's already in Detroit, it doesn't hurt to cover all the bases and put the border on alert for a terrorist cell.

I put feelers out to every legitimate and many illegitimate places. Some will have to wait. I'll have to visit in person, but I can only make those visits in the dark of night. I call in every debt, every marker from here to New York looking for the trail of al-Hakeem.

I then turn to the intel reports that Carrie briefly summarized during the meeting. It covers all the major players for this op, and I wish I'd been able study these earlier. I start with Sheppard's. I need to know more about him than he knows about himself.

Calvin Samuel Sheppard, fifty-two, only child to Ariana Jessica Toomey and Samuel Richard Sheppard. Mother is a retired agent with a stellar career, father a retired judge with conservative leanings. Divorced from wife Cynthia last year, two kids, grown and estranged from their father. Hmm, wonder what's up there.

Fluent in all avenues of investigation from cybercrimes to gangs to bank robberies and human trafficking. He has an impressive close rate of ninety-four percent. He moved easily through the ranks from Special Agent, Supervisory Special Agent and Senior Supervisory Agent and was promoted to Assistant Special Agent in Charge three years ago taking over the seat vacated when they promoted Sean Spencer to Special Agent in Charge of the Detroit Field Office.

His displayed excellent skills as a leader and his loyalty has never called into question, until now. What happened suddenly to make him so obsessed with my uncle and me? I need Carrie to dig deeper on him. I want to know about the rift in his family. I need to understand this sudden shift.

Next up Isley, Donald Jason Isley, forty-two. Middle child of five siblings to Constance Ann Riley and Harold Franklin Isley. His mother a successful and well-noted hair stylist to the stars, his father a director and producer of award winning documentaries. He's single, never married. Not much else on the personal end.

He began his career in the field, easily able to blend in with any group he needed to infiltrate. He was able to get in deep with several different factions across the globe. His successes soon propelled him into a handler position. His uncanny ability to come up with intelligence where no one else could helped him move up the ranks fast. This tells me he's a slithering snake.

He's able to get people to act against their nature giving him what he wants then turns on those he no longer needs or likes. He has a masterful lethal tongue and his file tells me I need to worry about him. He'll manipulate people and situations until he gets what he wants. Thing is, I don't know exactly what it is he wants with me.

Malcomb Jerome Davis, the youngest of two sons to Charlene Leticia Jones and Jeremiah Davis, both officers with the Detroit PD retired. Brother Jeremiah Jr. in and out of jail and rehab, turned to gangs and perished in a drive-by shooting. Little brother then went into law enforcement due to lack of interest in his brother's case. He eventually solved his brother's cold case in the beginning years of his career in the FBI, doing so on his own time.

Married thirty years with three children, two daughters and one son. He took on the parenting role of one Jessica Ann Caruthers when her parents passed away. Hmm, early age for parents to be dead.

Fluent in all avenues of investigation he steadily moved up the ranks. Big hitch when shot in a drug sting where two others lost their lives, a husband and wife team. Strange to be married and on the same op, it just doesn't happen. The couple that was killed Marlena and Benjamin Caruthers. Oh merda! Jessica's parents. Light finally dawning in this fogged brain. No wonder she understood me as well as she did.

Yes, I remember hearing something about it toward the end of my time in Detroit's Juvenile Justice system. They were in deep with the Mob, deeper than anyone ever achieved, when someone betrayed them. At least that's what I heard. I don't think a drug sting is the true nature of their death. Merda, I hope to hell my Uncle didn't have anything to do with this.

You don't kill cops. You go after the men in the family so you can get what you want out of them and put them on the payroll. I'll have to dig deeper on it later, after this terrorist business we have to deal with. Va fanculo! This is all we need. Putting it on the back burner, I continue into his background.

Okay where was I? He couldn't solve the one case that's haunted his career as justice for the murders of his friends went unclaimed. Everything else on target for a Deputy Director who spent his life in public service. I don't buy it. He knows how to play politics and somewhere in his sterling career he had to have turned. I know it like I know the sun will come up tomorrow. Obviously, I need more intel on Mr. Davis.

Jessica Ann Caruthers. I hesitate opening her folder and argue with myself about prying where I shouldn't. Does her knowing everything in my file actually give me a right to study hers? Shouldn't I get to know her through personal experience? Oh please, you know that's never going anywhere Andiamo. Just do it. She's on the team and you need to know all you can about those who are using you.

So, Jessica Ann Caruthers. Thirty-seven, daughter of Marlena Cardeux and Benjamin Alan Caruthers. Murdered during an undercover operation when Jess was fifteen. She became emancipated and, supported by Malcomb Davis, she graduated high school and went to college and law school. She passed the bar on the first go around and joined the Feds at the age of twenty-five.

Fluent in all avenues of investigation, she spent much of her time undercover. Her career took big hit when her lover, also an undercover female agent, lost her life when the gang they'd infiltrated found out the truth.

She was transferred to Alaska, ouch, and made comeback after being reassigned to Arizona. She transferred here to Detroit as the youngest Assistant SAC in Detroit history. She made her bones in human trafficking, turning gang and mafia members.

What kind of courage does it take to come back not only from the death of her parents but the death of a partner and lover? I find myself admiring this woman's dedication and bravery. She's gone through a lot and is still empathetic; still has heart. How did she end up amongst this bunch of numbnuts and not lose her core values?

When I finish studying all the packets hours later, I buzz Miss Edna and ask for any messages. She tells me Jessica called twice and it's important for me to get in touch with her as soon as possible.

***

Jessica heads to her office to type up her notes and make copies for everyone. Then she contacts the Wayne County Coroner's office to give them the identity of the body they're currently hosting. Next, she contacts Deputy Director Davis as he left a message for her. He gave his assurance he and Special Agent Spencer will be at the briefing in ten minutes.

She takes a few moments to catch her breath, rubs her face to get the tired out, grabs herself a cup of coffee, and heads to the conference room. She's sitting in the middle of the table going over her notes as others stagger in. Malcomb comes in and shines a smile at his favorite Agent. Jessica returns it, standing to greet him with a hug. Underlings around her are staring with their jaws on the ground wondering why she's giving the Director a hug instead of a handshake.

Jessica speaks briefly with Special Agent Spencer and as they finish, Sheppard walks in, a shocked look on his face.

"Director Davis, Spence, what can I do for you?" Sheppard asks trying to sound like everything's perfectly fine.

"Ah, just the man I was looking for. Calvin, I'm a bit confused on some points which I believe you need to clarify for us." Spencer sounded calm enough. The Deputy Director choosing to hold back, let his SAC handle his subordinate.

"Sure would you like to come to my office, Sir?"

"Here's fine Sheppard." Spencer turns and addresses the room. "Everyone except Caruthers and Isley if you would leave us please," and he waits for the room to clear.

"Would you care to tell me what you were up to last night?" he asks.

"Sir?" Panic nearly takes hold of him.

"You heard me, Sheppard. I want to know how attempting to intimidate a civilian and accosting her at her own home, someone we've enlisted to aid us, is going to help get this terrorist."

"I-I...," he stammers for a brief second. "She's withholding valuable information regarding her uncle sir. I believe he's heavily involved in this terrorist plot, as is Ms. Andiamo, and that they should be held over for questioning. Ms. Andiamo shouldn't be the one we use to go after a terrorist. We can do that without her, sir.

"We should be using her to put her uncle behind bars and in turn, herself. Agent Caruthers here fails to see that as she's carrying on an intimate sexual relationship with Ms. Andiamo. I'm not going to go as far as to say she's in their pocket but...well...just putting it out there, Sir."

Jessica knew this could happen but didn't believe he'd do this to her or go so far as to accuse her of being on the take. They'd worked side by side together, fighting the good fight. She really thought he wouldn't, couldn't do this.

"I'll deal with Agent Caruthers in just a moment," Spencer said. "Mr. Isley, are you in agreement with Agent Sheppard?"

"Special Agent Spencer, I must admit having Big Tony would be a coup. As much as I'd like to be the one to put him in a hole and throw away the key, I do believe that Ms. Andiamo's insight and hunger to make right what happened to her in the past makes her an excellent and most valuable asset. We would be ill-advised not to use her exceptional skills on this task force." He abandoned Sheppard without remorse.

"I happen to agree with you, Mr. Isley. Agent Sheppard, Ms. Andiamo has expressed interest in pressing charges against you."

"Sir?"

"Did you or did you not go to her home, enter the grounds without a warrant, demand she produce her uncle and then proceed to attack her?"

"Well sir, as I've just explained..."

"There is no explanation for your conduct Sheppard. If she chooses to press charges, you realize your career is finished? Was that worth it? Was this lapse in judgment worth everything you've worked for? You and I go way back, Cal and this isn't like you. You run the Counterterrorism Department so why your sudden interest in Organized Crime? I thought I could count on you." Sheppard, red-faced and angry, turns to Jessica with murder in his eyes. It doesn't escape Spencer's notice.

"Don't look to her, Calvin. She didn't rat you out. I received the phone call rather early this morning from Ms. Andiamo herself. Agent Caruthers has absolutely nothing to do with this. You chose to act in a way that is unprofessional then you unabashedly try to put Agent Caruthers head on the chopping block. To say I'm extremely disappointed Calvin is an understatement. I don't understand how this task force prompted such behavior but it is unacceptable." Sheppard is speechless.

"Now, Agent Caruthers what is this about you having an intimate sexual relationship with Ms. Andiamo. Is it true?"

"I would hardly call it a relationship sir. We had sex a couple of times. When I found out she was the civilian we were dealing with, I sought council with my Uncle. As far as the inference that I'm in the pocket of the Andiamo's, I challenge you to find a single shred of evidence. You won't because there isn't any.

"I will provide any and all financial documents as I recently had them run and certified by this office. Anything that comes up different would be very suspect. Finally, I would be happy to cooperate to the fullest in any investigation into this matter should one be warranted. I've served this Bureau with honor and distinction, sir. My reputation is above reproach even when it's cost me personally."

"Sir is this correct, she came to you in a personal conversation," he addressed the Deputy Director.

"Yes, it is," was all that the Deputy Director had to say on the matter.

"Alright Caruthers, I wish you had come to me about this but we'll see if we need to get into this matter further or not. I need you to contact her and ask her to meet with us. Does she trust you? Are you two still sleeping with each other?"

"Not since I spoke with the Deputy Director and the only reason she will speak to any of us is because of our connection. It's the reason she chose to filter information through me to the task force and the reason I have a report to give you today."

"Alright, fine. I'd like you to cultivate that relationship if you can. How soon can you get her here?"

"As soon as she'll take my call but let me say, Sir, I'm very uncomfortable with this, using Ms. Andiamo in this way."

"Noted Caruthers. Sheppard, you will sound contrite and deliver a believable apology to Ms. Andiamo. We'd all like Big Tony permanently behind bars but we do this above board and by the damn book in order to make it stick. Do you understand?"

"Yes, sir," Sheppard said.

"I believe we'll sit in on the briefing as soon as Andiamo can make it here, now if there's nothing else, I'll be in my office. Let me know when she's in the building." They leave the conference room in an awkward silence.

"Well gentlemen, copies of my report are on the table. I'll leave you to it. I have to try to reach Ms. Andiamo in hopes she'll answer," she leaves the room without a word from Sheppard or Isley.

***

I dial the number Jessica left. It's not her cell phone. She answers on the first ring.

"Special Agent Caruthers," she sounds frustrated. I play it cool, guessing it's her work extension.

"Agent Caruthers, this is Toni Andiamo. My assistant says it's important. What can I do for you?"

"Ms. Andiamo, thank you for getting back to me. I know you have a lot on your plate today, but we'd like your presence at our offices today, in approximately twenty minutes. Can you make it?"

"That doesn't leave me much time." She must have found a bug on her phone or she'd tell me what's going on.

"Good, we'll see you then. If you have any questions you know how to reach me, good-bye Ms. Andiamo," with that she hangs up.

I let Miss Edna know what's going on and ask Karl to bring the equipment I need, moving to the ready room to check my communications with Mitch. Out the door and on my way in less than three minutes, I call Jess' cell phone. She answers on the first ring.

"It's about time where have you been? I've been trying to get hold of you for hours."

"What the hell's going on?"

"Shit has hit the fan here. When they found out what happened between you and Sheppard last night, Spencer had a fit. They called Sheppard on the carpet. He tried to take me down by telling Spencer about our us."

"I knew that weasel would turn on you."

"Yeah, you were right about him. I'd already told Cal about us and I'm glad I did. He backed me up, thank God.

"The bastard went so far as to say that I'm on the Andiamo payroll. I told them to run my financials and if they have to investigate this matter, I'd be happy to cooperate."

"Oh damn, Jess, that's a low blow. Well, we know they won't find anything. I think I might have to get a little nasty with Snidely Weasel and watch him self-destruct."

"At this point I think I'd enjoy seeing that.

I'm coming up on your office now, so I'll see you in a few minutes. Ciao Bella."

Oh, "bella" is it now? I shake my head at my own

Before I head into the FBI building, I check with Mitch to make sure my earwig is working. Good thing I did, too, because they're on me walk into the building. Once I'm in the elevator, I pump myself up for the meeting ahead.

CHAPTER TEN

My Feeb escort leads me to the conference room as if I were a death row inmate walking to the execution chamber. They frisk me again, run a wand and check me for bugs. I smirk to myself when they find nothing. Great job, team.

"Ms. Andiamo..." I turn to see Isley, slimy and slick like the snake he is, dressed in another fancy suit.

"Well, if it isn't Isley, Donald Isley." He turns a little red but holds his tongue. You have to admire that kind of control.

"Ms. Andiamo, thank you for coming at our request."

"More like a summons you mean. You know Isley you've got a way of pissing me off." I move to the table where everyone's looking comfortable, including Snidely Weasel.

"You really don't want this bastard, do you? You're just fishing for something you can use to get my uncle. I wouldn't put it past you to make up this whole scenario to get at him. It wouldn't surprise me in the least if you set me up and that would mean you caused the death of my family. No. I wouldn't put it past you for a minute. And now your little scenario is backfiring."

"Now, Ms. Andiamo you know that's not the case. We would never do anything to harm your family. Why would we do that with someone as dangerous as Al-Hakeem threatening our country?"

"Really? Well, you could have fooled me with this Snidely Weasel doing everything he can to keep him from meeting his fate. He's obsessed with catching my uncle and trying to put the both of us down permanently."

Sheppard goes on a slow burn, trying to hold back his temper and the color of his face told me he wouldn't hold for very much longer. My objective is to keep pushing him.

"Ms. Andiamo, yes I want to put you and your Uncle away for good. You're both criminals and cold-blooded murderers. I have no doubt you'll both face justice, however, this mission must take precedence."

"You dare sit there and call me a cold-blooded murderer? I killed for you. I killed for the CIA, the military and as a merc for this government, yet this man tortures people. He trains others to torture and kill. He trains terrorists. He *is* a terrorist. Our government even used him as an asset until he went rogue. You think you don't need me? You couldn't find him if he stood up and bit you in the ass."

"That is not true and entirely beside the point." Good. He's starting to lose it. Keep pushing it now, let go of some pent-up frustration.

"Really? You have my file. How many people have I killed on behalf of our country? Go on; tell me how many people I took out for God and country and then tell me Agent Sheppard, how many of my fellow comrades I had to lose because of idiots like you? You compare him to me when considering my character? You'll find there is no comparison. But you, sir, are just despicable."

Silence fell across the room. I feel heated right now, and I unleash the fire of my feelings and frustrations on this fool. He tries to come to his own defense, but I cut him off and continue my tirade.

"If you really are after al-Hakeem, then why were you waiting for me at my home, lurking in the shadows? Why did you enter my property without permission, threaten me and my family and tell me to turn over my uncle? Why wouldn't you just talk to him yourself? Did you really think I would give in to your threats? If I'm a cold-blooded murderer, as you allege, then what's to keep me from killing you to keep you off my back?" Now he did lose it.

"You threaten my life in front of all these agents in here?" he yelled and jumped up out of his chair. "How dare you. I'll have you arrested. I don't have to stand here and take this. I'm the person in charge here. Spence? Malcomb? You heard her threaten my life. You heard the way she speaks to me. Can I arrest her now so we can get down to business without this criminal?"

Yes. That was almost too easy. Looks like I just sealed Snidely Weasel's fate. I'm a bit disappointed that he didn't put up more of a fight.

"Malcomb!" he yells. "Why isn't she being dragged off and chained like the dog she is?" My rage begins to boil, and I stand to get in his face, but the Director speaks up.

"Ms. Andiamo, please accept my apology on behalf of the FBI. Not all of us feel as Agent Sheppard here. I personally thank you for your service in the military and other operations for the good of our country you participated in over the years."

"Director, you're commending her? She's nothing but a thug. She's a cold-blooded, murdering thug. She's just the same as her uncle. Scum! Hiding under the guise of a military hero." He looks at her with disdain, thinking the Director would have his back.

"Shut the hell up, Sheppard," Davis says between clenched teeth. "Sit down and shut the hell up before you do something to flush what's left of your career down the toilet." Stunned to silence, he plops in his chair, looking like a kid whose mother took away his favorite toy.

"I am sorry, Ms. Andiamo. We have no wish to railroad you or your family. We just want Mansur al-Hakeem before he does more damage," Isley states.

"Well, if that's true then we need to stop worrying about my uncle and start worrying about what we've found so far. I'm sure you all have Agent Caruthers briefing."

"Yes, we've read Agent Caruthers' report, Ms. Andiamo and it's very thorough, as far as it goes. However, we still need to fill in some blanks. Would you answer some questions for us?"

"If I can, Mr. Isley. Ask away."

"For starters," he begins, "in Agent Caruthers' report, it states your uncle refused to do business with him and his group. We find this hard to believe. Why would he refuse?"

"Why? The guy's a terrorist. You are aware of what I went through with him, correct? I would think that's a no-brainer. I'm sure you already knew the answer to that question so why ask it? Aren't there more important issues we need to discuss?"

"You're quite right, Ms. Andiamo so let's get down to the progress report. Where does your investigation stand?"

"Well, if you've read Agent Caruthers' report then you know the progress of this mission. It's not an investigation so let's not sugarcoat it. Agent Caruthers has already provided this information to you. You already know that I have a string or two that I may be able to pull. I have people in place and sketches to every contact I could think of.

"My investigation into what happened to my family is ongoing. I keep up to date with the Detroit P.D. and the ATF. If you want them to brief you as they do me, you know who to talk to. Now, tell me what you've done to bring this mission to a successful conclusion?"

"Ms. Andiamo," he began through clenched teeth, "I thought you'd be more cooperative. I could have you arrested for obstruction. I'm sure we'll be able to find al-Hakeem ourselves." I laugh so hard I almost fall out of my chair. I love pissing off feds.

"Et tu, Mr. Isley, I'm sure you'll have no trouble in almost acquiring your target, just as you have for years. You won't catch him. As I told you before, you've got too many leaks in your organizations. He'd have a field day with you. Go ahead and lock me up, lose your bait, see where you get. I can carry on my investigation into my parents' and sisters murder from inside if need be. But, let's be honest here, you, the CIA, have no power to arrest me. The FBI? Yes. Local PD? Yep. Unfortunately for you, I've done nothing to warrant that arrest." I reply, staring him down.

"When I get out, I will know every person responsible. I'm a very patient woman, Mr. Isley. I'm filtering the information I hand to this task force because your house has leaks. You'll get it all, eventually, but not here and not under the gun.

"And, you wanna know what I think? I think it's you who are being uncooperative. You're the one who's not sharing information so you can take your 'need to know' BS routine and shove it up your ass."

Isley studies me. His silence causing his control tip on its edge. Every person in the room looks to him, waiting for an answer.

"Very well, Ms. Andiamo, we shall play it your way for the moment. Agent Caruthers will disseminate what information we have. Make no mistake; I will only go so far before I yank the chain back. Your mission is still one of capture. Do you have a problem with this, Ms. Andiamo?" He expects a positive response. He thinks he's got my number. He's sadly mistaken. I sigh and shake my head at him.

"No, I don't have a problem with that at all Mr. Isley. My karma would be happier and I prefer it that way. Contrary to popular belief, I am not a cold-blooded bitch who would just as soon kill you as look at you" I steal a quick glance at Sheppard. "Now, if you'll excuse me, I've got work to do."

Ms. Andiamo, could you wait a moment please?" Spencer asks. "Give us the room, please. Caruthers, Sheppard, Isley, you stay. Director? You're welcome to stay as well." They wait until the room clears before addressing me again.

"Ms. Andiamo, again, please accept my apology. I find Agent Sheppard's conduct reprehensible."

"Spence, I'm not the criminal..."

"*Agent* Sheppard, you would do well to keep your damn mouth shut," Spencer's frustration with Sheppard showing.

"Ms. Andiamo, do you wish to press charges against Agent Sheppard for entering your premises without cause, without a warrant and accosting you at your home?" Sheppard's face again turns purple with rage but Spencer's glare in his direction keeps him from saying a word.

"I haven't decided. If you take this seriously and deal with it properly internally, then I'll decline. If it's not handled to my satisfaction and he comes after me again, you'll have one helluva situation on your hands."

"Rest assured it will be dealt with harshly and swiftly. Thank you, Ms. Andiamo. Now, if you'll excuse us, we'll take this to my office."

He leaves and I head out, glad to be out of there and able to breathe the fresh air again.

"Did you get everything, Mitch?"

His disembodied voice comes back to my hidden earpiece. The burst microphone looks like an ordinary button on my blouse. The bug detection blocker I carry looks like a satellite phone and silently vibrated while they searched me. A device recently created by my development team and the reason they didn't pick up on any of my comm devices. Sometimes, it's good to have your own R&D department.

"Sure did kiddo, you're just as sweet as always. They dropped a bug on your clothes, but Karl took care of it. Karl said it's easy to jam the main signal but there's a secondary signal piggybacked onto the main. Much like the one you have; it's set at a higher frequency. Advanced technology, to be sure, but still a bit behind what we've developed. Yah, that one took a bit longer to block without blocking yours at the same time. It's jammed now but he had a bugger of a time doing it."

"Can he track the source? If we find it, we might be able to find al-Hakeem. Do we have any activity on the tracker I planted? Something ain't right here but I've got no choice now but to see it through. I have to meet Caruthers as soon as finish her ass-chewing and give her orders to get as much out of me as she possibly can."

"Right. I'll get him on tracking that technology, but it'll take some time. He says it's some of the best work he's seen in a while. No activity on the tracker yet but I'll let you know as soon as he moves."

"Okay, keep Karl on it. I'm off the grid for a bit then I'll be at the ristorante."

Carrie's there in the parking garage to prevent a possible tail by the Feds. I cut her loose and head up Jefferson Ave to look at the mansions along the river. My dad and I used to do this when he knew I needed to vent, still do get out now and again. Well shit, we won't be anymore. That thought makes me turn around and pull into the abandoned parking lot that leads to my private little bit of dirt by water, the "beach" where I took Jessica that first night.

I plop my ass down and stare out at the river. It seems a lifetime ago that Jess and I made love here that first night. Watching the river flow by helps clear my head. Blurred pictures float through my mind.

Slowly they start to focus getting sharper and moving faster like a movie. They're mainly about a time with my family; the time we fished and had a family picnic at Selfridge Air National Guard Base; my mother teaching us how to swim at Lake St. Clair; my younger sisters in a musical, they had beautiful voices. So many memories coming fast and hard. Tears well up and fall like raindrops. I was an idiot to treat my family the way I did when I was younger, and I feel the pain of it now.

As I head back to my car, the wind kicks up and it starts to pour. I'm taking these fond memories with me, happy to have what I did with my family before somebody cut it all short.

Shaking my head to clear it and wiping my face dry, I set off to meet Jessica. It's time to teach people they can't extinguish my family without paying the consequences.

***

She's sitting in my usual corner booth and flashes a short smile at me. God, she takes my breath away. I take the seat opposite and lean back in the booth.

"You're all wet. Where'd you go?"

I shrug my shoulders not wanting to get into it as my bug blocker in my pocket buzzed its silent warning.

"Sorry, didn't mean to sound like an interrogator grilling a suspect. I just got curious. Find any of the answers you're looking for?"

"No, just more questions." At that moment, Franco comes out with the telephone, drops off the usual appetizers, and disappears into the kitchen again.

"Si," I talk into the receiver.

"It's Mitch, wanted you to know they put a big bingo on your babe. She was transmitting like a beacon from a lighthouse. Karl has them jammed. You know, it's strange that only one of the three has the secondary signal on it. Makes you wonder how she got hers."

"Thanks," I reply. Jessica stares through me as I hang up.

"They got one on me, didn't they? Damn it! I thought I escaped unscathed."

"Three is hardly unscathed, but don't worry, they're jammed."

Pissed off at the idea they were able to place not just one but three bugs on her unnoticed, she takes it out on the unsuspecting Italian bread, ripping it apart and slamming it home in the olive oil and garlic. As she stuffs it in her mouth and closes her eyes, I can tell she's beginning to feel better. Italian food *is* comfort food.

"Don't worry, they managed to slip one on me and I was looking out for it."

"Oh, well, that certainly makes me feel better." She rolls her eyes.

I carefully consider her as she laughs at herself, seeing nothing that would give me pause. Just as I catch my breath, Franco comes out with our food.

"Grazie, Franco." Franco seems almost frightened to speak but he does.

"Signorina Andiamo, I'm a so sorry to hear of the trouble with you famiglia. If a there's anything I can a do for you, just a call."

"Grazie Franco. You're catering the reception after the funeral?"

"Si, Signorina. I make a da food. I shall leave you now."

Once again, I thank Franco and off to the kitchen he goes. I turn to Jess as she gobbles down her lunch.

"You're not hungry or anything are you?" I watch her in amusement. She smiles back at me before replying.

"I can't help it when it comes to good food, especially good Italian food." She gobbles more and sips her wine.

"So," she brings me out of my trance. "Sheppard is no longer the SAC. He's suspended pending an inquiry," she pauses, looks me in the eye with the color of storms in hers.

"Toni, he's going to come after you, you understand that don't you?"

"Yes," an evil feral look surfaces, "I know he'll come after me. I planned on it going in there today."

"You're scaring me, so I won't ask what you plan to do. Just promise me one thing, will you?" Her tone has me looking at her curiously.

"What's that?" I suspiciously answer her.

"Think about the consequences before you kill him, please?"

"You know, I expect better from you Caruthers." My temper crackles. "I don't go around dispatching people for the hell of it." She stares at me, not in the least worried about my tirade.

"I don't go off half-cocked and kill any time my temper fancies it, no matter how much I'd love to. I'm not a sociopath or a psychopath or whatever the hell your profilers call me. I do have a conscience, Agent Caruthers, and standards such as they are." Never taking her smiling, amused eyes off me, she put down her fork, to sip her wine.

"Are you finished riding your high horse, Ms. Andiamo?" She holds up her hand to stop the rage from spilling out of me.

"I don't believe you're a sociopath or a psychopath. However, I know what you feel inside when it comes to your family and how raw and testy you are now." Hmph. Didn't know I was that transparent.

"All I ask is that, when you do come across Sheppard again, and I have no doubt you will, take a minute to think about what you're doing. Make damn sure it's to avenge and not for revenge. You, I have every confidence, know the fine line between the two." Well, I'll be damned.

"You know, I believe that was the most pleasant ass-chewing I've had in quite a while and believe you me I've had a few in my day," I reply calmly.

"Really," she shrugs.

"Of course, it balances out because I've chewed a few asses in my day too."

"Well, while I do so enjoy being around you, you didn't yet make that promise, Ms. Andiamo." She drums her fingers on the table. I sigh.

"Alright," I hold up my hand. "I promise to think before I act when I next see Snidely Weasel. However, if he steps onto my property uninvited again, I won't be as gracious as the first time. Will that do Agent Caruthers?"

"Yes, that will do Ms. Andiamo. Now I suppose we should get down to business. I guess you want to know what happened after you left." When I nod, she continues.

"Okay, after you left, it got interesting. First, they ripped Cal to pieces; told him he was very lucky you weren't pressing charges for assault and trespassing; questioned his reasoning for going to your home without a warrant. H said he believed I was in your pocket, wanted to catch us red handed, doing something illegal and that he got a tad over enthusiastic when confronting you. I don't think they bought it. They did grill me about us and our relationship. Believe it or not, it's still very bad to be a homosexual in the FBI."

"I get you," I nod.

"I reiterated what I told them earlier and followed up with certified copies of my financial records and statements from our friends on how and when we met. I also told them any time they want to put me on a voice stress analyzer I'd be willing and happy to do the polygraph. They jumped right on that and scheduled it for first thing in the morning.

"And, that's when they told me once my poly clears, I'm to be the new SAC of the task force. I wasn't expecting that, and I guess I'm still buzzing about it. It's a big responsibility and an honor. So, I know they need to dot the i's and cross the t's when an accusation like this is brought even if it is just a deflection. Anyway," she took a breath.

"Since they've always known about my sexual preferences and they know you're gay, they decided that sleeping with you is in the best interest of the government. I told them I was uncomfortable using you that way but would do it. So now they think I will sleep with anyone for my country." She tilted her head, smiled and took another sip of wine.

"I doubt you'll let that go on after this mission is over." I think I detect a slight nod as she continues eating. Doesn't seem like she wants to deal with that right now.

"They're impressed with the information I gathered so far and, even though al-Hakeem remains the prime objective, they still want to see your uncle's head on a platter if they can manage it. It goes to the back burner, but I'm to try to gather as much about him as I can."

"I figured that." I got very serious for a moment and creased my brows.

"Jessica, you know I won't compromise or rat out my uncle, not even for you." I look her in the eyes, those gorgeous eyes. She answers by taking my hand, keeping eye contact.

"I hope you know I would never ask you to do that," she reassures me. I keep my eyes locked with has and nod.

"I believe I do. Thank you." At that moment, I see a woman afraid of losing everything and strong enough to go on regardless. Such courage. Such conviction.

Such power she holds over me. I feel a bit awestruck. You're going down in flames, Andiamo, down in flames.

"Okay, where were we? Oh right, they were also impressed with the size of the file you had. They were thunderstruck that you'd give it to me since none of them could to get anywhere with you."

"I can imagine the look on Isley's face."

"He harped on me about getting the names of your sources. He figures you wouldn't even trust your own family with that kind of information."

"I imagine he's looking to plug up leaks in his own organization without letting anyone know. You can tell him the information is out there. It's just a matter of putting it all together in one package. That's all it took for us."

"Sure, he's really gonna buy that. I can just see him now. He'll fall off his chair laughing at me while I see my career being flushed down the toilet following Cal's."

"He can laugh all he wants, it happens to be true, though I will not tell you how we accessed all that information."

"That's more like it. I think I'd flip if it was that easy."

"Did they say anything valuable such as the whereabouts of al-Hakeem?"

"No, but they did have a few rumors about what he's doing in the United States. He doesn't want to hit New York again, but he's found, and I quote 'easy access in Detroit'. What he wants to do here is beyond what little they know. I've been trying to follow his movements using satellite photos and cameras through the most likely routes from New York including through Canada. I've also kept up on any chatter out there and have a few things to go over with you."

"Okay great," I reply.

She finishes the last bite of food as I finish mine. And just like that, Franco's there with our cannoli. I start to tell Jess something and look up to see her staring at the cannoli, her eyes huge.

"What's the matter?" I ask, laughing.

"I've been in this city for the last three years and I was born and raised here. Why didn't I know about this restaurant? How could I miss the best food in the city?"

"That's because you didn't know me."

She looks up from her cannoli and shakes her head. "Well, I guess I do now. I've found a new favorite place to hang out."

"Sure, just do me a very big favor and don't mention that you're FBI." When she chuckles at that, I say, "I'm not kidding. Franco'd be upset if he lost three-quarters of his clientele."

"I promise I won't tell anyone but Franco. He deserves to know," she scolds me.

"What else did they discuss?" I'll have to take her at her word.

"Well, not much more. They're mostly sniffing after the trail of crumbs you're leaving them and the few things I could come up with on my own. We need to discuss what we're going to do about the Caniff situation sometime before we deploy tonight." I look at her and she rolls her eyes. "No, I didn't include that in my report."

"Right. I decided I'm going to send in one of my sources, put him under."

"You trust this person?"

"No, I don't, but I need someone and he's the most believable person I have. I already planted a burst transmitter on him. They shouldn't be able to find it." She looks concerned.

"What? They're hard to detect. Your people didn't find the one I had on me today." At that, she chokes and sputters on her cannoli.

"You had a bug on you? Why didn't you plant one in the conference room as long as they can't detect it?"

"I thought about it, planned on it but then decided against it. I thought it might undermine you with your bosses what with all the bullshit you went through to convince your them that I have a measure of trust in you. And, for reasons I cannot fathom Agent Caruthers, I actually do trust you."

"I know that didn't come easily for you, so I'll just say, you honor me."

"The viewing starts tonight," I change the subject. "I know your people want agents there, but I don't want them inside, even with proper creds, they're too easy to steal or counterfeit. You'll be there if they must have someone. That'll also help us keep up our little display."

"Alright, but you know they'll also have a surveillance van."

"I guess that'll have to do as long as they allow us to grieve in peace. I don't want them to go after my family, including my uncle while we're at the funeral home. I won't have my parents and sisters dishonored by that kind of scene."

"I will personally speak to them about that," she agrees. We finish our cannoli and Franco comes back with the phone.

"Si."

"Toni, don't say anything about anything anymore. That second signal I told you Karl found got through the jam. He had to shut down the whole works. I suggest the two of you come to the office most rikki tik to deal with this."

"You got it," I reply.

Jessica looks at me strangely. I reach my arm across the table and put my finger on her lips. "Baby, I guess it's time to get back to it though I can think of about a dozen other things we could be doing instead."

"Oh yeah?" she looks at me with a gleam in her eye playing her part so well my legs go weak and my belly twitters. "I'll get the check and we can head someplace for a more appropriate dessert."

"My dear, Franco won't accept any money from anyone that sits at my table. I send him a check once a month with a huge gratuity. He would feel very humiliated if you offered him anything above what I already provide."

"Oh, okay." We stand to leave the ristorante and Franco comes to clear the table.

"Grazie, Franco, everything was bennissimo as always."

"Prego, Signorina. I see you soon." He disappears quickly into the kitchen and we depart.

Once outside, I pretend to have a coughing fit in order to let Mitch know I was back on comm. He sings in my ear.

"Okay, kiddo. We managed to jam the signal again but whoever's on the other side is working just as hard to make sure he gets through. Karl is swearing up a storm. I didn't know he could put that many words together at the same time," Mitch chuckles.

"This worries me, Mitch. This could mean someone listened in on the conversations at Fed Central." Jessica looks concerned and I hand her my back earpiece.

"Hello Mitch, please repeat that last remark."

"I came across a second signal on one of your bugs and on the one that was on Toni. We're having trouble blocking the son of a bitch. While we've managed it now, I don't know how long it'll last. There's a chance one of these was planted in the conference room during your briefing."

"Shit, this is not going to sit well with my bosses. You know I'm going to have to tell them there may be a bug."

"Yeah, I know," he responds. "When you get here, I'll set you up with some equipment that'll detect it. It's more sensitive than what you Feds are using. It'll be powerful enough to pick up just about any signal, but not quite as good as they ones we use at Storm HQ."

"Am I going to be allowed to tell them where I got this equipment?"

"Sure. They're for sale at Andiamo Security Concepts, Inc. We'll be happy to work out a contract with them."

"Oh, they'll love that," she laughs.

We part ways to meet up again at my office instead of hers. She understands I don't want to be there after the meeting we had. Plus, she needs to pick up the new counter surveillance equipment needed to find that peculiar bug.

***

Jess and I are with my team in the main SCIF looking at the transmitters we removed from our clothing. Two are standard and no problem to trace back to the owners through their serial numbers. The other two, though, they're a mystery, total custom jobs with no serial numbers or ID of any kind. We'll have to dig to get any intel on the maker.

We got as far as we can with those right now and settle in to try and track al-Hakeem. We pour over copies of reports from the Feds IT department as well as satellite images and photos from cameras at traffic lights. I pull up a large map of the U.S. on the wall screen and study it.

Miss Edna brings in a tray with coffee and tea not knowing what Jessica prefers, along with an assortment of cakes and cookies. I thank her and she leaves silently.

Jessica hurries over and fill one of the largest mugs with her usual two creams and two sugars and picking up two cookies from the tray. She sighs enjoying her first sip. I smile to myself as I do the same but keep mine pristine – straight black.

"There's just too much to go through. Are your people narrowing this down even a little?" I'm the first to break the silence.

"Some. They're using face-mapping and facial recognition software but it takes time. They've eliminated quite a bit but there's still a lot to go through," she nibbles on her cookies.

"Okay, maybe we can whittle it down some more here." I pick up the photograph studying the dead eyes of my nemesis. My eyes blue and I'm struck with the pain and nausea from a fresh concussion. The heat of the desert drips into my eyes stinging my already blurred vision. Sweat rolls down my back and between my breasts. The stench of tightly packed sand floor, stained with the piss and blood of others that came before me, fills my senses nearly making me lurch.

"Shit, Mitch, she's gone. Help me bring her back ..."

The excruciating pain in my head was almost unbearable. I feel someone behind me and send a fist flying in their direction. I elbow someone else as another grabs my arms trying to hold me still. I struggle and spit at the one in front of me. I feel his knife slicing through my flesh and sting of his whip on my back. I struggle, yelling out my name, rank and serial number over, and over again. Then a scream as he slams the broomsticks home and then, darkness.

I vaguely hear someone telling me it's alright, it's okay, to come back. Come on back now. Safe, you're safe now. I feel someone stroking my face and I collapse into them, trying to escape the pain. Jesus. It hurts, so real, so fresh, like it just happened. I feel myself breath and my eyes flutter. The pain seems further away now, foggy, like a dream. I vaguely see Jessica's face and hear her voice again as she takes me to the ground and cradles me in her lap. "Damn, she has the glow of an Angel," I say to myself. I pass out. Several minutes later, I wake up, still on the floor, my head still cradled in Jessica's lap.

"Welcome back," she gives me a warm smile, her voice gentle.

"Shit," I choke out, my voice grated. My ego has me trying to spring up and shoo everyone away but my body is definitely not willing to do what I tell it to. So much pain, my scars are on fire.

"Easy, that's it, lay back and take a few minutes." She tells me when I try but fail to get up. She wipes away my angry tears then lays a cool washcloth across my forehead. I feel her strength, her gentleness. I'm safe. I feel safe. This is good.

Miss Enda has me sip water. Then I close my eyes and shut out everything but Jessica's caress as I shiver and shake the flashback away.

"Ok, this is embarrassing," I try to move again a few minutes later and Jessica helps me sit up.

"It's alright. I imagine your people have seen and helped you before," She says, still softly stroking me.

"Yeah, well I...," I croak out. Jessica understands the silent thank you and I let my eyes wander the faces of my partners, my friends, my comrades. I spy the beginning of a bruise on Mitch's cheekbone.

"Ah shit, Mitch."

"You just grazed it. I consider myself lucky you didn't break my nose," he laughs it off, his face still one of concern and strain. "You got Agent Caruthers with a good elbow. She took it like a pro and didn't blink an eye when you spit in her face."

He helps me to my feet, impressed with the way Jessica handled the situation. I could tell it shook him up and I know he still gets them. Still has the flashbacks, the nightmares. We don't really talk about it, but we know. In a way, I'm kinda glad I punched him, probably kept him here, grounded, not back in that hellhole with me.

"Damn." I look to Jess with embarrassment once again and she smiles telling me it's ok. Shit. This is a big blow to my tough facade. I hate this crap. I clear my throat.

"I think we can all get back to work now. We need to find this son of a bitch before he wreaks any more havoc." Everyone takes their seats and Jessica squeezes my hand before parking herself right next to me at the head of the table.

"Where exactly in New York was the photo taken?" I ask and take another look the photograph of the man who brought so much pain.

"It should be marked on the back," Jessica states softly.

I quickly flip the picture over, this time dismissing the face. I rattle off the GPS coordinates and a marker shows up on the smart screen with a map of Queens, NY.

"Ok, this says it was taken, um, looks like a week before my parents were killed. He had plenty of time to get here or activate certain cells." I highlight all the possible routes via highways in the US, Canada, as well as shipping and fishing lanes and flight routs.

"I agree. I told my people to concentrate on the most likely route from New York through Pennsylvania, Ohio then into Michigan. Of course, he could have gone into Canada and came through Windsor into Detroit via the Ambassador Bridge or the Tunnel or by way of the Bluewater Bridge into Port Huron but best not to cross the Canadian Border and not twice. He'd be taking an unnecessary risk that way."

"Yeah, I think you're right there. I think we can rule out travel through Canada. It's easier to move around the states than going through two border crossings. He could also use the waterways and travel by boat following the coast of Lake Erie or the shipping lanes and up the Detroit River. You have no other sightings of him since this photo?"

"No. We were lucky to find this one and to cover the waterways I'm having our staff comb through all satellite images and facial recognition on every port and fueling station between as well as shipping and fishing vessels. We pulled all security camera footage of Customs and border crossings and all camera footage from New York to Detroit along the three most likely routes. We're also pulling all flights from every airport and private aircraft that's taken off from New York and vicinity or airports along the way."

"Agent Caruthers, I must say you are very thorough and mapped this out much the same way we have. But we've done about as much as we can for now. Not much more but wait and see if we get a hit. If we can find possible targets that'll help us narrow the search considerably. We must know everything that'll be happening here in the Detroit area no matter how obscure. I think that's the best way to trap these guys – we have to identify their targets."

"I'm working on that as well." Jessica confirmed. "Since we're in the middle of the Stars and Stripes festival leading to the Fourth of July, it's going to be hell finding what's *not* going to be a target. Now that Cal's out of the picture, though, it should be easier to gather the intel on potential targets."

"I believe they have more than one cell active and that he's kept them separated, each one getting details about their target only. That means there must be a logistics cell as well, running the different legs of this though that one's probably wound tight and compartmentalized, too. Say you might have a one or two person cell from logistics working the financing, and other cells handling the weapons needed for the operational cells. Then another of the logistics cell would be handling transportation and so on. It's because of how compartmentalized these cells are that we have difficulty finding them before they act." She rubs the tiredness in her eyes.

"The operational cells, the ones carrying out the master plan, have no idea who the others are. The exception is for one contact in logistics that gives them their orders and that one contact may only have knowledge of the people in one or two cells.

"Others would have knowledge of one person in that cell and with another entire cell and so on. So, no one knows the full breadth or scope of one single operation. Simply put, if one is taken down another is activated to take its place which is why we need to find the head of the snake so we can get *all* that are involved."

"You also have to deal with the fact you still have a mole trying to thwart your efforts and it's not Snidely Weasel. He, unfortunately, was just a conduit. A pawn easily manipulated," I tell her.

"I know," she turns downcast. "It's just hard to believe that anyone I work with could actually betray everything we stand for. I'm not saying it doesn't happen because it does, but these are agents I've worked with for years. I trusted these people with my life as they trust me with theirs."

"I understand how hard it's going to be for you but I'm sure one way or the other you'll stand," I tell her and she gives an affirmation.

"Anyway, I should be on my way and see what they have for me." She hesitates, trying to decide what to say, something, anything. "Thank you for the meal and coffee," she decides on. "Oh, and for removing the bugs from my jacket and the equipment I need to keep mine safe," she says meaning her people.

"No problem. I'll see you this evening?" I ask hopefully though I couldn't tell you why.

"Yes, you will definitely see me this evening." She picks up her things leaving all her copies with me and quickly departs.

CHAPTER ELEVEN

After Jessica departs to deal with her own house, I sit at my desk studying Mansur al-Hakeem. I want to know him as well as I know myself and as well as he seems to know me. I read the file backward and forwards, forwards and backward for the next several hours, recounting everything I remember about him then reading everything added to his file since.

I scrutinize and then narrow my focus little by little. I scan for little things that don't add up. Usually, people look for the major thing that stands out and end up missing what's been in front of them the whole time.

Piece by painstaking piece, line by line, I go through his file and begin to notice things. Small breaks in surveillance here, a missing report there. Several small things that lead to names and hours later, I put the file down. I'm able to name a source or two in each of these agencies. I finish writing my notes and buzz Miss Edna.

"Yes, Ms. Andiamo?"

"Miss Edna, I have some notes that need typing and call a meeting as soon as you finish. I found some things."

"I'll get right on it, Ms. Andiamo. I'll be right in to pick up your notes." She breezes in to pick up the notes.

I turn my chair around from the window to give her the papers. I murmur a word of thanks. As soon as she leaves the office, I click the locks in place and start pacing. How am I supposed to tell Jessica that her mentor, the man who took her into his home, raised her as his own, put her through school and helped her with her career, that he is in this up to his eyeballs. I decide to deal with it later and lie down, dropping immediately into a restless sleep filled with the nightmare that is Mansur al-Hakeem.

***

I wake on a sandy dirt floor my head pounding as if a herd of elephants stampeded from one ear to the other inside my skull. There is an incessant buzzing in my head driving me crazy. I groan, try to see if I can sit without throwing up. Ok a bit nauseous though I need to lean against the wall, so I don't fall over.

My vision slowly clears, and I take stock of my surroundings. There's no furniture and there are two windows about neck high if you're on your feet. One in the wall above me the other is in the wall to the left of me. I hear someone calling out my name. Mitch and Murray are on one side of me, and Carrie is sitting up along the wall to my right. I hold my head in my hands trying to get rid of the buzzing and I answer.

"Yeah, I'm okay. Where the fuck are we?" I query pulling myself up to look through the hole to see a bruised and bloody Mitch looking back at me. Murray, equally bruised and bloody, sits against a wall throwing stones at something in the middle of the floor. It doesn't bode well that there's an underlying smell of urine, blood, and cordite permeating my nose. Buzz, buzz.

"Damn Evers, you look like shit," I tell him holding the side of my head to make sure it stays on.

"Gee thanks kid, you don't look so pretty yourself," he chides and I let out a humph.

"He's here kiddo. Mansur al-Hakeem, the one we're looking for," he whispers.

"Oh fuck," I reply. "We need to figure a way to get him then get out of here." Buzz, buzz.

***

I struggle to breathe as I come out of my dream, realizing it's my intercom doing the buzzing. "Yeah," I croak into the squawk box.

"Are you okay Ms. Andiamo? I've been trying to reach you and you didn't answer when I knocked or buzzed you." Miss Edna is concerned.

"Great, just great," I clear my throat. "I dozed off a moment Miss Edna, that's all. No big deal."

"I finished the notes and the conference room is ready for you," she states not wanting to accept my short explanation.

"Thanks, Miss Edna. I'll be there in five." Heading for the bathroom, I splash cold water on my face trying to wash away the ghosts of my past. Flashbacks and nightmares. Damn him. He's not going to win. I won't let him win. Scars burning, I walk into the conference room to start destroying his network.

"Miss Edna," I start and she pops up to pass around the freshly typed updates.

"We finally have a few avenues to pursue in our efforts to find Al-Hakeem." While they quickly scan the reports, images, pictures and my notes, I continue.

"As you can see, I listed those I suspect are the leaks. We need to run these people down and find out what they know. I want them all under surveillance within the hour and make sure we wring every bit of intel we can. Clone every phone, set up infinity bugs so we can to turn on cameras and microphones and have eyes and ears on each of them. Find them, rough em up, scare em, so they run to handler. We can turn them over to the Feds later, when we get what we need."

"I want to know when they eat, sleep, pee, fuck, and with who. I want who they know, who they talk to on the phone, on the street, in the gym, in the shitter, everything. I want to crawl up their asses and camp out. Squeeze every bit of information we can before the FBI gets to them. Capiche?"

Everyone nods heads as I look around the room. They're still busy taking notes and making lists and I feel a swell of pride in my team. We mesh. Each one is an expert in their field. They all know what to do. Someone pounds on the door and the monitor shows Frankie getting ready for another door pounding. Shit, I keep forgetting he's around. Miss Edna lets him in, knowing we're wrapping up.

"Hey, was' popping," he looks at me with a hopeful question in his eyes, like he's hoping he'll get to join the team and work on a real assignment.

"Hey Frankie, sorry, we lost track of time. Are you doing okay at the shelter?"

"Yeah," he shrugs and that's all he says about that. I stare at him a moment considering if I should pursue the conversation. He seems tense but and I decide it's not the right time. Better to let him think his way through for a bit. Then I switch gears.

"Do you own a suit, Frankie?"

"Huh? What? Suit? Naw. Why?"

"Well we're going to fit you with one, and while you're wearing it, you will be on your best behavior, capiche?"

"Shit dawg, you gonna tell me why I gotta wear a damn suit for?"

"Yeah, later," I turn to Karl. "Karl, show this kid some computer work. Let him learn how to find the people we're looking for." Karl acknowledges.

"You got it, Sarge."

"For reals? Shit yeah," Frankie perks up. "You for real goin' to show me stuff? Hot Damn!"

"Frankie."

"Oh. Yes, ma'am. Sorry, I got all excited and forgot myself for a minute."

"Miss Edna, show Frankie where he's to be set up." I wait until they're gone then go into another aspect of our findings.

"Now about this place on Caniff, I have someone going in undercover. I don't trust him as far as I can throw him. I want him controlled twenty-four seven. Agent Caruthers and I will be on the scene after my family's viewing to make sure insertion goes as planned." At my nod, Mitch brings up a map of the area on the computer's wall screen.

"Get surveillance set up on the house itself and let's see how we can possibly put eyes and ears in the home and on the cell phones. We'll have a better chance to learn something. "We then go over appropriate actions if they discover him or if he uncovers evidence that we need to hand over to the Feds. I wish Jess were here, but I'll fill her in at the funeral home.

Two hours later we have everything planned. I head out, Frankie in tow to buy him a suit and take him over to my place to get ready.

"Damn girl."

"Okay, head up to the guest room, take a shower and change." He stood staring at everything around him, taking.

"Where you get the scratch to live like this? You born with it?" I blast out a laugh before answering.

"No, I worked my ass off. I grew up poor until I left the military and started my own business. I took some lessons from my Uncle, now I can do pretty much whatever I want to. You can do the same if you put your mind to it. I'll help you. I was going to show you the house I grew up in but they blew it to smithereens. Maybe I should still show you." I tell him turning to face his questions. "You work hard and be smart you can do the same."

"Sorry 'bout your peeps. Feel ya dawg. My blood died from a drive-by. He was in the life ya know? Moms was a druggie and od'd. That's why I live with my Grams." Wow, did he just open up to me? I try to keep my face neutral and nod my head. Now I know the story behind the tough façade. "So's how come you watchin' out for me?" he asks.

"Cause I used to be you. I was always the one in trouble, especially with the law. I could be spending my life in prison instead of doing what I'm doing now if it weren't for my Uncle who straightened my ass out. I owe him my life, so I figure the best way to pay him back is to help someone else as he helped me. You got brains, Frankie; you have some of my talents, you also remind me of myself when I was your age, so you got elected."

He gives me the eye, not quite knowing if he could believe me. I turn myself back to the bedroom when he gives a curt nod of thanks then turns to disappear into the guest room.

"Frankie, you seemed to want to say something about working with the shelter earlier, what's going on? Is everything okay?"

He nods his head. "Yep, jus' fine. Jus' reminds me is all, but it's okay," he shrugs his shoulder. "Is it okay to keep doin' that after I don't have to anymore?"

"You bet. I think they'd be grateful if you kept giving them a helping hand," I say, feeling proud of him.

He gives one curt nod, then disappears into the guest room. I shake my head. It's probably the first time anybody but his Grandmother believed in him. I head to my shower to get ready for death's rituals.

Twenty minutes later, there's a buzz from the gate. Jessica. I buzz her in and get to the door just as she pushes of the doorbell.

My heart turns over at the sight of her. She's breathtaking and I gruffly give her the third degree to hide this crush.

"Agent Caruthers, what are you doing here? I mean how do you know where I live?"

"Ms. Andiamo, I am in the FBI. I know things. I thought we could catch up," she retorts.

"I don't like people coming to my home uninvited," she lifts her brows at me.

"We're supposed to be having a torrid affair so I think it would be more than appropriate to be in your home, don't you think?"

"Yeah, I suppose you're right," I acknowledge. "and I'm actually glad you're here. A lot happened since you left the office." I turn and head up the stairs toward my office leaving her to catch up. Frankie stands at the top of the stairs staring at Jessica, eyes wide and mouth open. I can't blame him. That tight little black dress shows off all her curves.

"Frankie, you're being rude. Pick up your jaw, wipe your chin, and say "Hi." to Agent Caruthers. You remember Frankie, Agent Caruthers?"

"How are you, Frankie?" Jessica looks more confused than Frankie does right now.

"Frankie, finish getting ready. Jess," I start up the stairs, "with me." Damn, why does she have to look so good? It's distracting to no end. How am I supposed to give her bad news with her looking like that? All I can do is treat rough, though I know it'll make her curious, override any potential anger.

When we get to the office, she shuts the French doors behind her, leans back and gives me an 'alright I'll give you one shot to tell me what the hell is going on' look. I couldn't help but laugh at her. She scrunches her eyebrows in anger.

"You know babe, you're awfully cute when you're riled up. I love staring at the storms in your eyes. They fascinate the hell out of me." Really? Did I just say that?

"I'm so glad I could provide some entertainment for you, but for now will you please explain to me what is going on?" She lets her frustration show.

"Certainly, I'm sure you remember that big file on Mansur al-Hakeem. Went through it finally. We did it Jess. We found several people we suspect are moles various organizations." The spark of enthusiasm in my eyes catches her attention.

"You're not shitting me, are you?"

"No. Things are going to happen fast now. Some of these people are here in the area and are under a watchful eye as we speak. After the viewing tonight we have one to deal with ourselves, someone from your own office," I turn serious. I could see her defenses slam into place like a wall of stone

"Who and be prepared to prove it." She softly murmurs. She doesn't fool me with her quiet. Underneath is anger that someone other than Snidely Weasel could betray everything she believes, everything on which she built her sense of duty and honor. Taking a deep breath, she braces herself from a blow I'm about to deliver. I suddenly hate the fact it's me that has to deliver it.

"Your Deputy Director, Malcomb Davis," I quietly tell her.

"No! No way in hell that's true," she whirls around in disbelief. I thought she was going to leap over my desk and wail on me.

"I'm sorry, but there's no doubt in my mind that Davis is a mole. I don't know exactly when he turned but from this file it seems like quite a long while ago. I suspected it even before my run-in with Snidely Weasel because he was the only one who knew about us. It explains Sheppard's surprise that his boss treated me the way he did, why they didn't have much of a file, and why there were so many roadblocks to all the information. It explains Isley's surprise at the thickness of the file. He received his copy from Davis."

"Is Isley dirty?"

"Damn it, I don't think so, but I'm not one hundred percent certain. He's a sleazy snake and if he is dirty, he covered his tracks well. I'm going to have to deal with him. I'll have to live with that for now; however, someone very close to him is a mole. I'll let him deal with his own house, but I'm asking you to let me deal with Davis."

"No. I appreciate you want the opportunity, but I will deal with this myself. *If* he is dirty, which I highly doubt, I have to be the one dealing with it. I need to talk to Spence and we need to do this right and by the book. I'm not a shrinking violet and I won't act like a pansy." Her voice takes on the edge of a sword and her eyes are the color of its steel. I just accused her mentor of doing something that's not just against the law but morally reprehensible.

"I don't doubt it, but this guy means the world to you. Anyone with half a brain can see that. I'd rather be the one asking the questions. I'm not saying I don't trust you, but you might choke up and we can't risk any chances right now. You're too close." She sighs, knowing I'm right. It doesn't mean she likes it, and her manner definitely lets me know it.

"I have to be the one questioning him. Otherwise, the higher-ups will take him to Quantico where he'll disappear, and no one gets answers. I will list you with me. It's highly unusual and I'll probably catch flack again for being in your uncle's pocket but it's the best I can do. I do not believe this is true, not for a moment, but I can't ignore it. Not if you have proof and it better be pretty damn solid." Shit. I hate her having to take flack because of me, the shit she put up with already and will put up with once this is over. Fuck it. She's a big girl.

"Jess," I wait for her to turn around and face me, "he knows it won't be long before we connect the dots. He's either going to try to bury his involvement by getting rid of everyone he's connected to, or he's going to take off and disappear. Either way, he's a danger to you. What I'm telling you is watch your backside." Okay, so I feel better watching out for her. Down in flames.

"Don't worry about me," she quips. She takes out her cell phone to place a call. But, I am worrying so it frustrates me even more. I mentally roll my eyes. Man, get the fuck over this puppy dog crush.

"What?" She asks frowning at me when she hangs up.

"Nothing. Umm, what else did I need to tell you? Oh yes, about Frankie. I'd rather keep an eye on him than wonder what the hell he's up to so he's coming with us to the viewing tonight. Would you appear in front of the judge with me to explain some of this? I know we can't give them details, but at least we might be able to get a delay until after this is over." She hesitates a moment before answering me.

"Of course I will. No problem. Well, are we all caught up now?" Her mood had taken a downturn.

"No. We need to check on my guy tonight. Make sure he's in place and I got a message to meet Stutter too. You in the mood to kick some ass?" I offer a release of the tension caused by throwing dirt on her uncle.

"You really know how to treat a girl," she sighs. "How could I say no to some ass kicking?" At that she comes over, picks me up and plants a kiss that sucks the brains

right out of my head. She puts me down and let's go as I
fall back into my chair. Fottimi! Fuck me!

"Damn, what sparked that?" I scowl. Once again, I look
up to see Frankie's open mouth at the door. I'm not used
to closing doors in my own house. Wait, Jessica closed the
doors when she followed me in here. I roll my eyes and
sigh.

"How long have you been standing there Frankie? Don't
you know it's rude to watch others play kissy face? We
need to have a chat about you knocking."

"Uh, sorry dawg, but I's ready to go. You know, I ain't
known no gay folk before feel me? Is it the same when I
kiss my bae when I have one anyway. I mean, you know."
I shake my head and rub my face with my hands. I don't
need to get into a debate about this right now or explain
to him why I am the way I am when I sure don't know.
Jessica just laughs.

"Yes Frankie, I would imagine it's the same feeling," I
respond. Jessica's laugh has not subsided and I give a look
her way.

"Well, are we ready to go? I'm sure you'll want to talk to
your uncle before it starts. I'll fill you in on my phone call
afterward." She turns on those heals and heads out the
door. Frankie and I stare after her.

"Frankie, my man, I think for the first time in my life, I
bit off a little more than I can chew."

"True that. If you need help, I be more than willin."

"Thanks, Frankie, no offense, but I think I'll keep this one to myself." We do a long, convoluted handshake and follow Jessica.

***

The funeral home reeks of flowers and the smell of the dead. For as many funerals as I've been to throughout my life, it's hard to get through that scent. Beautiful stained-glass windows line the front of the building.

In the center is a sitting area with artwork from local artists, shelves lined with books, and photos of the owners. The restrooms are on either side of the sitting area with a bereavement room on each side and a food and beverage area for each.

We're set up on the right side of the first floor, turning both rooms into one big room. At the head of the room are the closed caskets of my family arranged in a semi-circle. A picture is on an easel at the head of each casket and flower arrangements placed around them. Pictures my parents and youngest sisters are scattered around the room. A sofa and chairs for the family face the caskets with rows of chairs behind them. More sofas and chairs line the walls.

I introduce Frankie to what remains of my family and they take him under their wings while I check in with the security detail.

As I head out, Jessica comes in. I know my lights up like an electric light parade. I take her around and introduce her to my family as well. My glow isn't lost on my sister Beth who gives me a knowing look as I roll my eyes at her.

I take Jessica to pay respects to my parents and sisters promising to share the pictures with her after dealing with our duties and we go our separate ways.

I with the outside team, make sure everything's going smoothly, then make my rounds inside. On the way, I grab a coffee and small sandwich from one of the platters Franco brought over then head back to join my family. They're busy greeting people when Uncle Tony and his entourage walk in.

"Buono sera, Padrino," I greet him. We move aside so I can explain Jessica being here and to keep business to a minimum. Though I know we did a thorough sweep, there's still the possibility of extra electronic ears trying to listen in. As we finish, Frankie walks up.

"Oh, Godfather, let me introduce you to Frankie Tee. Frankie, this is my Godfather and Uncle, Antonio Andiamo."

"Ah, so you are the Frankie my niece has been telling me about."

"Yeah, I mean," Frankie can hardly swallow his spit. "I heard of you dawg. Oh not from Ms. Toni, I mean she tells me a cool story about her blood and all, but not who you is dawg." My Uncle laughs.

"I'm glad it was a cool story. When all this sad business is over, we'll sit and have a long chat, da uomo a uomo, man to man. It was nice to meet you, Frankie. Ok? Ok, ciao."

Frankie, so impressed with my Uncle, doesn't argue about the dismissal. He just trots off happy as a clam. I stare after him, surprised at how he handled himself. My Uncle chuckles to himself.

"Wow. I can't believe it. No mouth, no attitude, it's like he's a different person. He's certainly impressed with you. I wonder what he's heard."

"It would be interesting to find out wouldn't it?" He looks amused. It's good to see him amused at something. "Well, I'll let you get back to it then. Be careful out there tonight. I worry about you."

"Padrino," I say as he kisses each of my cheeks. I make the rounds checking up on my people again then set out to find Jessica as I wonder where Frankie headed. I find both of them with my sister Beth. It looks like Frankie's keeping her on her toes. I slip in quietly behind Jess and put my arms around her. She stiffens then relaxes remembering we have to keep up appearances.

I'm just in time to hear the punch line of Frankie's joke. Everyone within earshot bursts into laughter. I shake my head. Laughter at a funeral home, what this world is coming to I haven't a clue. I take Jessica around to each picture, sharing my family memories with her. She's introduced one family member after another, keeping up the ruse of a relationship between us. I can't believe I'm introducing her like she's my wife. I'll definitely be glad when this is over.

Just as we head out for another perimeter check, a loud crack blasts my ears. The floor shakes suddenly and shards of stained-glass rip through the room. I hit the ground making sure those around me are safe and protected. When I'm sure nothing else is coming, I get up and look for my family and Jessica. She's on her phone, her clothes shredded by flying glass and debris. Looks like she has a few cuts and scrapes but nods her 'okay' to me. Next, I look for Frankie and the rest of my siblings.

Well, so much for Frankie's new suit. It's a total loss. He assures me, in a flourish of curses, that he's just fine. The caskets remained steady, though the pictures and easels ended up on the floor. Flowers shredded; their petals mixed with colored glass on the floor.

When I know my family is okay, I run out to the street where a few cars are ablaze. A little kid comes up to me and hands me an envelope. I look at it and shove it in my pocket when I see several feds approach, weapons drawn. Their van is not among the vehicles burning. Damn. Jessica comes from behind me to talk to her colleagues and tears them new assholes. I look around for my outside security, not seeing them.

"Secure the perimeter, damn it!" I order the remaining security. "Find out what the fuck happened to the rest of our people! Why didn't the FBI surveillance pick up anything?" I call Mitch to come back, he and Andrea had left fifteen minutes earlier, and see Murray, Carrie, and Miss Edna running up to me. I give them assignments; grateful they aren't injured. Beth waddles up to me.

"What the hell is going on, Sis?" I motion to Frankie and he comes running up to me.

"What ya need?" he asks eagerly.

"Take my sister to the rest of my family Frankie. Stay with them until we can get everyone safely out of here." I look Frankie in the eye. "I'm counting on you, Frankie." He swells up with pride.

"Toni, Toni, what the hell is going on?"

"It's alright Sis, I'll explain in a little bit. Right now, I need you to go with Frankie until the cops come and clear everything, okay. Please Beth," I plead. Beth looks at me, sighs.

"For now, but you will explain what's going on around here." She turns on her heel her belly leading the way.

I look around and find myself alone, so I slip the envelope out of my pocket. Inside is a letter. I read it and feel all the blood drain from my face.

"Merda," I exclaim shoving the letter back into the envelope looking around for the little girl who gave it to me. I find her and gently quiz her about it. After she runs back to her mother who is, I believe to be one of my cousins, I turn to seek out Jessica. Shit. She's too busy reaming her Jr. G's asses. It's not until hours later when we stagger back to the office, that I remember the letter.

***

"Which one of you is going to explain what the hell just happened here and how these guys got past you to plant something as big as this is on these vehicles. Johnson, you start and it better be damn good for me to let this go unpunished." Johnson swallowed his spit.

"We're awfully sorry Special Agent Caruthers but we had a situation. Special Agent Sheppard came crashing into the van. We were doing our jobs, staying vigilant, and watching every person and every camera we set up."

"Why wasn't I notified the moment Agent Sheppard surfaced and how the hell did he get in the van?"

"We were about to notify you when the cars blew. Honestly, if anyone planted anything here we would've caught it," Johnson pleads his case. Someone walks up to her and whispers that a couple of Toni's security personnel were just found deceased.

"I want every second of every camera frame by frame scoured, Johnson. We have a couple highly trained security personnel dead!" Jessica walks away in disgust. She feels responsible for the devastation. Toni trusted her.

"Crap!" Johnson watches his boss walk away and turns back to the van.

She demands an update from ATF and when she's finished with them, she finds the local police and pries what they found out of them. She'll be damned if this is going to happen under her watch again.

CHAPTER TWELVE

Thursday 2 July

I'm sitting in my office, gazing at the lights on the other side of the river, when Jessica walks in. She shuts the door and leans against it, rubbing her face, steeling herself to face me. I watch her reflection in the window as she walks over to lean against my desk. Putting her hands on my shoulders to rub away the stiffness, I lean my head against her arm, and we stay for a while.

"I put each of them in safe houses. Well, all but Uncle Tony. His place is a fortress." I finally say. "The Rosary won't be said tomorrow and my family won't be buried until this is over. I can't believe this. I can't bury my family right now." I fall silent again.

"I'm so sorry Toni. I know what it's like to feel like you've lost everything near and dear to you. I wish I could wave a magic wand and bring them all back or make the pain go away." I stay silent but give her a slight nod of acknowledgment.

"You need to know that from what I saw your people put up a hell of a fight at the Funeral Home," Jessica continues. "I think they picked up on something, saw somebody who didn't belong and went to help or confront them. I can't confirm that at this point, but my guys are going over the footage. We'll find something. Sheppard appeared and made a scene, which is why they missed

what was going on with your people. They were getting
ready to notify me when the cars blew."

"Merda," I reply. My rage at Sheppard intensifies and I
plot his fate.

"I believe the cameras picked up what happened or at
least picked up the faces of those that set this in motion.
I'm hoping to have confirmation soon." Jessica continued
when again I gave a curt nod.

"Toni this was more organized, more planned out than
any so far. These bombs weren't your average fuel oil and
ammonium nitrate pipe bombs. From what I found out
through the ATF so far, the three bombs look like they
were set off using cell phones. They used military grade
explosives. They're still investing to see if they can find a
signature that'll lead us to the maker. Mansur al-Hakeem
is here. He's directing this symphony of murder and chaos
and he's directing it right at you."

For several minutes, there was an awkward silence in the
room as I soaked up everything, she told me. Could it be?
Could it be that al-Hakeem brought in his expert
nicknamed Sanie Qanabil? If the Bombmaker's here, this
is not a good sign. What's he up to?

"Jessica if that's true, then you'll likely find the signature
belongs to Qadir Nasr Hosni aka Sanie Qanabil, The
Bombmaker. He's the top man al-Hakeem uses for major
operations. If he's here, then this is going to escalate and
fast. He'll use several cells to create distractions and draw
our attention away from the main goal."

"I'll let them know. Let's hope your guy can find us someplace to start looking for him," she answers. I stand to contemplate the river once more sticking my hands in my pockets and finding the forgotten letter.

"Oh, he sent me a little love note, you know," I tell her as I grab it out of my pocket tossing it on the desk. She picks it up and reads it. The color of her face cools to match her eyes.

Miss Andiamo,

I hope I will soon see you personally. You and your Uncle, I am afraid, are on the wrong side of this Jihad. He should have been a more cooperative businessman. You are a woman and should not be involved in such matters. Only a man may truly do the work of Allah. I had hoped I drilled that into you, so to speak, when last we met.

If you get in my way, I will set explosives under all your family vehicles next time and several others in the downtown area. Your police will be chasing their tails trying to put everything out and trying to find us. I am able and will destroy Detroit and it will no longer, how do you say, be on the map. I look forward to the day we will come face to face once again, but not before my work is complete.

I wish to send Mr. Davis greetings. He will meet his fate soon, as will you, Miss Andiamo.

Yours in Allah,

Mansur al-Hakeem

"How...? Who...?" She can't speak.

"He used an innocent little girl who was there with her family to pay respects, a cousin of mine. Don't bother. She's just a little kid who received a few silver dollars to deliver it to me. Funny thing though because nobody pays kids silver dollars anymore. I remember my grandparents saving silver dollars for us kids a long time ago. Anyway..." I go back to staring at the lights across the river.

"He's made contact with you directly Toni. This isn't a game anymore. He's trying to blackmail you with your family."

"I know. It will not work. He continually takes the wrong tack with me. And this means we must find him and find him fast."

"Damn. We need to talk to some of these people in order to do that. I need to have a few words with Malcomb. I have him under lock and key by the way. Have you talked to the others yet?" She sounds frustrated.

"Yeah," I simply say. "You know this is going to spill over to more than my family before it's over."

"It already has. I'm sorry this is costing you so much on a personal level. I know there's nothing I can tell you that'll help the ache in your heart, but I can do my job and make sure the others around me do theirs. We're going to get him before he has a chance to fulfill this letter, Toni. I won't give up until we have him."

Oh, we'll get him all right." My quiet words don't fool her. She knows I'm a ticking time bomb inside. How does she know that after such a short time? How does she see right through my defenses?

She gently turns me around and catches the violence in my black eyes. I watch the storms in hers. In that moment, we see each other for who we are. I'm cold, a calculated killer. She's hard, rigid, an arm of the law. I kiss her then. A kiss of rage, unleashing all my frustration, torment, and temper on this woman who seems to handle everything I throw at her. How? Why? Why would she want to? These and other questions fuel my fury.

I tear at her clothes as we unleash the wild within us. We snarl, growl, claw, and wrestle, finally releasing a howl I'm sure could be heard across the river. Breathless and barely sated, we lie on the floor beside the desk. We start again but soften to a soothing tenderness I didn't know I could give. I stand, gather her up in my arms, and carry her to the couch. Is it possible that this newly found tenderness could douse a fire of pure rage?

She understands what I need and softly caresses my cheek then lets her hand continue down my throat to my chest. Her gentle touch lingers over my heart feeling its pounding beat. Painfully slow this time afraid to let this moment end. Her touch sets fires along its path. My shaking hands try to remember every inch of her features as tears silently fall. Her kiss sprouts little tendrils that touch me deeply, reaching to my darkest depths, breathing new light, new life to my shadows. I try to give her something of myself the only way I know how. I reach her core. She tangles her fingers in the back of my hair and pulls me in closer releasing a small cry.

Time stands still and the worries of the world melt away as we melt the glaciers in each other. Kiss by tortuous kiss I continue tasting until I finally settle to drink of her sweet nectar. I let myself drown in her pleasure and it doesn't take her long for the tremors to break into an earthquake. My heart twirls and thumps as I hear her yell my name.

Before she can catch her breath, she flips me, and I feel her in my bones. She touches me, and I join her with my own pleasure. This intensity, this connection with another takes me to a deeper level of intimacy than I knew possible.

As we lie in each other's arms, temporarily spent, I think about everything and nothing. I think about my Army unit, the times I was a mercenary and the faces of the dead that I sent to hell.

I think of my parents, my sisters, my family. I think of my Uncle and the work I do for him. I think of Frankie. I think about Calvin Sheppard, Malcomb Davis, and Mansur al-Hakeem. I think of all the ones I lost throughout the years, the young men and women who didn't have to die.

I ponder all of this while I hold onto Jessica. My arms tighten around her not wanting to leave this little slice of safety and peace.

I think of my parents' relationship and what it took them to stay together for so long, how much love they had for each other. Was I capable of it, of that kind of love?

I never thought my heart could be satisfied with one person, not again. I never thought to want it again. I'm satisfied with the way I am. Aren't I? Damn Andiamo, you really are going down in flames. What in the world, are you thinking? A Fed? Really? Talk about self-sabotage. Still, she brings a feeling of calm seas, a safe port from the storms of my life.

We dress and I watch her. Tattered nylons, ripped dress, God, she's beautiful. I turn to look at the river once again, knowing this could never be. She comes and puts her arms around me, hugging me close. Steeling myself from the torment in my mind, I turn to face her.

"Ready to deal with Davis?" I ask to head off any other conversation. She shakes her head and her eyes cloud.

"He owes me some answers," she said, sounding far away.

"Jess," I grab her arm as she leaves the office. "We'll get answers. I have no doubt of that. They just may not be answers you want to hear."

"I'm aware of that," she snaps ripping her arm out of my grasp. Then, realizing what she did, takes a deep breath and lets out a sigh.

"I'm aware of that," she says in a much calmer voice. She looks me square in the eye with the most fearsome look on her face. "Let's go." I nod and follow her out.

***

I follow Jessica through the hallways running deep underground. Areas requiring palm prints and chip readers to gain access. Walking in silence and marking out the security measures, I realize how easy it would be to breach. I think I'm going to put together a security package for the building. I'm thinking of retinal scanner with voice print and code panel along with the palm plate. But that'll have to go on the back burner for a while as we finally come to a series of soundproofed rooms where once again Jessica uses her ID and prints to enter.

Inside are a couple of agents at a console viewing another room. Here they regulate everything from lights to air temperature, monitor body temp, pulse, voice stress, and anything other pertinent details. She tells them to keep cameras off and not to record our conversation until she gives the go ahead. We then pass through another door where we stand face to face with the man who raised Jessica. He doesn't look like someone who would betray his country, but then, they never do. I've seen traitors come in all shapes and sizes. He's confident and strong of will. We are about to change that. Jessica takes the lead.

"Deputy Director Davis, tell me there is no truth to Ms. Andiamo's revelation that you are the one helping to keep Mansur al-Hakeem from being brought to justice."

"Jessica..." and the look on her face shut him down.

"Director, I need you to answer questions regarding this matter." Silence.

"Please Uncle Mal," Jessica pleads. He slumps in his chair and continues that silence. Jessica nods over to me and I take up the conversation.

"Davis. Give me what I want so I can tell him I received his message."

"You might think me a fool to think I could keep everyone in the dark. I knew I had a short timeline when the Director wanted you personally, Andiamo. Well, I won't give you what you want. You'll have to find him on your own."

"Davis, I know you. I've known men like you my whole life. You manipulate and use others and don't think about the lives you play with as long as you can keep the illusion of power. That's all it is you know, an illusion.

"Now, you know me. You know that even if they put you in the deepest, darkest hole, I will find a way to get to you. You know I will. So, it's up to you. How do you want to go out, Davis?" He wasn't smiling anymore. His eyes dart from me to Jessica back to me.

"Say what you want, Andiamo, you'll get nothing. You can't play me like you do with others," he says.

I laugh. The sound is harsh and cold, and Jessica stares at me if just for a moment.

"What makes you think I play with my meals, Davis? You are going out one way or the other so it's up to you how. Are you man enough to face yours?" Deathly pale and, though his facade shows a few cracks, he remains solid. How wide can we make the cracks before we break him open?

"I won't be the only one who wants you." I pull out the letter and throw it in front of him on the table. "He knows I figured you out. He'll find you, too. It's going to be a race to see who gets to you first. You think you're safe in here? I saw several different ways to breach this place, more than I can count on my fingers and toes."

I lean and whisper in his ear. "Frankly, I hope he wins because he's not like me." I laugh again. "He'll eat you bit by bit while you scream and beg. Trust me on that. I really think you should choose me, Davis, but you look too tough to want a clean death." He looks to Jessica leaning against the wall with her arms crossed.

"You're going to sit there and let her threaten me aren't you?"

"I'm extremely disappointed, Mr. Davis. You betrayed everything we stand for, what they stood for," she referred to her parents. "You not only betrayed the job, you betrayed me. Frankly, I don't give a shit what happens to you," Jessica responds taking the knife that was in her heart and jabbing it at him. She looks away her heart bleeding.

He took her under his wing when her parents died, murdered. He raised her, vetted her, and taught her everything she knows. Now he's cut her to the quick and in the seconds it took to learn of his betrayal her world came crashing down around her. All she can do now is try to catch Mansur al-Hakeem. She's sick to her stomach.

"Jessica."

"Don't start with any sanctimonious bullshit. It won't do you any good. It doesn't mean anything anymore. Ms. Andiamo, please continue your explanation to Mr. Davis." She looks away from him.

I could tell that stung him more than I anything I'd said or done so far. Maybe I should have let her do this interview. Her heartbreak is palpable in this little interrogation room but maybe her disappointment is breaking him. I continue my barrage.

"Thank you, Special Agent Caruthers," I turn back Davis. "She's calling you Mr. Davis now. Uh-oh! You're taking backward steps here fast. I'm sure you're familiar with how these people work. You didn't make it to Deputy Director by being naïve. You have my file, Mr. Davis. It's much more extensive than what you've lead people to believe, but you know everything don't you?"

"Yes, I know everything. Only Isley and I know everything about you. I do know what you're capable of. I also know what he is capable of, so forgive me if I don't tremble with fear at your threats and innuendos," he weakly states not quite convincingly. He's trembling and Jessica's disappointment in him weighs heavily. He keeps looking at her. I push him more trying to take him over the edge.

"That's because, Mr. Davis, you haven't seen me work in person. I am more brutal than our friend al-Hakeem ever could be and it's because of him that I'm that way. You think on that Mr. Davis. Both of us will have fun with you. Of course, that is, if he lives."

"Ms. Andiamo, I have no doubt that he'll be the one victorious if you two happen to meet in a dark alley," he says trying to hold onto some pride.

"That's just rude Mr. Davis. Now you've gone and hurt my feelings." He sits, stoic. I shrug my shoulders.

"Then this conversation is moot. I shall leave you to your own devices. However, things turn out between al-Hakeem and me, you will not live to find out. So, even if I lose, I win. Good-bye Mr. Davis, good luck." I turn to follow Jessica.

"Ah, wait a moment Ms. Andiamo. Jessica." Bingo. Obviously, Mr. Davis was not ready to shake off his company so soon but *I'm* not naïve either. He's playing his game. So for now, we'll play along.

"Mr. Davis you made your choice. You told me you're not afraid, so I'm taking my leave now. What else is left to say?"

"Now look…"

My voice slices the air with the sharpness of a well-honed knife, "I don't play games Mr. Davis and I dislike being played. I'm sure Agent Caruthers shares this feeling," Jessica sharply nods her head in agreement. "You crossed too many lines for me to have any sympathy for you. Now, you will tell her what she needs or we will feed your carcass to the rest of the pack after I get through with you."

He looks at Jessica who's once again leaning against the wall with her arms crossed. She looks down at her nails then gives him a look that I hope never to be on the receiving end.

"This is your last chance Mr. Davis, you're damn lucky it's me you need to deal with. Quantico won't be in as generous a mood," she coldly states. He appears to break. I have my doubts he'll give us anything of substance.

I sit in the control room now as we spend the next hour making sure that the little bit of information this puke is spewing is on the record. I can hardly stomach it. We make sure it's all legal like with a signed waiver of his Miranda rights and Jessica's interview on tape so there won't be any trouble when the higher-ups take their turn.

Most is double speak, he says nothing of importance. For me, it was too easy to break him. He's the Deputy Director of the FBI. He definitely has his own agenda and he's snowing Jessica, but he does confirm what little we know. It's pretty much a wash.

Ripped to shreds, Jessica leads me to her office. She's worked for the government long enough to know that you need to cover your ass. She had to expect that there'd be people who'd betray her and the work, but I don't think she expected it to come from the one person she so obviously admired, so obviously loved.

"You alright?" I worry. I'm not sure what to do. I've never really comforted anyone before.

"Great. I'm just peachy. Wonderful," she quips back at me.

"You, my dear, are full of shit." I walk over and grab hold of her to enclose her within my arms. She fights me at first then lets her head fall on my shoulder taking deep breaths. I rub her back hoping I'm helping.

"Talk to me Jess, please."

"I grew up believing he was sort of the favorite uncle, you know. I remember my parents, Malcomb, and I hunting and going to the shooting range. They believed that being female didn't mean I shouldn't know how to defend myself or survive off the land if I had to. He's the one who taught me how to fight and to prepare for any situation.

"When they killed my parents, Malcomb was the one that came to tell me. They worked together on a sting that went terribly wrong and though he was hurt and still bleeding from a fresh bullet wound to the shoulder, he knew he had to come to me and be there." She chokes up at the memory of her parents' death.

"Malcomb made it possible for me to stay in my own home until after high school. I went to college getting my Criminal Justice and Law degrees, took the bar and signed up for the academy the day I learned I passed. There was never any question of me going into the FBI. Since my parents couldn't be there, Malcomb was the one to hand me my badge when I graduated. He mentored me every step.

"Now, I wonder if the sting went as wrong as he claims, or did he turn somewhere else along the line. Every moment since their death is now called into question, everything I believed all these years," she states, her breath hitching.

"I'm not quite sure how to help you Jess, all I can do is tell you we can right it again by getting *Him*. We will make it right again. I promise Jess," and I never welch on a promise.

"I know we'll make it right. It just doesn't feel very right at the moment." She sighs heavily. She holds on for a few moments not wanting to let the connection go. Taking a deep breath, she reluctantly lets me go, ready to get back to work.

"Let's follow up on these leads." My phone vibrates. I look at the message that scrawls across the screen and scowl. Shit.

"We need to get to my office. Mitch has something. I set Frankie up in the same safe house as my sister. She's going to have fun with him. He went kicking and screaming all the way."

"Your office then," she quietly walks to the elevator.

"I notified Tyrell to ask for a continuance and to ask the Judge for an in camera once we settle up. We can't let him out of the safe house right now. I've called his Grandmother to offer her the same protection. She wanted to know how I got her grandson into more trouble than what he was in. She's not happy with me and told me to stuff the safe house but to make sure nothing happens to her precious little boy."

"We'll make sure he's safe."

"Yeah, right now we're playing by his rules and he's coming at both of us. He could know about our ruse. If he does, then he'll be taking a run at you next Jess. I won't let that happen." I look at her square in the eye as she looks at me.

"Well I won't let anything happen to me either and I won't let anything happen to you. So we're watching out for each other. Let's see what we can do about this situation."

CHAPTER THIRTEEN

"What's up, Mitch?" I ask when we walk in. He's not looking happy.

"Our boy just claimed responsibility for a bombing in Toronto," he returns.

"Damn! Do we know what was bombed?"

"A power plant. But it was a distraction for what he really wanted."

"Which is?" Jessica asks.

"He stole what amounts to nuclear waste from the imaging department at the University of Michigan's Hospital."

"What?" Jess and I replied together.

"Yeah, it doesn't quite make sense," Mitch replies.

"Yes, it does," Jessica states and it hits me at the same time.

"Dirty Bomb," we say together.

"Damn. Okay, we've got to move fast, figure out where he plans to strike. Now we know why the Bombmaker's here. We need to ID what would be his choice to detonate this thing. Everything that's happening in the city during the holiday week draws good-sized crowds. We've got a lot to go through and not much time to do it."

"Murray, Carrie, and Karl will be here as soon. Miss Edna will be back in about an hour. Charlie's grumbling and she went to tell him off. Want to place a bet on who wins that fight?"

"No, I don't take sucker bets, especially where Miss Edna's concerned. She'll eat Charlie alive," I answer. At Jessica look of confusion, I explain. "Charlie is a champion grumbler. He grumbles if one hair on his head is out of place. Since Miss Edna's been spending most of her time here at the offices lately, he's got a lot to grumble about."

"Ah," she grins at me. "From what I've seen of her here, I have no doubt she'll set him straight in no time. All right, what needs doing? Point me in a direction and put me to work."

"You got it, kid. Here you go." Mitch hands her a stack of papers.

"Great, I'll get right on it," she groans and rolls her eyes.

"Careful what you wish for kiddo," Mitch pats her on the back. I have to smile. Mitch has taken a shine to Jessica. It didn't take much, and he fought hard against it, but he can't hide it now.

"Meet you in the conference room, Jess. Mitch uno memento per piacere?" As soon as Jessica leaves the office I turn to Mitch.

"She got to you. She found a chink in that armor of yours and got to you."

"Yeah well..." he turns a little red.

"Softie," I say.

"Kiss my macho ass," he laughs.

"Not in this lifetime, thanks." I turn serious now. "Mitch?" I didn't have to say anything else.

"I hear ya, kid. I'll meet you in the conference room."

"Thanks, Mitch." He walks out as I sit to call 'Isley, Donald Isley'. I don't trust him, but I need him on board if we're going to find al-Hakeem. He answers as if fresh out of the starting gate. Asshole.

"My office ASAP," I snap and hang up. Let's see how fast he makes it here. I make a few more phone calls then join everyone in the conference room.

***

"Okay I want everyone here before we start. How long before they get back?"

"They should be on their way now," Mitch answers.

"Okay, I've invited a newcomer to our little party. We're not going to get much further without his CIA access and extra ears to the ground. So, we'll waiting for Isley as well as our own."

"Hey guys listen here," Jessica says from behind a report she was reading. "Do you realize that in every major city along the path we thought he'd take there are reports of break-ins at dental offices?" Jessica pipes up.

"That means what exactly?"

"Dental offices have the same radioactive material that the university has but on a much smaller scale. If he hadn't stolen from the University of Michigan, we might not have discovered his mission to detonate a dirty bomb here. He must not have gotten enough material in time to pull this off so he resorted to stealing from a University. I think he finally made a mistake."

"Then I'm betting you're right." I say. "I wouldn't have looked twice at it and if Mitch didn't give it to you, we might have missed it altogether. Lucky break, maybe the tide is finally turning our way for a change."

Just then, the rest of the team walks in followed by Isley. He's not a happy camper. He opens his mouth to say something to me when I cut him off.

"Hold your hot air, Isley. I'm letting you into this op, or whatever you want to call it. So sit down and shut up." Miss Edna gives him a report and his jaw drops as he reads. He looks up with confusion in his bloodshot eyes, not looking as fresh as he sounded over the phone. I feel better now that I see him.

"How'd you get this information?"

"Right." I turn away. "What have you got Carrie?"

"Well, we did as you said. We have some leads we still need to follow," she hesitates, and I give her a go-ahead nod, "but the biggest goes back to the house on Caniff. Most wouldn't talk, but I think we scared them enough to report up their leadership chain. If they put them back in play, we'll be all over it."

"Good job, Carrie. Murray. Karl. What have you got on Caniff?" Isley interjects a question.

"Would somebody kindly explain the details I seem to be missing?"

"Certainly," I turn to Jess. "Agent Caruthers, would you please update Mr. Isley?"

"Of course, well Mr. Isley, we've run every lead into the ground, talked to informants and sources and that led us to a place on Caniff in Hamtramck. We've had them under surveillance since we found the location. Ms. Andiamo was able to place a man inside.

"We found several listening devices, which is to be expected. However, the two were different. There was a transmitter planted on Ms. Andiamo and one on me that carried a secondary signal piggybacked on the original. We're working to trace that source. I'm sure you were scanned when you got here."

"Yes, some snotty young punk wouldn't let me in otherwise."

I jump up and run out of the room making Mitch and Jessica laugh. Isley 's confused.

"What did I say?" he asks.

"Frankie's our resident juvenile delinquent," Mitch says. "Toni saved him from the 'savage streets' and he's supposed to be in a safe house. He must have escaped and made his way back here. I knew there was something I liked about that kid,"

"She saved him from the streets?" Isley inquires.

"It's a long, amusing story, Isley. We'll tell it to you sometime," Mitch answers back. "Meanwhile Jessica, why don't you finish while boss lady deals with Frankie."

***

I find Frankie sitting at Miss Edna's desk waiting for me.

"Frankie I swear to God I'm going to put you in a straitjacket and shackle you in the basement of an abandoned crack house. What the hell are you doing here? You're supposed to be in the safe house with Beth. How the hell did you get here?"

"Chill dawg, ya know I don't deal with being caged. I know your blood be cool, but she be all pregnant and shit, and I'm not doin' nuttin' and got all bored, knew I wasn't doin' no good jus' sitting on my ass and figured I could help out."

"Frankie I'm going to choke the shit out of you. You still have a fucking foul mouth. You are fucking going back to the safe house if I have to drag you by the fucking short hairs." Frankie flashes that little boy innocent smile at me.

"I'm not the only one wid it," he points out. "You drag me back to the safe house, I jus' leave again. You not leavin' me out in the cold dawg, cause I won't go. You know I won't." He crosses his arms in front of his chest his chin sticking out in stubbornness giving away his young years despite his toughness. I sigh and pull my hair.

"Shit, kid, you're giving me a fucking headache. I do okay with my fucking mouth when I'm not around you. I promised your Grandmother nothing would happen to you, Frankie. I've lost too much. I can't afford to lose you too."

"You ain't gonna lose me, I'm too good-looking," he says with a smirk and I snort.

"Alright, this is how it's going to go kid. You will do exactly what I tell you when I tell you. You'll always have one of the team with you. If you don't, I'll have the judge put you in protective custody so I know you won't be able to go anywhere." Frankie pales at the notion of going back to Juvie.

"Do you understand all this Frankie? Do you understand what could happen to you if you don't learn and be smart and listen? I'm not calling your Grandmother in the dark of night to tell her you're dead." Frankie swallows hard, losing the smile.

"I got it." I shake my head and head off toward the conference room, Frankie close on my heels.

"Idiot! Only an idiot would be happy to be hip deep in a pile of shit," I grumble. Frankie, grinning from ear to ear, trots behind me. As we enter the conference room, Jessica is just finishing her briefing. All eyes zero in on Frankie.

"Miss Edna, I hate to tear you away, but I need you to supervise Frankie in the electronics room. He's doing well tracking that second signal. Oh, and call the safe house to let them know he's okay and they'll be moved shortly."

"No problem, Ms. Andiamo." Miss Edna gets up and shoos Frankie out.

"He'll be safer here than on his own. Murray, I want you visit Beth's safe house fire every fucking one of those idiots on duty. Take another team, make sure they know what'll happen to them if they lapse while on the job. Then supervise the move to a new place."

"You got it, Sarge," Murray sings back to me.

"What are you so happy for? This is a chink in the security. I don't think I'm being paranoid these days, am I?"

"No Sarge, you ain't paranoid. I just like firing people is all." Murray pretends to be more somber.

"You're a sick man Murray, a truly sick man," I joke, and he flashes his pearly whites in his best 'salesman rocking his cigar between his fingers grin'. "Alright, how far along are we? Are you up to speed now Isley?"

"Yes, I am, and I have a few questions for you, Ms. Andiamo, if you're willing to answer."

"Okay. Now that we flushed out most of the moles, I think I can speak more freely One rule: whatever you hear in this room stays in this room."

"I'll agree to that. I understand why. Okay, where to begin? Let me start by asking how you were you able to find these moles when no one else was able to put any of it together?"

"Simple, Mr. Isley. Once we had the whole file, I sat down and studied it. I mean a line-by-line, in-depth study. Little things started to stand out and I pieced them together. If you'd studied the full file, you would've seen them."

"I gave the file to a trusted colleague who's on your list, which explains several things in my domain. He'll be dealt with severely."

I have no doubt his co-worker will face an even darker future than the Deputy Director will. They'll probably throw him in a deep dark hole where no one will see him again.

"Then Agent Caruthers and I had a few words with several of our informants. The one recurring theme was this place on Caniff. All of them were scared to talk. Fortunately, some were more afraid of us." Isley sat thinking for a moment or two.

"You trusted a Fed with your sources?" That's the first question on your mind? Lame, Isley, really lame.

"They didn't know she was a Fed and yes I trust Special Agent Caruthers. She's one Fed I know I can trust with my life."

"Fine. So how did you link the theft from UofM and the bombing in Canada? No one else put it together."

"I have connections." He doesn't need to know they're in the Prime Minister's office. He's not the only one who can play the 'need to know' game. "And, they did put it together. As for the rest, you can thank the Bombmaker making an appearance and Agent Caruthers knowledge of dirty bombs."

"I see. So, you're saying that the Bombmaker is here? Why do you think this?" he sits straighter in his chair.

"Because of the bombs planted at the viewing for my family. I'm sure the ATF will find his signature once they sift through all the evidence."

"Well, this is not good news. Next to al-Hakeem, the Bombmaker's next on our list. It would be a definite coop if we could capture him in all this.

"And what's your uncle's role here? You can't think I'd believe that crap in Caruthers' report. I'm not stupid."

"I don't care what you believe. I told you before, he's off limits." Isley raises his hands in an 'I give up' gesture.

"Okay, okay. Don't get riled, you know I have to ask. I'm just doing my job." He grins.

"I get you. Just remember, my family is off limits and so is Frankie - off limits." I look hard into Donnie baby's eyes. Though the smile remains on his face, it loses its luster.

"I get it, off limits. So, what else do you have?" He looks around the table. Everyone stares silently. Now it's my time I smile.

"What else do we have?" I ask.

"Well, we tracked our guy from the Caniff location. He went from there to a location on Grand Ave. where we lost the signal. He hasn't checked in and we searched the last known location to no avail," Murray reports.

"Right, that's not good. Why didn't you tell me sooner? How long's it been since last contact? Did you let the cops know what's going on?"

"Yeah, they said they'd keep an eye out and let us know if they find anything. I sent a picture over, so they'd know who to look for."

"Okay. Shit, he was our best shot, so far. Why did we lose signal? Did they find it or did it malfunction, what?" I ask.

"We haven't been able to determine yet," Karl speaks up. "But working on it now."

"Damn it, what about these other leads? Karl, find out what's going on with our man, and find the damn source of that second signal."

"Ja, Sarge," he nods then walks out.

"Murray, get to Hamtramck after you square my family in a new safe house. Set up camp in the cop shop, quietly. I want to know the minute they find out anything."

"You got it, Sarge." He follows Karl out of the conference room.

"Carrie, you're with Mitch checking out these other leads."

"Roger that, Sarge."

As they leave. I turn to Isley. "Mr. Isley, if you'd talk to your sources and search your databases, personally, I'd appreciate any information you and your people can give us. Anything relevant, the chatter or especially if the chatter stops, you know what we need." Everyone knows that when the chatter stops, something's about to happen.

Also if you can light a fire under some asses and get us a list of important happenings or gatherings or activities it would be greatly appreciated."

"You got it, Sarge," his laugh drips with slime and he slithers out of the room. I pick up a scanner and run it around the room - nothing.

"Well, at least he knew enough not to try," Jessica says. "He's got a crush on you. I don't know what to feel about that."

"Nothing to worry about. It's not a crush. He wants me for wet work again and if he can find something to turn me, he won't hesitate to use it. We need to hit the streets. I got a message from Stutter while I was dealing with Frankie, need to meet him in about an hour. I need to speak with Miss Edna and then change out of these rags. You might want to do the same. I don't know why but I find I like having you alive and kicking. And, though I thoroughly enjoy watching you take out street punks, your current look'll only invite trouble. We don't need that distraction now. There's too much at stake."

"I believe I'll accept that change of clothes."

***

As we head out of my office, Isley catches us. Damn, my timing is usually better than this. I've been a little off my game lately.

"Ladies my, my, my, where are you headed dressed like that? You look positively edible." He whistles and pats his heart; his voice is dripping with venom. I grimace. Jessica frowns.

"Well now, Isley, that's none of your business. We'll be in the field, back in a couple of hours." I wink at Miss Edna. She knows to keep an eye on him. We head out again leaving him with his jaw hanging.

CHAPTER FOURTEEN

3 July 0130hrs

"Stutter doesn't usually keep me waiting this long," I say checking my watch as I lean against the alley wall. I push off and pace. Jessica looks concerned.

"You think he could have asked too many questions? Maybe asked the wrong person?"

"Maybe. I don't know. We'll wait a little longer then go look for him. I don't like it, though." I said, pacing back and forth while Jessica leans against the wall, arms crossed. Five minutes later Stutter walks into the mouth of the alley. I let out a sigh of relief.

"Damn it, Stutter, why the hell are you so late? You're cutting my time to the bone here. What'd you find out?"

"S-s-sorry S-Storm. I g-g-got caught up in someth-th-thing." He hands me a crumpled piece of paper. "Th-th-these are the ones you want. They're the ones that k-k-killed your famil-l-ly. I have to go," he turns on his heel and I grab his collar.

"What's going on Stutter?" I ask concerned at his behavior.

"It's-s just th-that this is r-wrong. My people aren't like th-this. Muslim people I know are faith-f-ful and p-p-peaceful. I d-don't like this b-b-business and I d-don't like

t-t-turning on my own. I wouldn't have d-d-one th-this b-
but th-these g-guys g-give us a b-bad name and it was
your f-family." Stutter's stuttering becomes worse the
more upset he is.

"I know how difficult this must be for you. I know you
and your people are peaceful and loving. I wish this wasn't
necessary, but you know there's always the bad sect as
with any group or religion. You also know I'll do all I can
to bring an end to all this. You have my deepest gratitude
and appreciation, Stutter. I take care of mine. You know
that, right?" He shrugs his shoulders and nods. "You need
a place to hole up until this blows over?" I ask.

He nods again and I pull out a piece of paper with another
hundred and a key from my pocket and hand it to him. He
murmurs thanks and was gone.

I look at the sheet of paper Stutter gave me and study
names and addresses. It's time to call out the man who's
very good at getting information from people. I shudder as
this man gives me the creeps. Unfortunately, Jessica
notices.

"Look, Toni, I know what you want to do but we need too
much information from them. I need you to let us handle
this. We need to do this swiftly and legally. Toni I'm
asking you to trust me to do this for you. They will be
brought to justice."

I walk down the alley a pretending to think about it as I
covertly take a picture of the paper Stutter handed me. I
know I need to let Jessica handle this but one of these men
is going to disappear, temporarily or permanently. Which,

I haven't decided yet. I turn and head back, willing my face to show nothing.

"Alright," my throat tightens not wanting to agree. It felt wrong to go behind her back, but I knew it was the only way.

I turn to leave, and Jessica grabs me from behind. I instinctively tense then relax just a bit letting her hold onto me. It's surprising, this willingness to let this woman hold me.

I feel safe with her, yet I know it could never work. I try to pull away, angry about these feelings. Jessica pulls me back, holding on a few moments more before we head our separate ways.

***

I take the hidden elevator that opens inside my office. I called Mitch on my way back and he's there waiting for me when the doors open. I needed to talk to him before we call our expert in. I don't want to do it but see no other way around it. As Jessica said, we have no time left.

"We need to call in Dr. Grill," I get right down to it. We call him Dr. Grill for two reasons. One is his more unique skills lies in his ability to push people for information and get everything he needs. Second is his use of a certain chemical cocktail that essentially grills them from the inside out.

He started with the CIA in '71 working in the MK Ultra program. He impressed them with his abilities, and they used him for years to obtain the information they needed.

They eventually sidelined him, publicly declaring his methods inhumane. It looked good for the Congressional Oversight Committee charged with overseeing them, though I have a feeling they keep him on their payroll for, shall we say, more difficult questioning.

I've seen him work. He has no feeling. He feels no pain, literally, so others' pain has no meaning to him. He's devoid of all things that make us human. He carries no remorse.

"Oh, Jesus kid, are you sure?" he asks as the color drains from his face.

"I got a list of the ones responsible for the murder of my family. We're out of time. We need answers and fast. Jessica thinks her people will get what we need. I'm not as confident as she is. They're staging a raid on the Caniff house and the place on Grand Avenue as well. I hope they find more than a few expendable people but this way's faster. We only need one to talk to get the information we need."

"We need to find another way, Toni. We can't do this."

"I'd be happy to find another way! Don't you get it? I just can't think of anything else to do, of any other way. Believe me, I didn't come to this decision lightly. I'd prefer to take care of these people my way. It would be a lot messier and gain me much satisfaction but may not produce the results we need and would probably take too long.

"We can't take that chance, Mitch. I wish there was another way. I debated it all the way here, hoping you could come up with something, anything, so I wouldn't have to make this call."

"Shit kid you know I can't. You sure you want to do this? It's very 'last resort' stuff here, kid. There's gotta be another way."

"We're wasting time. Just do it, Mitch. Make the call. I want him ready when we pick up. I need the team in here fast so we can find these men."

"I'm on it," he sighs and leaves the office to make the call and gather the troops.

I head to the conference room and start a search for each name on the list. One by one, their pictures and information pop up on the wall screen. As they do, my team comes in.

"These are the men responsible for the murder of my family," I start. "Study them, find them. We need the most experienced of the group. The most experienced will have the most information. The rest we'll deliver to the FBI. I'm bringing in Dr. Grill." I hear gasps across the room.

"I know, I know. If there were any other way, I'd use it, but he can gather information quickly without leaving a trace. He knows how to leave his prisoners with no memory of him or the interrogation they went through. Any questions, complaints? Good. Go." Everyone scrambles and I have no doubt that they'll deliver.

***

3 July 0500hrs

Jessica sets up her board in the conference room as she waits for the others to file in. She studies the plans for the two homes they're hitting and commits them to memory. She woke up a judge to sign the no-knock warrants and hopes that something is still there by the time they arrive. That those who killed Toni's family are brought to justice as promised.

She's a team leader for the FBI's Special Weapons and Tactics team (SWAT). She's also one of few specially trained as an Enhanced SWAT Agent to assist the Hostage Rescue Team (HRT).

There are approximately forty members of Detroit's SWAT team that includes local law enforcement who train with the FBI. She has a couple Special Agent Bomb Technicians (SABT), ready to participate as well as ATF Agents. She goes over different tactics and strategies in her head as her people walk through the door.

Isley stops in front of her. "What's going on Caruthers?"

"We're staging for a couple of raids, Isley. Sit down and we'll go over everything." He scowls but takes his seat as she begins to address the room.

"We've finally received a few leads. In the folder in front of you are the men responsible for the explosion and murder of several members of the Andiamo family. I have arrest warrants for them and no-knock warrants for these two residences, but we need to move fast.

"Johnson, you're taking the lead at the Caniff residence, I'll take point at the Grand Avenue location." She displays satellite images of the Caniff location and surrounding area on the big screen, pointing out a parking lot next to an empty store.

"This is where you'll stage," she points to a parking lot next to an empty store around the block from their target. "This is the target. There are two doors, one here and here. There are three windows in front and two in back to avoid, two other windows on each side to watch. We don't want anyone to use them to flee once you hit the doors. Any others inside besides our suspects are bonuses. We bring them in for questioning. Inside," she clicks the remote bringing up floor plans for the inside of the house. She methodically goes through every step with both residences.

"We're going in fast. Quiet and simultaneous," she says, wrapping up. "Any questions?" she asks. Finding none, she dismisses them. Johnson lingers waiting for the others to file out.

"What's up, Johnson?"

"I just wanted to say thanks for this after the funeral home fiasco," he fumbles.

"Look, we all messed up there. Besides, you're a SWAT agent and I figure you deserve a chance at payback."

"Damn right," he perks up.

"Also remember that we're looking for a civilian who's undercover and missing since last night and watch for suicide/murder. They might try to take everyone out rather than be caught."

"Let's get to it, then." He heads out. Jess follows closely but Isley blocks her at the door.

"Why wasn't I briefed before the meeting, Caruthers?" He slithers.

"You were notified of this meeting as soon as I had intel. You and I were at the same briefing at Storm Investigations. This shouldn't come as a surprise.

"Sorry, I wasn't around to lead you by the hand." A sneer on her face. "We've been busy here, with no help from you. So, I suggest you back off." Her nose inches from his as she stares him down, allowing her disgust to show. At that, she heads to the staging area to suit up and go through the steps one last time.

***

3 July 0345hrs

I turn in my seat looking through a small window to the back of the van where Dr. Grill is setting up. We're in a black panel van with quick-change Canadian plates. In the back are two stainless steel fully reclining swivel seats, one with removable cushions for comfort. A table folds down from each wall. His equipment and chemicals meticulously perched for easy reach. Stainless steel rods are bolted into the ceiling with steel stoppers and clamps where he hangs the IV bags. Soundproofing material wraps around the entire area so no one accidentally hears him at work.

Mitch is driving. The plan: drive the freeways while he works, gather as much intel as we can. Karl and Murray are at the Caniff and Grand Ave. houses waiting on Jessica and her team and making sure the others don't rabbit. We're on our way to Carrie who found our man and slipped him a roofie; the head of the cell that terminated my family.

We pull up and corral him into the van. Carrie takes off not wanting to have anything to do with Dr. Grill. I toss our guest into the swivel bucket seat, the one without cushions, strap him down, and roll up his sleeves for easy access. The doc administers a paralytic right away, so he doesn't fight, then starts an IV to deliver his cocktail.

He has a list of questions I want answered. He likes to start with simple conversation then move into more pointed questions adding different drugs based on his willingness to answer. He puts them under, questions them as they're coming out, then puts them under again, creating a cycle and adding other chemical cycles until he gets what he wants

He adds amphetamines to bring them up and then brings them back down. He makes their insides burn and then flushes them. He makes them itch then flushes that. He pumps them up and slams them down without batting an eyelash. I guess you could say the same about what I do. While I have no compunction about what I am and what I do, I know he's in a class of being all his own.

I'm here in case something goes wrong and he needs help. The seat is fully reclined, and I watch as the good Doctor prepares our guest. IV's in both arms begin to flow. Our man, who'd been quite chatty, starts to slur and then he's out. Dr. Grill injects the contents of a syringe in the IV line and our man screams as his eyes fly open. And, so it begins. I take a deep breath and let it go steeling myself for what's to come.

***

3 July 0630hrs

Jessica and the SWAT teams are in their staging areas when word reaches them that one of the subjects is wandering into the target zone looking like he's drunk. She gives instructions not to interfere, that they'll breach once he opens the door. She takes stock of her agents one last time, waiting for word that he's opened the door.

When the word does reach her, Jessica calls for breach at both places. They move like a well-oiled machine. Jessica leads her team through the door with one of her members securing their main subject. Room-by-room they secure and clear. Jessica heads up the stairs and left to clear a room when a male subject appears in the hall with a weapon. Someone takes downs him, secures the weapon, and secures him as well. He needs a medic after that takedown. Continuing to clear the area Jessica and her team move through the house and secure the premises.

Johnson reports in that they're cleared and secured with no incidents. She heads out, her MP5/10 hanging around her neck and armpit, lifts her goggles onto her helmet and removes her gloves, stuffing them in a pocket.

Now's the tricky part: secure the subjects into a vehicle, secure relief for her medics still working, and make sure nothing is touched until cleared by her SABT. They've deployed a robot here and at the other residence as well.

Next comes the documentation of evidence and analyzing each piece thoroughly. Everything takes time. "Too much time." She thought.

Outside, she waits for the all-clear from her tech and spies Toni leaning on a police cruiser looking calm and cool. A fact she finds curious, given the circumstances. She heads over to speak to the woman that's slowly capturing her heart.

***

3 July 1230hrs

Trying to look calm leaning against this cop cruiser and I spot her, looking damn sexy in her tactical gear. With all that's going on, this is what comes to mind. My decision to use Dr. Grill isn't sitting well. Granted, we extracted an extremely important piece of information but that was it, just one piece of the puzzle.

I'm here to see what Jessica came up with, if anything. At least that's what I tell myself. I want to make sure the man responsible for killing my parents doesn't remember what I just put him through.

I see a body bag and wonder if it's my guy and then I spot him being led to a transport vehicle with a couple of others. Relieved, I wonder what happened, who lost their life tonight. Then my wonder turns to worry as I see Jess. I look her over thoroughly, satisfied she has no wounds, and breathe another sigh of relief.

"Hey," she says leaning on the police cruiser next to me.

"Hey," I answer back. "What happened to that one?" I nod at the coroner's van.

"He decided to point a weapon at someone and found it was a bad decision. Stupid. We tried like hell to save him though, to get some answers," she scowls shaking her head. A thick strand of hair came loose from her ponytail and she forces it back behind her ear, looking frustrated.

"It's going to be awhile before we can get inside to sort through everything. I did identify bomb-making materials and weapons. Who knows what else is in there? The bomb techs are checking to make sure it's safe for us to process." She stops as something comes through her earpiece.

"Shit." I hear her issues quick urgent orders for her people to evacuate everyone in the neighborhood and move them to a parking lot several miles away.

"Ricin materials," she tells me. "I'll let you know when I can meet you. We're going to be here awhile."

"Alright," I say but she'd already turned to head back.

***☐

3 July 1300hrs

Sheppard sits in his car outside of Big Tony's home and its sprawling grounds waiting for the man to leave his haven. The longer he waits, the more he thinks about why he's suspended and why that bitch of an agent isn't. He blames the past week on Big Tony and his niece, and, of course, Caruthers.

After waiting for hours, he realizes this man has no reason to leave and decides to provide him with one. He checks that his weapon is loaded and the safety off, a Glock 23 .40 cal, one of his personal weapons. Hefting the Glock adds fuel to the anger burning in him. They took his badge and his duty weapon. "They shouldn't have taken my badge," he thought.

He steps out of his car and saunters to the front gate where he's immediately greeted by four security guards. They'd alerted their boss hours ago that Sheppard was watching the house and radioed that he was heading for the gate. Word came down to turn him away.

"I need to speak with him," Sheppard told the guards as if they should let him pass because of who he is.

"He's not in Sheppard," the biggest and beefiest spoke up.

"Of course he is. I saw him pull in several hours ago."

"He's still not in. You're not welcome here and need to leave."

"You open this gate right now and let me talk to him or by God he and his niece will face dire consequences. I'll see to it personally." The big guy laughs, knowing it's an empty threat.

"We have no doubt, Ms. Andiamo, is able to handle herself and as for Mr. Andiamo he had a good laugh over you and he's still not in. Good day to you Agent Sheppard," as more guards joined the formation at the gates.

He decided to keep arguing even though his words fell on the men's deaf ears. He kept up for several minutes before stalking away. Back at his car, slams the door and continues his vigil of the Andiamo estate.

Half an hour later, a flurry of vehicles pass through the gates. Sheppard takes photos of the cars hoping to capture a face, gathering plate numbers to run later. One of the guard's marches through the open gates and motions for him. He drives up wondering what's going on.

"Your boss change his mind and decide to have a chat with me?" Sheppard asks. The guard smiles.

"Yes, Mr. Andiamo would like to have a friendly, private chat, Agent Sheppard. If you could park your car in the space provided just inside the gate a cart will take you to him."

Sheppard does so and is quickly shuffled into the cart and whisked away. No one notices later when it's not Sheppard driving away in his vehicle.

CHAPTER FIFTEEN

3 July 2100hrs

After dealing with the Sheppard issue and dealing with possible scenario's, we search for possible targets to release Ricin or set off a dirty bomb. I'm working in my office when Miss Edna comes in with some information I need. "Thanks, Miss Edna, anything else?" I ask noticing her reluctance to leave.

"About this message," she hesitates to hand over the piece of paper.

"Yes?"

"I don't want to interrupt you with trivial business but this is bothering me."

"It's okay Miss Edna." I hold out my hand for the message and she fidgets for a moment or two more before handing it to me. I unfold it and read.

"Is this for real?" I look to her perplexed.

"I'm afraid it is, Ms. Andiamo. I didn't want to bother you with it but just couldn't throw it away. I thought it best for you to decide what to do."

"Okay, alright, no problem. I'll deal with it. Thanks, Miss Edna."

"Can I do anything else for you, Ms. Andiamo?"

"No, I think everything's handled thanks to your efficiency."

"It's easy when it's for you and your team. I don't have to explain things. Get some rest, Ms. Andiamo, you need it."

"I know and I will. Thanks." She makes a move toward the door. "Oh, Miss Edna, did she say why she's called? I mean, I don't hear a word from her for, what, five years now? Then she calls out of the blue with all that's going on? I don't like it, not one bit. You know how I feel about coincidences."

"Yes, I do, Ms. Andiamo, you don't believe in them and neither do I, not with this one. She didn't say why she was contacting you though she did sound a bit tentative, as if she were relieved that you weren't here. She happily left her information and rang off quickly."

"Hmm, I wonder what the hell she wants?"

"Do you want me to call and tell her you're not interested in speaking with her?"

"No. As happy as it would make me to be that petty, it has my curiosity up. I'll find out for myself, though, thanks." I turn to my window as Miss Edna slips quietly out the door.

Shit, this is all I need right now, yet I couldn't help but contemplate what Maggie could possibly want. We had a great relationship or so I thought. We were together for five years when she walked out to get smokes one night and never came back. I know, but it really happened that way. I had no clue anything was amiss in our relationship. I certainly wouldn't have believed she was doing drugs and stepping out on me. Shows you how much I paid attention.

I tracked her down and found her shacking up with somebody to get free drugs. She threw away her life and ours for to stuff up her nose or smoke. She lost everything she had as well as just about all I had. I rebuilt my life stone by precious stone, but she'd taken every morsel of trust. She stripped every string of pride away and it nearly cost me my life. She nearly lost hers.

A couple of years ago, I heard she finally got her shit together, found a job in a law firm and started practicing again. I finally quit wondering about her when I heard she was dating the mayor's daughter. Go figure. That's why the rest of my relationships haven't been relationships, just a series of one-night stands that last a couple of days maybe a week rarely two.

Until now. Until I met Jess. Has it only been a week? Something about her pulls at me, makes me crave her, makes it near impossible to concentrate around her. I have to find out what it is that draws me to her. What makes me always want more? I find myself with a need I didn't think I could experience. Especially not after Maggie. Damn it, I'm back to Maggie. I sigh heavily, pick up the phone, and dial the number she left on the message.

"Haltom, Biggs and Dally, how may I direct your call?" The receptionist answers.

Halton, Biggs, and Dally are one of the top law firms in the Detroit Metro area. What is she doing in a place like that? She must have really put her life back together.

"Margaret Valens please."

"May I tell her who is inquiring?" Inquiring? Jesus.

"Toni Andiamo from Storm Investigations returning her call," I say rolling my eyes.

"Just one moment please," she responds and puts me on hold. At least the music's decent.

Maggie's voice fills the phone. "Toni? My God, I never thought you'd call me back. I thought you'd written me off long ago."

"My mistake, I should have thrown the message away, but curiosity got the better of me. I swear it'll be my downfall one of these days. So what is it you want?"

"That's my Toni, tough exterior, soft interior, and always straight to the point."

"You know there's nothing straight about me and I'm not your anything. I'll ask you again, what the hell do you want? You've caught me in the middle of a difficult case, one that's already cost me dearly."

"I know, I heard. That's why I'm calling. I just wanted to say how sorry I am to hear about what happened. I know how close you are with your family. I stopped by the funeral home hoping for a chance to talk to you, but it seems a pretty brunette was taking up all your time. I left when I realized I couldn't catch a moment with you.

Then, of course, I hear about the explosions when I get home. I'm sorry Toni, precious."

"I didn't see you there, but then again I wasn't exactly paying attention either. I didn't exactly expect to see you there. Matter of fact I didn't expect to ever hear from you again. You clearly didn't want me around anymore."

"Look, Toni, I know we didn't leave things on the best of terms ..."

"The best of terms?" I shout over the phone, interrupting her. Calm down. Just get through the call and say your goodbyes. I take a deep breath.

"Sorry. Let me begin again," I say more calmly. "You cost me everything. Do you really expect me to be happy and say 'Hi, how are you doing? Has life treated you well since you fucked me over?"

"No, I suppose not," she replies.

"What in the world possessed you to call me after all this time, Maggie? I can't believe it's just to express your condolences for the murder of mi famiglia."

"I've thought about you a great deal over the past couple of years. I straightened myself out, gained back some of what I lost. I realize what I miss the most is you."

"Oh please. You don't think I would actually believe that do you. Besides I thought you were with the mayor's daughter," I choke out.

"I hope you'd believe me. It's the truth. And, Mimi and I split a while ago. I see your investigative skills haven't suffered. Still have your ear to the ground, huh?"

"Always and obviously not close enough. Look, I'm sorry about Mimi, but I don't see why you'd want to have anything to do with me. If I remember correctly, you called me a bunch of names, none flattering, when I found you with I don't for the life of me even remember the sleazy bitch's name. You were crazed, hopped up on whatever, and almost took my face off.

"I came awfully close to ripping your throat out and I put your little plaything in the hospital holding on for dear life. This type of behavior is not conducive to 'It's all a misunderstanding dear, can't we just forget about it and move on?' What's your real motive here, Maggie, because I don't play games anymore, especially not with you?"

"Well, I guess I deserve that. Look, I worked my ass off to turn my life around and get back on the right track. I'm trying like hell to apologize to you for the pile of shit I left you in and to ask you to forgive me." Her voice softens, takes on a pleading tone, "I'm so sorry my precious." Yeah, I'd do whatever she wanted when she called me that back in the day.

"Don't call me that. I don't want to accept your apology, Maggie. Don't know if it's in my heart to forgive what you did. I don't see myself as available to you anytime, never actually." There, I said it.

"I see you still know how to torture me. It's not going to stop me from trying."

"Try all you want, it won't get you anywhere. Look, all this sentiment is really getting to me but as I told you at the beginning of this conversation, I'm in the middle of something here that's more important than this sad reminiscing so I really must bid you adieux. I finally get to do what you failed to do when you left so goodbye, Maggie."

"Toni wait."

"What's there left to say?"

"There's plenty left to say, Toni. I'd just like the chance to get together and say it. I just want a chance, okay?"

"No, it's not okay."

"Alright, but we will be seeing a lot more of each other because I just bagged your uncle as a client." Great, that sorry ass son of a bitching whore piece of shit fuck. I'm going to tear him a new asshole if I ever find this al-Hakeem mother fucker.

"Fine, but don't expect to have me falling at your feet. I won't be. Goodbye Maggie, I need to get back to work." I hang up the phone as she tries to reply.

Damn it. This is all I need. My uncle playing matchmaker with my ex-druggie, ex-girlfriend. Bald face mother fucking piece of fucking shit. I think Frankie's not the only person who brings out my foul mouth. Maggie always did and now my uncle and I are going to have to have a little chat about matchmaking.

I sit staring at the river, brooding, craving sleep that wouldn't come. With everything I put the man that killed my family through the only thing we came away with was a date and time: the 4th of July, dark thirty.

I'm still having a hard time reconciling what Dr. Grill did to him, at my request. He killed my family. Get over it, Andiamo. What's done is done. At least we now have a date and time to go with the 'how' and I hope Jess comes up with the 'where'. Just then my cell phone rings, and Jess tells me to meet her at the office as soon as I can get there.

I let Mitch know where I'll be as I rush out the door. I must tell Jess what I found out and I know she'll ask where I got it. Do I tell her? This weighs more heavily than the method I employed to get that information.

***

I make the short trip to Jess's office and once again go through the long task of getting through security. Is it just me who gets this treatment or does everyone go through this kind of attention, I wonder? I seriously doubt everyone goes through this amount of crap. I head to the elevators. As I exit on her floor, she steps out of her office, spots me, and nods toward the conference room.

"We need to talk," I whisper as I meet her at the door. She nods her agreement and I take an empty chair waiting for others to file in. I notice one of her Jr. G's is missing. Probably out doing his boss's bidding.

"Alright everyone, settle down. We have a lot to go over and very little time. The Caniff residence looks like it was the logistics cell. They did the planning, recruiting and gathering resources there and we found detailed plans for several locations around the city. They have several operational cells in the area with three to five people in each. Captain Stubinsky, please select which officers you want to work with my agents and put your SWAT teams on alert. We muster as soon as we know the when."

"I can help with that," I interrupt Jessica. "This takes place tomorrow, the 4th of July at around 2100 hours." Jessica's look is one I hoped never to earn.

"Okay, this doesn't give us much time so when we're done here, gather everyone for briefings and assignments. The Grand Avenue residence is where they put the equipment together. Ms. Andiamo was right about The Bombmaker. His signature was confirmed at Terrorist Explosive Device Analytical Center (TEDAC) and from the looks of the materials found, there's a massive undertaking underway by Mansur al-Hakeem."

"They have Ricin which must not be allowed to become airborne. There's evidence of Improvised Radiological Devices (IRD). From the report on the UofM and dental break-ins, we could be dealing with at the most three devices. We also have evidence of several Improvised Explosive Devices, (IED) mostly vests and pipe bombs." Jessica turns as the door opens.

Someone whispers in her ear and she whispers a few questions back. I'm close enough to hear that Malcolm Davis escaped and the person who helped him, Special Agent Jake Barley, is dead. Probably a Jr. G's. That explains his absence from our little gathering.

"We'll reconvene in two hours. Gather your personnel and be ready for assignments. Andiamo you're with me." She dismisses the room then turns on me.

"When the hell were you going to tell me about this? It would've been great to call the teams in to set up assignments right away instead of waiting for fucking hours on information I should've already had. Now I need to deal with Davis' escape," not to mention that one of her Jr.'s was working for and reporting to the Director. She turns and heads to the holding area leaving me to follow.

"Jessica, look I took one of the guys responsible and gained the date and time from him then sent him back to you, none the wiser. You won't find a mark on him with exception of a couple of needle holes." That stopped her dead in her tracks.

"You chemically interrogated him," she said quietly shaking her head. "I thought we gained a measure of trust going through all this, Toni. I thought you trusted me to take care of this for you." Her quiet demeanor spoke volumes. She continues down the hall as I try to keep up with her.

"For reasons I can't fathom I find I do trust you. That's why I'm telling you at the first opportunity you've had to hear it. You've been busy. I didn't think we had that kind of time and I did this in the span it took your guys to get in place to raid those houses. I didn't kill him, though I could have. I turned him loose to be picked up by you and now we don't have to waste precious hours hoping someone will talk." I grab her by the arm, but she shakes me off, the storms in her eyes dark grey and dangerous.

"Jessica …"

"Look Toni. I understand your reasons. I don't like them
and I certainly don't agree with them. I think while I was
with you at the scene there was enough time for you to
provide a heads up. I'm pissed and I'm hurt Toni and it'll
take me time to process, but right now I have to deal with
this situation." She resumes her path to the holding area,
and I'm stunned into silence, merda.

Crime scene techs are busy photographing every angle of
the mess that was made of Agent Barley when we get
there. I hear Jessica take a deep breath and let it out with
a sigh. This can't be easy for her.

"Talk to me," she barks. "Where is Tivac? She's supposed
to be manning the cameras and who's supposed to be on
guard duty?" A guy standing near holding a cup of coffee
stares at Barley splayed all over the floor. He lifts his
blank eyes and his hand. Looks like he's in shock to me.

"He told me I could take a break. I had to use the
facilities, so I took him up on it. I wasn't even gone ten
minutes. I'm so sorry. I just had to use the bathroom and
I got a cup of coffee." He goes back to staring at the body
in disbelief. Jessica shakes her head.

"Hiller go wait over there for someone to take your
statement. I have no Doubt OPR will be all over our asses
for this. Where's Tivac? Did someone clear the camera
room?" she asks again then heads that way. A tech yells at
her for walking through their crime scene unprotected but
she ignores him and prepares to enter the camera room,
hand on her gun.

I shake my head; they give me a hassle every time I enter this building and they don't even know how to clear a crime scene properly? Feds.

Inside she finds Sarah Tivac in a heap on the floor, blood dripping from her head. Jess checks for a pulse and calls out for an ambulance.

I rush in and move her out of the way, using my combat skills to assess and provide what little treatment I could. Once the paramedics arrive, I text Mitch to get the team up here for assignments and to get ahold of my brother as well. Spencer arrives and Jess turns away from me to deal with him. He came down to check on things and ended up reaming quite a few asses, Jessica's included.

CHAPTER SIXTEEN

3 July 2345hrs

Alex and I are in Jessica's office as he relays what he's uncovered. He found two cells that activated very recently. He gave Jess the run down on each location and was able to provide a head count along with names.

"I believe they have explosives as well as significant firepower. These guys are extremely well-financed, Agent Caruthers," he says, pacing her office.

"Call me Jessica, please. Are you alright, Mr. Andiamo?" she asks concerned with his obvious agitation.

"Yes, I'm okay and, please, call me Alex. It's just being cooped up with the Feds is not my idea of fun, makes me nervous," he tells her. I know exactly what he means. Jessica lets go a laugh that breaks the tension in the room.

"Your sister has the same problem," she looks to me and I give her a half a smirk.

"Do we have time to take them out before they deploy? Alex do you have eyes on them?" I ask.

"Of course," he answers me.

"I'll see what I can do. Now if the both of you wait in the conference room, I can begin," Jess kicks us out of her office and we to run right into Isley. I nod to my brother to head out without me.

"Ms. Andiamo how fortunate I should run into you." Yeah right. He was probably waiting for me.

"What do you need, Isley?"

"We need to have a chat. Please join me in my office?"

"We don't have time for this," I address him.

"Please," he holds his hand out for me to precede him. He's a slick snake and I let him pass me so I can follow him down the hall and to the elevators. His office is in the CIA field office two floors below Jessica's.

"What's going on Isley?" I ask once we are in his office.

"Ms. Andiamo, it's come to our attention that you were in Chicago when a certain accountant passed away from an alleged drug overdose."

"And…"

"Come now, Ms. Andiamo, we both know he didn't end his own life and it wasn't an accidental overdose. We both know it was you who helped him," he accuses.

"Really? Hmm, interesting. And you know this because?" I ask not giving anything away and quickly replaying every move I made that night. Was there a camera I didn't see, a surface I didn't wipe down? Relax; he's just fishing, trying to make you doubt yourself, make a mistake. You didn't miss a thing.

"You're in Chicago, someone dies. It seems wherever you go death follows." I bust out laughing.

"I believe people die every day no matter where I happen to be even here where I live. How many have died today? I can assure you I haven't dispatched anyone. Yet, you sleep comfortably when others are busting their asses trying to put this guy away, a man that you let roam free." Isley didn't like that.

"You were once an asset for the CIA Ms. Andiamo; I want you to work for us again, and only you, not your team. Work for me exclusively."

"I feel an 'otherwise' coming on," I say, feeling something isn't right here. Why would he want me to work for him? What's his agenda? Curious.

"Otherwise, we go to the FBI about Chicago and others we know of." Again, I burst out laughing. He scowls, apparently not happy with my reaction.

"And what is it that you know, Isley? You know I was there for business meetings with a few clients. I'm sure you verified this. I'm sure you also confirmed that after my meetings I was in the company of a bouncy brunette or was it a busty blonde or a racy redhead. I have a few in Chicago so it's hard to keep track. Whichever, I'm sure they had a wonderful time. I like to please the women I'm with." I lean in and lower my voice. "You can't prove anything, Isley, because there's nothing to prove. So, go ahead, take it to the FBI. I've done nothing," I get up to leave but Isley stops me.

"Are you sure you want to play it this way?" he asks with a fake smile.

"Do what you're going to do. You don't scare me, Isley. I won't be threatened into working for the Company again," I turn and leave shutting the door behind me.

Once in the elevator, I lean against wall for the moment taking a deep breath, letting it out, and clearing the look on Thorstein's face out of my head. Good thing there's no longer a body available for testing. I paid a pretty penny to have everything else either destroyed, cleaned or sanitized. I know Isley's not going to give up. He wants me as his personal weapon, and I know I need to prepare for a fight there. I shake my head to clear it and head back to the conference room with my brain now focused. Time to concentrate on what we have yet to do.

***

4 July 0030hrs

Alex and I are huddled in the conference room corner by ourselves quietly discussing our plans in code. We're discussing how to prepare for the confrontation with al-Hakeem and how to deal with Sheppard when we both get a message that former Deputy Director, Davis, just entered one of those locations we have eyes on. At the same time, Jessica flies in and we barely have time to take our seats before she begins to speak.

"I was just informed that the Vice President is arriving for a speech at the GM Towers in less than 24 hours. They're aware of our current situation and tightening security on their end but they refuse to cancel his trip. They're doing their requisite precautions and sealing off mailboxes and manholes. You know the drill there.

"We have several areas around the city we need to cover. HRT are wheels up and on their way. As soon as they get here assignments and staging will be handled."

Well shit. Now I know where al-Hakeem's going to make his big move. That's where our showdown is going to be. Davis forgotten for the moment, I go over what to do, where, and when.

"But, right now we have two more locations we believe are connected to this thanks to the Andiamo's. If we take these cells down that's more lives that will be out of harm's way. Same two teams stage here and here. We need to hit them now and hit them hard. We'll breach on my call. Remember we have a civilian informant still missing so be aware."

Jessica wrapped up and I was about to ask her about the Director when she was interrupted again. She turned to him, face hard as stone. He hesitated but swallowed his fear and continued, speaking so rapidly had to have him take a deep breath and start over. As he repeated his message a look of confusion mixed with concern slipped across her fact then went hard as stone. She fired a few quick questions then dismissed him. Alex and I look at our phones, and then each other, new texts showing on both.

"I've just been informed that one of our targets has been hit. It doesn't change our plans," she quiets the murmurs that went around the room. "Johnson, just like last time, smooth and by the numbers. My team, we secure and clear. Any questions? Good. Let's do it." She dismisses her team, and everyone leaves the room. I hang back.

"Jess, we have intel that Davis entered the premises shortly before it was hit. Don't know yet if he was still inside, whether it was him that blew it, or those inside because he showed up."

She grew quiet for a moment. I can only imagine what was going on, not knowing if this man whom she once loved was dead on the scene, if he caused it or if he escaped. Nothing I can do to help with this one. She took a deep breath and seemed to reach a conclusion.

"It doesn't change anything. You, your brother and your team have been invaluable Toni and I will make sure you get the recognition you deserve. We'll handle everything from now on." That sounded just plain wrong but it's out there now.

Guess she was more upset about the chemical interrogation than I thought. I freeze in place for a moment sure that my mouth dropped to the floor before I can muster an answer. Then, I explode.

"Excuse me? What the fuck, Caruthers, what's with the cold shoulder all of a sudden? With all the shit we've been through and everything we've done for you; all I get is a 'fuck you very much'? You're not cutting us out now that we're so close to achieving the target. You owe me better than that."

"Toni, listen, this is not my call. I came down from high up the chain. HRT is taking over and shutting out all but essential personnel. They're taking over the whole show and I'm probably shut out, too. Believe me, this is definitely not my doing and I will keep you informed every step of the way.

"I'm sorry Toni I know you want to do the takedown and I'll try to talk to them, but I can't and won't guarantee it. Right now, I have a job to do."

She turned to leave but hesitated, slammed the door shut, and turned back around to grab me. She kissed me heard, with the sharpness and skill of a razor and then she was gone.

Well, merda. When I'm steady, I nearly rip the door off its hinges as I leave, hoping to never see this place again.

***

4 July 0115hrs

"He's not going to go there at the last minute to plant this stuff, not with Secret Service and every law enforcement agency you can think of in place. No, he'll set it now after Secret Service have swept everything and before security is so tight no one has a chance to get by without heavy screening. He'll probably use a cell phone to set it off and possibly added a timer as backup, just in case. I hope we haven't missed him."

Now, back where I feel most comfortable, we're in the conference room going over where I believe al-Hakeem will place his Ricin and bomb. I'd sent my brother out to gather as many of our people as he could to cover the rest of the locations Jess outlined in her plan. I felt a lot better, now, after blowing off some steam about the HRT, FBI, CIA and every other agency involved in this fiasco.

"So, listen up, this is the plan. Carrie, you and Karl are going to be my eyes on the street so I can slip past whatever security is in place there. You'll also see to it that no one stops me when the shit hits the fan. Mitch, I need you in my ear to guide me to the roof here and guide Murray to this roof to be my spotter." Frankie was so quiet during my tirade and briefing that I almost forgot he was there.

"Frankie, look, I know you're not supposed to leave my side, but I must insist that for the next couple of days you remain with my sister. It's what's safest for you. Murray, you'll take him?" Murray nods and Frankie stands to leave. It worries me Frankie hasn't said anything. "Frankie?" He just nods his assent and disappears through the door.

"How soon can you be ready?" I ask, heading for my dressing area.

"As soon as you are," Mitch answers back. "You won't have a spotter until Murray gets back, Toni. I don't like it. You won't have anyone watching your back. We need to wait for the whole team."

"We don't have time. If he hasn't set it already, we only have a small window to pull this off. We must do it now.

***

4 July 0240hrs

I left a message for Jessica knowing it'd be too late for her to stop me when she finally gets it. She'll be too late to stop what I plan to do to one Mansur al-Hakeem.

Everyone's in place except for Murray who'll be along in another fifteen, twenty minutes. I'm dressed in a maintenance uniform carrying a bag of tools along with my weapons in a false bottom, hidden from search if I happen to be stopped along my way to the roof.

"You're clear this side, Toni. There's a skeleton crew for security and it looks like the advance team is fast asleep," Carrie whispers in my ear.

"Roger that. Karl how about your end," I whisper, keeping my lips still.

"Clear my end. The device is set outside the security perimeter. They'll never notice it."

"Roger that." Karl set up a device we developed that's the size of a watch battery. When placed within range of a camera, it'll disrupt the stream long enough for Mitch to run enough loops of empty hallways, elevators, and stairways for me to pass through and get to the roof.

"Mitch, cameras entrance," my words are short and to the point.

"Go for entrance and elevator two," he answers in my ear. I enter the building and head straight for the maintenance elevators and number two opens for me.

"Shit Mitch, how did you do that," I ask him once the elevator doors close and I'm on my way up.

"Magic," he whispers and I picture him smiling and wiggling his fingers. I snicker back at him. The elevator doors open and I head down the hallway toward the stairwell. The coded door opens at my will and clicks shut behind me.

Shaking my head, I take the steps two at a time and come to another coded door. After the faint click of the lock, I open the door to the windy and cool night air. Sticking to the shadows, I take off the maintenance uniform to reveal my black tactical clothing underneath. I add my utility belt and fill it with the weapons I selected. A collapsible baton, my Sig p229, knives, and tools to dismantle any device I might come across.

A search of the roof, including every vent, nook, and cranny produces no trace of a either the device or al-Hakeem. Thank God. Looks like I made it here before him. Outstanding. I have an excellent field of view from my vantage point. Now, I settle in to wait.

This particular roof is on the building where the Vice President will give his speech. Mitch whispers in my ear that Murray just arrived. A slight sound comes from behind me and to the right. I stiffen quickly scan the rooftop moving back into the shadow of an air conditioning unit.

Finally, I spot a figure bent over one of the vent fans. I'm facing his front. Suddenly he spins around. I see the spread of paint on his back. His front is probably full of paint now, too. Damn it, Frankie. You're supposed to lay low, stay out of this. Idiot! I quietly slip behind the dark figure.

Dark of Night

***

4 July 0230hrs

Jessica's team arrives at the smoldering ruins of the location they were set to take. Jessica had ordered the fire department to stay clear, but there was nothing left for them to douse. In fact, there wasn't much of anything left. She could do nothing until the robot and dogs did their work, bodies, if any, and hopefully not the Davis's, are taken to the morgue, and any materials found handled by the SABT and crime scene techs. She issued her orders and took her phone out to report in when she saw a missed call from Toni. The call to her boss forgotten, she listens to her message eyes widening as she does.

"Oh crap, Toni, no," she exclaims. "No, no, no, no. Don't do this, not alone."

She assigns two agents to work with the locals and crime scene people, pulls her SABT and the rest of her team to explain the situation, gives explicit instructions and left, full lights and sirens.

CHAPTER SEVENTEEN

4 July 0300hrs

"Well, hello, al-Hakeem, it's finally just you and me. I've looked forward to this for years." He looks from his clothes to me and curled his lip.

"Ah, Sergeant, you are a continuing source of wonderment." He referred to me by my rank when his men captured us. I was just a newly tagged Buck Sergeant at the time. "I've looked forward to this meeting as well. I did not plan for it to be this soon. You're ruining my paycheck and I don't appreciate the interference in my work."

"Well, I'm just shedding tears at your loss of income and I really don't understand why I'm such a wonder. I'm just like every other soldier who's been tortured, whose family's been murdered. I just want the sons-of-bitches that did it to pay."

"It's not personal, just business," he shrugs it off. I know it's a lie and call him out on it.

"Really. It sure seems personal when it's *my* family you tried to recruit into your arms deals, *my* family you stole money from, *my* family you tried to ruin, and only *my* family you killed.

"I am a warrior of Allah and you are a simple whore bitch. An Infidel. I cannot begin to fathom how you see yourself as anything but an abomination. Your kind always come up with something that satisfies your own mind."

"The only abomination is a murderer who kills innocents under the guise of doing it for Allah. Your own religion forbids it and no religion takes kindly to murder. Come on. No one's listening. You don't believe any of that crap you just spouted, am I right? You're in this for the paycheck. You're a hypocrite Hakeem. A sorry ass, son-of-a-bitch, murdering hypocrite."

"Listen to who, how you say, the pot calls the kettle black?"

"I kill," I shrug my shoulders. "It's a job. One I happen to be very good at. I don't kill cops or kids and I certainly don't kill innocents in the 'name of God'. He may not like me, but that's none of your business, is it? Let's quit pretending here, and get down to business. I don't suppose you're willing to surrender, are you?" I ask taking out my baton and extending it to its full length with a flick of my wrist.

"You amuse me so, Sergeant, surrender to you?" he laughs.

"I know, but for the record, I had to ask. I'm glad you chose not to give up so easily. I'm a little rusty and can use the practice." He bursts out again.

"Does this remind you of anything?" I raise the baton taking a few swings. "You know what I'm going to do with this right?"

I barely finished my sentence when al-Hakeem lunges for me, enraged. I easily move out of his way, expecting the move, pulling a knife with my free hand, a K-bar from my Army days. He pulls a second knife. We circle each other, a lion and a wolf. Two predators squaring off wanting a piece of each other.

I watch his eyes, feint to the left and come up ripping off a chunk of his ear, hitting his ribs with the baton, making him grunt and double over. He quickly straightens, feels his ear, looks at the blood on his hand, then at me. He nods then in a flash of movement lunges once again.

I lean back almost out of reach of the knife and not quite fast enough with the baton to thwart his attack. The cold steel bites into my right arm. I counter and slice his right cheek and bounce my baton on the opposite side this time.

He expels a short grunt with the loss of air as I hear the crack of a broken rib. Recovering quickly, he launches at me with a flurry of movements putting me on the defensive, using my baton and knife to stave off his attack. I counter with my own attack when I see a slight lull in his momentum. It's quiet. The only sound our breathing and the clink of metal on metal from knives and baton. We go at each other for what seems an eternity but, is only a few minutes. Slice, spin, lunge, hit, counter; a weird dance of death.

He pulls back and stops, standing with hands folded in front, his breathing labored. I stand at the ready not even breaking a sweat.

"Very good Sergeant, but not good enough," he wheezes. "You will be joining your family very soon."

A.M. Paoletti

"Not before I finish you." At that he feints left, spins right, and lunges. I move, losing my balance and falling to one knee. He comes at me again. I deflect his arm with the baton, and slash up through his pants and belt, deep enough to hit the bone of his hip, then swing the baton I blow out his right knee. He roars out his pain falling to the tar. I stand back letting him take in the gravity of his situation.

"Very good," he spits blood. "But it's going to take more than a few love taps to stop me," he snarls pulling himself up using a cement support from one of the vents.

I wait until he's fully upright before I head in easily staving off his knives and blow the other knee. He goes down again, screaming in pain. I rush him then, dislodge his weapon and pull his arm behind him, breaking it as his other knife plants itself temporarily in my right shoulder. The satisfying sounds of his cracking bones overshadow the pain from his knife, a mere mosquito bite.

I ignore his screams, snapping his last limb with satisfaction. Shredding his clothes and his dignity, I leave him with nothing but his boots. Now, for my grand finale, I stuff my baton where the sun doesn't shine.

I slowly withdraw then slam that puppy home again and again, counting out the number of times he did the same to me. I take his knives, carving him as he carved me, and then his whip. Hearing him shriek and beg gave me a pleasure I never felt with *any* kill in the past.

I am wrath. I am vengeance. I am fury unleashed as a storm born from Hades himself. When I finish I grab him up under his shoulders as he simpers, dragging him to the edge of the roof. He tries to wriggle away when he realizes what I plan to do. But he can't escape what's in store. With my boot on the stick up his ass, I push his broken and degraded body off the roof.

"Go to fucking hell," I scream and collapse against the roof wall. It took several seconds but I watch as he splats on the pavement below, the pre-dawn light just beginning to brighten the sky. I pick myself up. My shoulder is searing and every muscle scolds me from exhaustion. I stumble trying to reach the place I saw him leave his package.

***

Jessica arrives at the GM Towers barely putting the vehicle in park before she jumps out followed quickly by the rest of her team. A scream pierces the morning quiet and, barely a second later, what she assumes to be one Mansur al-Hakeem, splatters on the pavement.

She froze for a split second as blood, bone, and brain matter spray out then barks out a string of orders. "Find the Vice President's advance team? Where's security is? Lock this place down! No one in or out."

She wonders how they were able to get past all this. Where the fuck is all the security? She makes a mad dash for the roof, her tech in tow, hoping that Toni's alive, that she made it. "Please, Goddess let her be all right," she prayed.

"I'm sorry, Jess. He wouldn't surrender. I had to," she found me still trying to work my way to the package al-Hakeem had left. She helps me stand, seeing my ripped shoulder. I drop my head onto hers and as the grey closes in, I see a Martian with a big bubblehead then pass out.

"I know," Jessica whispers as she catches Toni slowly lowering her so her medic can do their job.

Now, she needs to pull herself together and finish the job.

***

7 July 0900hrs

I'm sitting in court with Frankie, my shoulder repaired, arm in a sling. In the hospital, I found out the team taking the second cell down encountered one who wouldn't go quietly. As he activated his vest, Sgt. Noonan with the local SWAT, threw himself on top of him preventing the killing of several in his path.

I'm making sure his family doesn't have anything to worry about from now on. They found the person in my employ, the one I had on the inside, dead. I'll take care of his family, too.

Jessica's people took care of the device that was to release Ricin through the ventilation system. The Vice President's speech went off without a hitch, and Jessica's HRT team took down the last two cells with little fanfare. Fourth of July celebrations went on as scheduled.

I expect to answer a slew of questions about what happened on that roof. They didn't want him alive but what I consider justice, they consider against their law. I'll deal with the consequences, whatever they may be.

Taking a deep breath, I sigh, thinking that I won't see Jessica in a personal sense anymore. While we're waiting for the judge, I scan the courtroom and do a double take as Jessica calmly walks in, takes the seat next to me, and squeezes my hand. Holy shit! I think I feel a bit light-headed right now. I know a stupid grin is plastered across my face.

A few minutes later the bailiff orders us to rise and Judge Grayson enters the room. About twenty minutes later, they call Frankie's case. Tyrell asks for an in-camera with Frankie, Jess, and I. The Judge looks at us as if we're crazy when Jessica rose to speak.

"Your honor may I approach?" She waits for permission then proceeds to the bench. She opens her Fed credentials and shows them to the Judge handing her a letter from Spence's office. "I'm here on behalf of the Federal Government, your Honor. Frankie recently helped us in a matter of National Security. We need to speak in camera due to the confidential and sensitive nature of this situation."

"I'll grant the in-camera, let's adjourn to my chambers." We rise as she starts to leave. The prosecuting attorney makes to follow but she stops them.

"Mr. Hubner, Mr. Jones I'm afraid the sensitive issue of National Security must be protected. If there's anything that needs to be directed and dealt with by you I will let you know and it will be put on record." At that, we file out of the courtroom leaving Mr. Hubner with a not so happy look as he flops back into his seat.

"Ms. Antonia Andiamo, it's been a lot of years since your presence graced my courtroom. I was proud you never showed up here again. Tell me why you're in my court today," she demands. I wonder how proud she'd be if she knew of the work I did for my uncle.

"Well your Honor, I'm sure you read my report." She nods. I continue, "So I won't repeat what's in it. During my questioning of the defendant, I saw something in him that reminded me of where I was at his age. I also remember somebody giving me a break, so I thought the best way to pay that back was to do the same. I turned Frankie in and started him on the community service hours at a church working with the homeless."

She interrupts me, "You turned him in? Why didn't you convince the hotel to drop the charges?" Hmm. A good question.

"I couldn't do that, your honor. The hotel hired me. Frankie also had to learn from his mistake. He couldn't do that if I just made it go away. All he'd learn is how to get away with it."

"I'm glad some of my speech stuck with you all these years, Ms. Andiamo." I blush and in front of Jessica, too. Talk about mortifying. "Sorry to pick on you but you're one of my success stories, though I suspect that's exactly what you learned, how not to get caught. You must be extremely adept at what you do. I hear all sorts of things."

"Your Honor…" I blush again.

"Relax, Ms. Andiamo," she laughs enjoying her toying with me. "Now, what's going on that needs to stay so confidential?"

This takes me back to my own sentencing eons ago. My uncle and his lawyers kept me from being charged as an adult. Judge Grayson set me on a difficult path to redemption that eventually led to mercenary school and the Army when I was old enough.

"That's harder to explain your Honor, I'll let Special Agent Caruthers take over from here," I defer to Jessica. Jessica rose to speak.

"Your Honor, I needed to take this opportunity to let you know what an asset Frankie was in helping us to not only stop a prolific terrorist but take down several of his cells as well. Moreover, while I cannot discuss the details, his intelligence, willingness to learn, and skills, such as what he allegedly displayed in this case, greatly contributed to a successful conclusion with few fatalities."

"Really, I'd be interested to hear how his skills as a paintball sniper contributed to the apprehension of a terrorist."

"Unfortunately, your Honor, all I can safely comment on is what's appeared in the news," Jessica reiterates.

"Understood, Agent Caruthers." She turns to Frankie. "Young man, what have you got to say for yourself?" Frankie looks at me with panic on his face. I nod back at him. He swallows hard. This is unusual for an in-camera but it's her courtroom and her chambers and I'm certainly not going to question her.

"Your Honor, I know I done bad. I learned lots from the B...I mean Miss Toni. My Grandma told me God gave me a brain and she raised me to know wrong from right and how it was up to me to decide how to use my brain for good or bad. I told her I'll use it for good from now on."

He expressed the same sentiment he told us at the beginning of the week. At least he didn't curse. The Judge is impressed anyway. She nods throughout Frankie's diatribe.

"You coached him well Andiamo."

"I swear your Honor, I did nothing of the sort," I laugh nervously.

"We'll go out and make this official with a plea. I hope that is amenable to everyone. I need to think exactly what I'm going to do. Okay, we'll take a five-minute recess. I'll see you in the courtroom."

We leave her chambers and return to the courtroom. I turn to Frankie. "Frankie, my man, I think the judge likes you. You impressed her. I'm proud to see you stand up and take responsibility for your actions."

"Damn girl, you don't have to get all teary and shit. I just doing the right thing like my Grams taught me."

I sigh heavily and audibly. "You know Frankie that mouth of yours has got to go. I'm glad you, at least, had enough sense to keep it clean in front of the judge." Just then, the Bailiff announces the judge and we all rise. After we take our seats, Tyrell remains standing addressing the court.

"Tyrell Jones for the defense your Honor, the defendant wishes to enter a plea of guilty to all charges."

"Do you understand what that means young man? You have a right to plead not guilty and have a jury trial. Is it your wish to plead guilty?"

"Yes, your Honor," Frankie answers her.

"You've discussed this with your attorney and those responsible for you on this matter and enter into this plea of your own free will?"

"Yes, your Honor."

"You have heard the charges against you Franklin Marvin Truset, how do you plead?"

Frankie winces from hearing his given name but he answers the Judge. "I plead guilty your Honor."

"That's very wise of you Mr. Truset. Mr. Hubner, you're awfully quiet over there, do you have anything to say?"

"Your Honor, what the defendant did was very serious. We're prepared to file to have Mr. Truset tried as an adult. That was nipped in the bud by Ms. Andiamo and her organized crime family."

"Your Honor, please," Tyrell jumps up.

"I agree. Mr. Hubner, this is not a setting for accusations without the offer of proof. If you think Ms. Andiamo and her family broke the law, then have the District Attorney's office bring charges. This case has nothing to do with the Andiamo family. This case is about a young man who has gone seriously astray," the Judge admonishes.

"I apologize, your Honor. As I was saying, the defendant, charged with very serious crimes, certainly warrants accountability. Since he will not be tried as an adult and is pleading guilty to these crimes, we think time behind bars to learn his lesson is warranted." With that said Trace Abner Hubner IV plops down in his seat.

"Thank-you, Mr. Hubner. Accountability is definitely a shared ideal. I also agree these are serious charges; however, I do believe recent circumstances should count for something. Stand up, young man." He does.

"Franklin Marvin Truset the court accepts your plea and I hereby sentence you to time served with a period of two years of probation, you will perform nine hundred hours of community service to include hours you've already performed.

"You will pay restitution in the amount of seven thousand dollars. I know that seems like a huge amount of money, but the circumstances warrant it and I'm sure a resourceful man like yourself will be able to pay this off soon.

"When I'm satisfied you have met all the requirements of this sentence, I will grant a suspended imposition of sentence and have your records sealed. That means young man if you screw up you will spend two years in the Juvenile Justice System, but if you meet all the goals I've set forth, then all will be good.

"The work you did for the government I hope one day becomes unclassified. It's good to see someone who actually cares about the direction of his life. Stand proud and be good to Ms. Andiamo. She gave you this break. I do not want to see you back in this courtroom again, got it?"

"Yes, your Honor. Thanks."

"That does it for me. Court is adjourned." The gavel sounds and the Judge moves swiftly to disappear into her chambers.

"Your Honor," she pauses by the door. "I'm surprised you actually remember me. I'm glad I can take this time to tell you, that without the opportunity you gave me I would not be the person you see here today." Who knows what I would've turned out like, I mentally snort and smirk.

"Kiss ass." She laughs, turns around and is gone. I laugh too. Damn, I hate being in a courthouse. I come up to Frankie, and we do the handshake.

"Congratulations Frankie, you impressed the Judge. I hope you'll continue to do well wherever you go. I'll miss the shit out of your mouth."

"It's okay. I ain't goin' nowhere, if you want permanent that is."

"You want a job Frankie, is that what you're asking me?"

"Yeah, I'm asking for da job."

"You got it. Now, let's get back to work." I turn to Tyrell. "Thanks. I appreciate you taking the case on your heavy schedule."

"It's no trouble at all, the easiest case I've had in a long time. Call if you need anything else." We shake hands and he leaves.

Jess walks up to me as I watch Frankie skip out of the room to join Mitch. It warmed my heart to see him so happy to work.

"You know, Jess, my whole life changed in this same courtroom." I'm not sure for the better, but it sure did change the direction.

"My uncle took care to see I didn't waste the chance I was given, just like I'll see to it Frankie doesn't waste his." Unobtrusively, she holds my hand and squeezes it as we walk out of the courthouse.

***

7 July 1300hrs

Jessica and I are sitting in my favorite booth at Bellisio's. It's hard to believe that just a handful of days ago I was in this same place reading a newspaper. So much has happened since then, essentially changing my life. After we order, there's an awkward silence. Both of us tried to break it at the same time. Laughing at the simultaneous blurts breaks the tension.

"Jess, look, I feel there's something that needs to be explored between us but not here with all these distractions and not under the heat of the moment."

"I agree. What are you suggesting Toni, because I feel more for you than I care to admit."

"I have an island ..."

"Wait, what? You have an island, a whole island?"

"I have an island and I'd like us to spend some time there, explore the island, the ocean, each other," My cheeks turn the color of the "Dago Red" wine we're drinking. I shrug my shoulders wincing in pain from my forgotten torn wing. She nods her head as she dips her bread into the oil and garlic herb mixture and contemplates her answer.

"Toni, I would love to explore with you," she finally answers and I let out the breath I didn't know I held. "There will be questions that need answering and debriefs up the yin yang, but I think after everything is done, I'm sure I can get away for a couple of weeks. I'm leaving tonight for Quantico and I hope to be back before the weekend."

"Great. There's also a matter of the funerals and Sunday's family dinner. Seems my sister is picking up the torch now that my parents are gone. Are you willing to endure it with me?" I ask. For some reason, I find it hard to look into those eyes that so fascinate me.

"If I'm back from Quantico in time, I think I'd enjoy dinner with your family, and it would be an honor to stand for your family at the funerals."

I do a mental flinging of sweat off my brow and we continue our lunch engaging in light banter, telling each other a bit about ourselves.

***

7 July 2300 hours

Former Special Agent Calvin Sheppard is waiting in an abandoned warehouse along the river. I come in with my shoulder bandaged and my arm in a sling. My brother looks up, sees me.

"Sis," my Brother nods.

I nod back and turn my attention to Sheppard, suspended from the rafters. I feel the rage well up inside me. He takes one look at my face and a puddle shows up on the floor beneath him.

"Tsk, tsk, tsk, Sheppard. You didn't think I'd actually show up here, did you? How in the world did you propose to escape my brother? Do you think he's not as angry as I am about our family's deaths, about so many unnecessary deaths?"

He shakes his head. I walk over and remove the gag from his mouth.

"You fucking bitch, they'll hang you and that bitch Caruthers for this." I let him bluster on for a few minutes.

When he runs down, I stare at him for a moment or two and address him calmly, considering the fury that's raging inside me. "My dear Agent Sheppard," I smile and move closer. "You gave the words to Malcomb Davis that had my family murdered. You stormed the surveillance van and the distraction caused two of my security people to lose their lives. Innocent blood is on your hands. You've destroyed lives and yet you still think this would help put you back in the good graces of the FBI. You really are mad."

"You think I'm mad? You're an assassin for the mob. You kill for money and sleep with women. You're the sick one, Andiamo. I will have your uncle. If I bring him in, they'll forgive me anything."

"You are a smug son of a bitch. My uncle had nothing to do with this operation. Y our hard-on for my him blinded you, *former* Special Agent Sheppard. Because of you, innocent people lost their precious lives."

"Innocent people, bah. None of you are innocent," he states.

"Why? Is that because they happen to have the Andiamo name? Two kids in high school are not innocent? My mother, a housewife, didn't have a care in the world, is not an innocent? My father, didn't have a clue about my business, worked for GM on a drafting board all day, is not an innocent? You are the one who won't get away with what you've done. It ends here."

"You're the one responsible for the killing of your family bitch, you and your uncle. They'll fry you if you kill me, and if you don't, I'll scream out everything I know about you."

"You don't scare me, Sheppard, you never did and who says I'm going to kill you. I highly doubt you'll be screaming to anyone."

He looks thoroughly confused at me. "I'll certainly scream when you let me go."

"Who says I'm going to let you go?" Fear slowly seeps into his eyes when the light turns on in his brain.

"Sheppard, I've wanted to kill you since the moment you stepped over the line and went after me at my home. You took my family away from me then you took my employees and if that weren't enough, you threw Agent Caruthers under the bus without proof or corroboration, nearly ruining her career, and put her through hell."

"That bitch should know her place. It's not in the FBI. The FBI is for real men, not sick, women who think they can be men." Rage paints my face and I try to keep my voice deadly calm when I speak.

"You know, Sheppard, you are one lucky son of a bitch. I made a promise to Special Agent Caruthers. I told her I wouldn't kill you to exact my revenge for the deaths of my family; that I could distinguish between an avenging angel and a vengeful rage. For me, killing you would be an act of revenge, to keep my promise to Agent Caruthers, I'm going to let you feel the wrath of my brother instead. He's made no such promises. You, I have no doubt, will be lucky to survive this day. Goodbye Sheppard, you lose." I turn and walk away, leaving the disposal of Snidely Weasel to my brother. I leave the warehouse to the tune of his screams and walk away with absolutely no regrets.

***

I don't see Jessica before the church service begins. She must not have made it back. The church is stuffy from so many people clogging the aisles and it feels claustrophobic. Frankincense permeates the air and chokes off my breath. I hate the stuff, but for some there's comfort in ritual. When we finally follow the caskets out to the waiting vehicles, breathing in the fresh air is a Godsend. The amount of security is staggering. I've made sure nothing, and no one will disturb these services today. I'm hyper-vigilant, constantly scanning the church from my seat with the family. Beth elbows me and I try not to fidget, leaving my security details to their own.

During the limousine ride to the cemetery, I keep vigil looking out the windows. Police block side streets and intersections. My people are at the front and rear and, where roads permit, protecting the sides, too.

The ride to the cemetery takes twenty-five minutes. I step out of the vehicle to check security as the rest of the procession files in. Jessica's here waiting for me. She leans on the limo, her fascinating eyes covered by Fed shades.

"Hey," she says her bottom lip slightly curled. She's wearing a smart black pantsuit.

"Hey," I answer back. "You made it."

"I drove straight from the airport. I'm sorry I missed the services. I here as fast as possible. I've posted agents all around the cemetery and I'm sure you have security posted as well."

"Bingo." I hesitate not sure what I should be doing or saying. "Thanks for the extra security and I appreciate the effort you made getting here." Her eyes remain behind her glasses and I can't read them. After several days of grilling at the hands of her compatriots, I'm glad she's here at all. She responds with a beam whose glow outshines the angels then takes my hand giving it a squeeze. We separate and I join my family while she hangs back to keep an eye out.

The cemetery chapel service was packed but thank God it was short. Our family waits until everyone leaves then we take the short drive to the gravesites for services there. Watching my family lowered into the ground brought a flood of emotion but I stand stoic, showing nothing. The limos take us back to the funeral home where we pick up our own vehicles and head to Bellisio's for the luncheon. Once again Jessica's there. Somehow, with her, I always feel safe and for a short time, my pain melts away.

***

I find myself at the head of a long table at my sister Beth's house for our Sunday family dinner. Jessica is on one side, Frankie and his Grandmother on the other and my brother sits at the other end. Miss Edna and her husband are here too along with Mitch and Andrea. Beth leads us in saying grace and then lifts her glass to make a toast.

"As we said goodbye to our parents and sisters, we say welcome to new family. While the pain of loss is still fresh, on nights like tonight, sharing memories will help ease that pain. Our family remains the heart of all things. Our family protects each other, fights for each other and loves fiercely. That's what tonight is about. So, it's with love that I say Una Famiglia, to the Family, salute" she raises her glass and we all drink a toast, some with wine, and some, the pregnant ones, drink sparkling cider.

We indeed share memories. For the next few hours we sing, laugh and joke around. All of a sudden, Beth's face changes and a hush falls across the room. Oh, shit. Oh, shit. Here comes the baby. We rush her and Jeffrey out the door with her hospital bag. Patricia takes charge of Ashley as everyone piles out to cars. Jessica and I stay behind to clean up. Once finished, we lock up and head out to greet new life.

EPILOGUE

I hear engines as I put the final additions on my file. I'm finally taking a few days' vacation following the Al-Hakeem matter and its aftermath. I finish with the file and put it away. The FBI and Isley interrogated me several times, for hours on end. It seems some of his injuries were inconsistent with his plummet to the ground. As I thought, there were questions about why a baton was partially sticking out of his mangled remains. Isley thinks he has the smoking gun that would make me work for him now.

Jessica was supposed to join me and we were supposed to be exploring. Unfortunately, something important came up at work. Since they made promotion to head the Counterterrorism Unit permanent, I suppose she had to answer the call.

Brooding, I shut down my computer and turn to the window looking for the source of those engines. Things are quiet in this place and I can often hear before I see what's coming. As the plane slowly comes into view, I send up a prayer that I can stay on vacation but feeling that it won't be possible. I came in late last night exhausted and in much need of rest, still trying to let my shoulder heal. Turning from the window, I break the hypnotic trance of the plane as it approaches. Damn.

Looking from the air, this island looks like a giant comma and the cabin I built sits in the larger end overlooking the cove where the rest of the island joins. Stairs carved into the bluff lead down to the docks and to the beach. A few different boats bob on the water representing the things I do to relax when I'm here. There's a fishing boat, one for skiing, a couple of Sea Doo's and a small yacht for entertaining, if that ever happens.

Virginia, aka Ginger, is my private pilot and lives on this island full time. She takes care of just about whatever's necessary to keep this place in shape and flies in any supplies I need. I met her on a trip to Belize. This place provides her with the anonymity she craves and she provides the services I require. She's bringing in my uncle on this trip. Very few people know about my place of solace or where it's located. Let's just say it could be somewhere south of Nassau.

The sky is particularly blue today with a few wisps of clouds tossed in to look like puffs of smoke from a peace pipe. The sun slowly drifts westward as I look around and sigh. The waves barely break as Virginia expertly lowers the plane and softly kisses the surface of the ocean.

My uncle's arrival here disturbs the peace and quiet of this place because coming here means only one thing, business. I dislike disturbances in my sanctuary. I come here to relax and try to forget about the rest of the world. But I hide my discomfort with a forced smile and walk down to the dock. Uncle Tony waves as he jumps to the floating dock while Ginger unloads our supplies and baby's her plane after the flight.

"Ah, buon giorno mi bella, Antonia," he greets me formally with his most charming smile and a big hug as I disappear into the circle of his arms. He pulls away and kisses my cheeks in traditional fashion, looking me over.

"Buon giorno, Padrino," my face softens into a genuine smile when I address my godfather just as formally. His smile is infectious. I turn to face Virginia. "Two hours and I'll be going back with my uncle."

"No problem Toni. She'll be ready." Her long ginger colored mane is in a ponytail today and it whips around with her when she turns and disappears down a path to her cottage carrying her supplies. I remember just how that hair feels from our brief affair moons ago and smile to myself. Coming back to reality, I turn to my uncle.

"Um, so, Padrino, what's the important business that brings you here?" I ask guiding my Uncle through the kitchen and into my office.

"A serious issue," my Uncle answers. "It must be handled swiftly and quietly." I nod.

"Ok, Padrino let's see what you've got and how we should handle this."

***

Jessica is in the situation room at the American Embassy in Riyadh Saudi Arabia. At Quantico, she faced a myriad of questions, debriefs, Voice Analysis Stress Tests all week long. She returned to Detroit to find herself permanently in charge of the Counterterrorism Unit. There was a package waiting for her when she returned, a package detailing every training camp and the locations of certain terrorists on the wanted list. There was also a tape explaining things from the day he ended up in the pockets of these people to his dispatching The Bombmaker. Though he could still be lying to her, she was secretly pleased her uncle didn't betray her parents and it was after their deaths he turned.

This training camp and prison is the place Toni met her fate with Mansur al-Hakeem and she's about to blow it to hell. She was surprised to learn it was still in operation especially given what happened. She was equally horrified that her mentor played a part in keeping it that way. Waiting on pictures from the SEAL team, her thoughts turn to Toni. She should be lying in the sun right now, sailing, fishing, exploring a new relationship. A devilish grin showed up on her face. She quickly squashed it when the SEAL team slowly came into view on the screen.

"We're ready, Mr. President," the Commander in the room speaks. The President gives his authority and the SEAL team goes to work.

"This is for you, Toni," she whispers to herself as she watches.

About A.M. Paoletti

Ms. Paoletti grew up in Detroit in a single-parent home. She learned first-hand how dangerous the city streets could be and developed a keen desire to help. Spurred by the crime and violence she saw growing up, she became a Certified Medical Assistant and joined the Army as a Medic and EMT 1.

During her service, she suffered an injury that made it impossible for her to continue to serve. She suffered through years of rehabilitation but always kept her desire to help others in mind.

Paoletti worked with veterans to make sure they received the care and recognition they deserved, became a voice for the LGBT community and took courses (Crime Scene, Internal Affairs, and others) that led to her volunteer work with various law enforcement agencies.

A lifelong writer, her work with law enforcement inspired the writing of her debut novel, *Dark of Night*. Seven years in the making, Paoletti promised her now deceased mother that she would see her book published; she's now made good on her promise.

Paoletti lives in Southeast Michigan with her wife and fur-babies.

MORE FROM MAD HATTER PUBLISHING, INC.

Available Now.

From our Minerva Press imprint

PTSD: Healing from Within by Sara E. Teller

SaraTeller.com

Sara E Teller brings yet another tough subject to the forefront of modern attention with style and sense of knowing that only comes with firsthand experience.

From the battlefields of the Middle East to the minefields of domestic abuse, PTSD has stealthily infiltrated our society for generations. Its impact is deep and complex, affecting everything from relationships to careers, communities, and beyond.

Teller not only brings light to this delicate subject; she also brings relief through a series of exercises and life-altering practices.

If you know someone who suffers from PTSD this book can be a life saver.

From Expansion Press

Billy of Flawn by Sammy Ogg

MadHatterPublishingInc.com

Billy's earthly life ended far too early. Struck by a car at only three years old, Billy is transported to Flawn, a magical land where all the children go when they leave earth too soon. The tragedy on earth created a door for Billy to enter the realm of Flawn – part of the domain of Elohim, the All-Powerful One.

Only Elohim knew that Billy was destined to be transformed into a formidable youngster whose mission he'd pursue with delight and energy in the land of Flawn. Elohim chose Billy above all the children for Billy's journey would decide an issue debated in the minds of men and angels since time began.

Follow along as Elohim guides Billy, his guardian angels, Kalos and others, to fulfill his destiny and help complete Elohim's plan.

From our Minerva Press Imprint

Narcissistic Abuse – A Survival Guide by Sara Teller

SaraTeller.com

Ms. Teller brings to bear her life experience combined with her intellectual and academic studies and presents a thorough reference book addressing the differences between healthy narcissism and Narcissistic Personality Disorder (NPD). Three distinct and separate sections focus on:

- Narcissism as an inherent humanistic trait versus pathological narcissism
- Victimization and the healing process
- Therapeutic intervention

☐

From our Sherwood Press Imprint

The Fabulous Feats of Mr. B by Bruce Weinberg

BrucePWeinberg.com

Mr. Bruce teaches children about creativity and imagination. Using relaxation and breathing, he takes his kids to a place that's peaceful and serene. Whether it's the top of a snow-capped mountain or a sun-drenched white sandy beach, Mr. Bruce transports your children and you can come along, too.

Try it at home, anytime, to help your kids relax and expand their imagination. Just have them close their eyes, inhale ten full, deep breaths (from your nose to your toes) and take them to any serene, picture postcard scene.

From our Motor City Press Imprint

Elephant Play by David Ryals

A novel that takes us on a journey into madness entwined with a glimpse into the gruesome and brutal ivory trade. An expressive work inspired by absurdity and satirized through vibrant caricature. Molded from the genius of the likes of F. Scott Fitzgerald, Vladimir Nabokov and Ralph Ellison (among others), Mr. Ryals emerges as his generation's most inspired novelist.

The strongest impression Elephant Play leaves on its 'silent readers' is that Ryals is not only a skilled psychological observer but also a strident moralist. His diabolic narrator is driven by a ghastly sense of helpless futility, born in the poorest part of America, but also a compulsive criminality that keeps his chance at fame in sight. It is a measure of the authors' power that he makes us live through that hideous dream and unlike his narrator, emerge from it illuminated. Or, bewildered. Or, diabolically amused.

See all our books and get on our mailing list for updates, events, and discounts at MadHatterPublishingInc.com.

Printed in Great Britain
by Amazon